AFTER

KILIMANJARO

AFTER KILIMANJARO

A Novel

By

GAYLE WOODSON

SHE WRITES PRESS

Published 2019

Printed in the United States of America

ISBN: 978-1-63152-660-2 (pbk)

ISBN: 978-1-63152-661-9 (ebk)

Library of Congress Control Number: 2019936488

For information, address:
She Writes Press
1569 Solano Ave #546
Berkeley, CA 94707

She Writes Press is a division of SparkPoint Studio, LLC.

Book design by Stacey Aaronson

To my husband, Tom:
Fellow Traveler, and the Love of my life.
Let the red carpet roll on.

"The first stage is seeing
mountain as mountain and water as water;
the second stage, seeing
mountain not as mountain and water not as water;
and the third stage, seeing
mountain still as mountain and water still as water."

—Qingyuan Weixin, ninth century

"To get lost is to learn the way."

—African Proverb

CHAPTER ONE

MIDFLIGHT CRISIS

I s there a doctor on board?"

Every physician's nightmare. Medical emergency in midflight.

The woman in the next seat grabbed Sarah's arm. "Did you hear that? They're calling for a doctor."

Why did she have to tell this nosey woman that she was a doctor?

There had to be at least one other doctor on board—someone who wasn't jet-lagged and sleep deprived. She had not slept a wink during the five-hour layover in Amsterdam. Besides, she was trapped in her seat by vegetarian lasagna. The other choice was salmon, and her mother always said you shouldn't eat fish on an airplane.

The PA system repeated the plea. *"Is there a doctor on board?"* The woman beside her snatched the lasagna and commanded, "Go!"

The plane was packed. Rows and rows of weary people. Just like the midnight crowd in the waiting room of the Philadelphia Memorial Hospital Emergency Room.

But this wasn't a hospital. Just a tin can, stuffed with hundreds of people, hurtling in an eight-mile high arc between continents. No X-ray. No EKG. No stethoscope. Probably no defibrillator.

Two flight attendants in Delft blue uniforms hovered over a foot projecting into the aisle at a peculiar angle. A familiar queasy wave washed over her, and she prayed for something simple. A hangnail, airsickness . . . even a nosebleed wouldn't be too bad.

Please God, don't let it be a heart attack.

The man connected to the foot slumped forward, face plastered to his tray table. Sarah grabbed his wrist. No pulse. But his heart had to be beating because he was breathing. Wheezing, yes, but still breathing. He wasn't dead. Yet. She tapped him on the shoulder. "Sir, are you having any chest pain?"

"No," he whispered.

A woman kneeling on the seat beside him brandished his food tray like a sword. "This is fish, isn't it? He's allergic to fish—he told you that!"

A flight attendant grabbed the tray. "He ate the salmon?"

"I thought it was chicken," he muttered.

Sarah glanced at the name badge. "Anika, do you have an emergency kit?"

"Yes, I'll go fetch it." Both blue uniforms fled to the galley.

Airway, breathing, circulation. The emergency ABC mantra.

He wasn't breathing so well, and his circulation sucked. No room to get his head between his knees. And if he needed CPR, he'd have to be on a flat surface. She lifted his head to stow the tray table. "Let's get you out of this seat."

He didn't respond. Floppy as a rubber chicken. She grabbed him by the armpits and tugged in a futile attempt to get him out into the aisle, but he was glued to his seat. His lady companion had disintegrated into blubbering and moaning, and a little boy with curly red hair and freckles in the next row peeked over the seatback and giggled.

Poor man, his life was slipping away, as surely as if he were being sucked out through a rent in the side of the plane. Sarah was his best hope, his only hope, and she was failing miserably. She locked her arms around his chest and pulled with all her might, but he wouldn't budge.

It was hopeless.

Until help appeared. A young black woman with closely cropped hair and a clipped African accent. "Golly, he seems in a bad way. Can I help?"

"Yes, please. Grab his knees." Not the world's smoothest transfer, but they managed to get him stretched out in the aisle without banging his head on something. Within seconds, his lips went from gray to pink.

"You're a Godsend," said Sarah. "He looks a ton better, just getting horizontal."

"What's your working diagnosis?"

"Anaphylaxis. He's allergic to fish."

Anika returned with the emergency kit, a black canvas bag stuffed with pills and bottles and bags and needles. Sarah snapped a tourniquet around his arm and searched for a vein while her colleague poked through the bag, muttering to herself, "Adrenaline, adrenaline, where are you?"

Anika tapped the African woman on the shoulder. "Are you a doctor?"

"Yes indeed. In fact, I am a surgeon." She pulled a colorful plastic tube from the bag and waved it at Sarah. "What's this?"

"An EpiPen."

"Pre-packaged adrenaline?"

"Yep. Stick it into his thigh. It's a sturdy needle. You can poke it right through his pants."

"Wow, this is very cool. We don't have anything like this at NTMC."

Sarah threaded a needle into a vein and popped off the tourniquet. "NTMC. That's Northern Tanzania Medical Center, right?"

"You've heard of it?"

"That's where I'm headed." Sarah connected the tubing and started the flow of sugar water into the vein.

The man opened his eyes and gazed up at the women bending over him.

Anika wrung her hands, "Should I ask the pilot to land the plane? He says he can stop in Khartoum."

Sarah tried to suppress a gasp. "Like . . . Sudan?"

"That's the closest airport."

The man sat up slowly. His blood pressure was 90 over 60. No need for an emergency landing. Sarah plopped on the floor and sighed with a blend of relief and exhaustion. Adrenaline had propelled her through the crisis, but now she was spent.

The African surgeon cleared her throat. "You're going to NTMC?"

"Yeah, I'll be there for a year."

"I guess we'll be working together." She extended her hand. "My name is Margo. Margo Ledama."

"I'm Sarah Whitaker. Now I know at least one person on this continent."

Anika pointed out that the man could not stay on the floor. "We must keep the aisle clear. Unfortunately, the plane is full. I have no place for him to lie down."

They helped him back into his seat. Margo rigged a way to hang the IV fluid from the overhead compartment and winked at Anika. "You should bump us up to Business Class for this."

"I wish we could do that. I can offer you some little rewards. And I need you to fill out some forms." In the galley, she presented each doctor with a business class amenity bag and a clipboard.

Margo paused in filling out the form, tapped the pen against her chin. "I'm not really a full-fledged surgeon yet. One more year of training."

"Me too. I'm taking a break before my chief year. Got a scholarship to study maternal mortality in East Africa."

"Ah—So you're the new OB fellow. You'll be delivering lots of babies."

Sarah shook her head. "I'm a surgeon—not OBGyn. I'll be doing research."

Margo raised one eyebrow. "Research?"

The plane began to pitch and bounce, and the pilot's voice rang out, "We're encountering some turbulence, so I'm turning on the fasten seat belt sign. If you're up and about the cabin, please return to your seat."

The woman in the next seat patted Sarah's arm. "It's lucky you were on the plane."

"I'm glad it wasn't something more serious."

"You're so inspiring. A missionary in Africa."

"I'm not a missionary. I'll be doing research."

"Either way, you'll be helping people. So noble. So brave. You could get Ebola or—"

"Africa is a big continent. There's no Ebola in Tanzania." Sarah did not feel noble or brave. The last time she felt like this, she was eight years old, standing on the high diving board, gazing down into cold blue water, a chorus of children taunting her to jump. It was too late to turn back.

The amenity bag contained a few useful items: lip balm, hand lotion, a sleeping mask, some cozy socks . . . She put on the socks and her noise-cancelling headphones and tipped her seat back as far as it would go. Sleep would not come. Outside, monotonous beige sand spread all the way to the curved horizon. She fiddled with the ring on her left hand. It still felt foreign. And it was loose. No time to get it sized. A ray of sunshine splashed onto the square-cut diamond, sprinkling little rainbow sparkles on the wall and on the seatback in front of her.

CHAPTER TWO

TOUCH DOWN

The nightly stopover of KLM 569 was always a major event at Kilimanjaro International Airport. Passengers poured out of the jumbo jet and stormed the tiny terminal, milling about, gradually sorting into queues, like steel balls in a Pachinko machine.

Margo scampered out through the East African Resident exit with her carry-on bag. Sarah was glad to be in the *Have a Visa* group because the *Need a Visa* line snaked and coiled around the room and extended back out onto the tarmac. She thumbed through her passport, browsing the stickers and stamps that chronicled her travels. Her father had lectured around the globe and sometimes took the family along. She had journeys of her own, like the mission trip to Honduras, the month in Europe with David . . . But she had never been to Africa before this. At the customs wicket, the agent nodded for her to look into the camera and put her fingers on the print analyzer. Finally, there was the satisfying *ka-thump* of the stamp.

The stream of backpacks and huge suitcases circling on the conveyor belt was continuously replenished as passengers claimed their luggage. On a huge video screen, a leopard swam across a river to pounce on a massive crocodile and drag it into the water. Then a buffalo gored a lioness and tossed her into the air. The walls were studded with posters promoting local tourist attractions. The woman who had sat beside Sarah on the plane pointed to an advertisement for The Tanzanite Experience. "It's a museum, but they also sell jewelry. I'm heading there first thing in the morning."

"What's Tanzanite?"

"A precious stone, found only in Tanzania." She pointed at Sarah's ring. "Tanzanite is much rarer than this diamond."

Sarah's luggage rumbled past. "I think I see my stuff." She caught up with her two massive bags, loaded them onto a cart, and rolled out into the cool African night, the air laced with hints of jasmine that buffered notes of diesel and charcoal. A horde of men waved papers with the names of passengers, some handwritten with Magic Marker, some professionally labeled. A glossy white placard emblazoned with "Abercrombie & Kent" in bright blue script welcomed the Patterson party.

The hospital was supposed to send a driver, but she didn't see her name anywhere. One by one, drivers and tour guides claimed their clients and the crowd gradually dissipated into the night.

The contact number at the hospital rang on and on. No surprise. That office would obviously be closed at this hour. If only David were with her. He would know what to do. A cool breeze sent a chill up her spine, as she recalled a story that her sister had found on the internet, of criminals posing as taxi drivers who force victims to take money from ATMs. She was about to call David when a man in a faded and torn Chicago Bears T-shirt seized control of her luggage cart. "Come, Mama."

Perhaps he was her driver. "NTMC?"

He grinned and nodded. "Okay. NTMC." He rushed the into the parking lot toward a crowded mini-bus. Obviously not a hospital transport.

She ran after him, "Wait! No!"

He ignored her protests and proceeded to load her suitcases into the back of the bus.

"No shillings." She pointed to her purse, shaking her head. "I have no shillings."

He waved his arm toward a nearby ATM.

"Sarah!" A figure sprinted across the parking lot, into the pool of light near the bus.

It was Margo. She stopped to catch her breath, grabbing her knees. "The driver doesn't have your name on the list." She pointed to a stocky man ambling across the parking lot. He had a thick neck and carried his elbows away from his torso, like a weight lifter with bulky biceps or a sheriff trying to avoid bumping against his gun holsters.

He bowed slightly. "*Daktari* Sarah? I am Tumaini. *Pole sana.* I thought you come last night."

She recognized the Swahili words for "doctor" and "so sorry."

After a few heated words with the driver, Tumaini retrieved her bags and led the way to a van marked with the logo of NTMC. He opened the passenger door with a flourish. "*Karibu* to Tanzania, Daktari Sarah. You are welcome. Where do I take you?"

"It's a hotel; let me find the name." She scrolled through her smartphone. "Kibo View Lodge."

Margo peered over Sarah's shoulder. "That's a nice place."

"What does Kibo mean?"

"It's the tallest peak of Mount Kilimanjaro. How long are you planning to stay there?"

"Just one night. I'm renting a house in the doctor's compound, but since it's so late at night, I thought I'd start out at a hotel first."

Margo nodded. "Very wise. You never know about the power. You wouldn't want to move into a strange house in the dark."

"Oh." Sarah had not given any thought to the possibility of electrical outage.

Tumaini glanced in the review mirror. "Daktari Margo. How was your safari to Amsterdam? Was it a good conference?"

"Excellent. We practiced surgery on cadavers."

"Daktari Sarah, where is your home? Somewhere in America?"

"I grew up in Texas, but now I live in Philadelphia."

"Fee—Lah, What?"

"Philadelphia." Sarah thought for a moment. "Do you know . . . Rocky?" She leaned over the seat and punched the air with her fists.

"Ah yes. Rocky!" He began to sing "Eye of the Tiger".

Margo put her hands over her ears. "Tumaini, please! Put on some real music. Maybe something to welcome her to Africa?"

"I think so you will know this." He popped a tape into an ancient cassette player and the opening strains of "The Lion Sleeps Tonight" filled the van. Tumaini sang along in his soaring tenor, Margo joined in the chorus, thumping in time on the seat back. Sarah's coloratura descant floated above it all.

CHAPTER THREE

A SOLO QUEST

The hot shower was truly a blessing after the thirty-hour journey. Sarah wiped the steam from the mirror and regarded her reflection. Her eyes were a bit puffy, pink-tinged, but not bloodshot. She had always thought that her neck was too long, but David said it was not possible for a neck to be too long. "It's just long enough to connect your head to your chest." He liked to say that she looked like a Botticelli girl, but not Venus, the naked lady on the shell. It was the "Printemps" painting. They were wandering through the Uffizi museum in Florence when he cried out, "Whoa! That's you!"

"They are you," would have been more accurate. The pale women in the painting looked like clones. It was a bit creepy. They all had the same straight blonde hair, aquiline nose, thin eyebrows . . . If only she had a more formidable appearance. Looking dainty was not an asset for a surgeon.

David, the man who had been central to her life for nearly six years, had not answered any of her calls or texts. She hadn't expected to miss him so much, so soon. She dozed off with her phone on the pillow.

The buzzing of the cellphone startled her awake. She could hardly wait to hear David's voice. But it wasn't him.

"Mom?"

"Did you have a good flight?"

"Not bad." She recounted a few highlights of her journey, leaving out the part when she felt stranded at the airport.

"Your father would be so proud."

Sarah chewed her lip. Truth was, her father had advised her against following in his footsteps. His exact words were, "Surgery is tough, Princess." She was still in medical school when he died.

"Better hang up now, Mom. I'm waiting to hear from David."

"Of course, of course. Call me back when you can. I love you!"

IT WAS THE foot. That's what had set her off. The man in the airplane's foot had been cocked at exactly the same angle as the foot of the blue-haired lady in the emergency room. Obvious hip fracture. Any first-year med student standing at the end of the stretcher would have nailed that diagnosis. Her blue hair was perfectly coifed, because she was just leaving the beauty salon when the car struck her. She was terrified, moaned that she was dying. Sarah offered reassurance and sent her off for an X ray.

When the blue-haired lady coded, her EKG showed the classic evolution of a heart attack: elevated ST segments, flipped T's, then V-tach. They took turns at chest compressions, shocked her again and again, but could not get a rhythm back. Sarah wished the sweet little old lady would hurry up and die.

Her advisor told her not to feel guilty for such thoughts. It was burn-out, an increasingly common problem among physicians. "It's not just the long hours, the life and death situations. It's depersonalization, loss of autonomy in this complex health care system—electronic records, more and more regulation. Taking care of patients can seem like shift work." She prescribed stress reduction and schedule decompression. As if Sarah had any control over her life.

David had a brilliant solution. He wanted to climb Kilimanjaro. "I could get a grant to work on that malaria vaccine project. We could spend a whole year in Africa."

"Kilimanjaro? Sounds extreme."

"It's not that hard. No technical rock climbing or anything that dangerous—just a long hike up the world's tallest free-standing mountain. Imagine the view from the top: three hundred and sixty degrees."

The concept of a break year was appealing. But she did not want to sit around idly during the hours that David devoted to saving humanity from a dreaded disease, so she scoured the internet for something constructive to do. Nothing seemed to fit, until she happened onto a statement that took her breath away.

PREGNANCY SHOULD NOT BE A FATAL ILLNESS

This was the vision statement of the Stanford Foundation, a non-profit agency waging war against the mortality of childbirth in sub-Saharan Africa. The website was replete with sad stories of women who suffered grievously in childbirth, preventable deaths, and disabling complications. There were heart-breaking photos of hollow-eyed orphans. The foundation sponsored scholarships for young American doctors to spend a year learning first-hand about women's health care in Africa. Each fellow was provided funds for a research project and encouraged to "think outside the box" for innovative solutions.

It resonated with her—a chance to re-ignite her compassion, to remind her of why she went to medical school in the first place. She did not feel qualified for the position—no training in obstetrics beyond medical school. But she submitted her application anyway and crossed her fingers.

She was stunned to receive an invitation for an interview. On a bright sunny day, she took a train down to DC and Ubered to a brownstone in Georgetown. The CEO, perched on a taupe velvet loveseat, reviewed the mission of the foundation. "Normally we sponsor young obstetricians. But Mrs. Stanford was very impressed with the passion in your essay. And she believes, as a surgeon, you could provide a fresh perspective. Will you accept the position?"

IT WAS A magnificent plan. She and David would be off on a grand adventure in an exotic locale, making the world a better place.

It was too good to be true.

Literally.

David didn't get funded for the malaria project.

He got the bad e-mail one night as they sat at the kitchen table. He slammed his laptop shut. "We'll just have to wait to go to Africa . . . someday when we're rich doctors."

"I can't back out now. I got all those references, the schedule is changed—"

"But . . . you wouldn't go without me, would you?"

"Can't you just come along with me?"

"What?" He scoffed. "Just goof off for a year?"

"I would have gone with you." And she would have. She would have followed him anywhere.

CHAPTER FOUR

THE MOUNTAIN

One would expect Kilimanjaro to be clearly visible from a place called the Kibo View Lodge. But when the sun came up, there was no sign of the mountain. Sarah wandered around the grounds, peering over trees and hedges and scanning the overcast horizon in vain. When her taxi arrived, she asked the driver to point out the mountain. He smiled and shrugged. "Kibo very shy today."

The road to the hospital seemed barely wide enough to accommodate two vehicles, but somehow it functioned as a multi-lane thoroughfare. Tiny three-wheeled transports trolled for passengers along the shoulders, and motorcycles streamed along anywhere they could squeeze through. The dominant vehicles were Dala-dala minibuses, each with a young man hanging out the door to recruit customers and a driver who felt completely entitled to claim the right of way at all times.

The taxi wove back and forth to avoid potholes, people, and goats. Small shops, vegetable stands, beauty shops, and bars lined the roadsides. Large displays of brightly colored cooking gas containers were arranged in splashes of orange, blue, and yellow. The air was saturated with the aromas of fish and corn roasting over charcoal. A small white coffin lined in pink satin sat in the dirt yard in front of one shop.

Children ambled alongside the road, clustered in groups of color-matched school uniforms, chattering, laughing, and somehow managing to avoid being struck by traffic. The most popular color was royal blue, but forest green was a close second, and there were smatterings of rust, maroon, and mustard. Each uniform, inexplicably, included a pullover sweater that could not be comfortable in this tropical climate.

SARAH'S HOUSE WAS like all the others in the doctors' compound: cream-colored stucco walls, red tile roof, and battered green garage doors. Built in the '60s, the homes had not been that well maintained. The linoleum on the kitchen floor was disintegrating and stains on the ceiling provided evidence of a leaky roof. But the house was spacious and clean. Large screened windows transmitted sunlight and jasmine-scented breezes.

Irene, the housing manager, pointed out the large sink near the kitchen door. "The housekeeper, Rosie, will wash your clothes here. You must buy washing powder. And she will i-ron your clothes."

"My clothes don't need ironing. They're wrinkle-free."

"You must i-ron the clothes. When the clothes are drying on the line, flies will lay eggs. You i-ron to kill the eggs. If you don't, they will hatch on your skin."

Sarah fought back the urge to scratch herself.

Irene gestured to a large electric kettle sitting on the counter. "You boil water for five minutes. Then you can drink it. Or you can buy bottled water." She inspected the kettle and clucked her tongue. "The cord is frayed. You must buy a new one." She gestured to a switch on the wall. "That is for the hot water heater. You turn it on for one hour, then you have hot water. But it uses much power. You give Rosie money for the power. Then she will go and pay it for you. And you must buy a tank of gas for this cooker."

Beyond the kitchen was a large room with sitting and dining areas. The veranda overlooked a large and lush but unkempt garden bordered by a hedge of brightly blooming bougainvillea. There were flame trees with crimson flowers, lavender laden jacarandas, and a family of monkeys rustled the branches of a mango tree. A privet hedge that wanted pruning encircled a large birdbath. The lawn was overgrown with knee-high weeds. Irene said a gardener would cut the grass.

"Can you see the mountain from here?"

Irene waved her arm northward. "The mountain is there."

"I don't see it."

"Too many clouds. Maybe this evening."

In the bedroom, a mosquito net dangled from the ceiling, tied in a loose knot. Irene shook her head. "This has net has many holes. You must buy a new one"

Information overload. It was a relief when the housing manager left. Sarah turned to the daunting task of unpacking and worked steadily, until she heard a loud squawk from outside. A weird green bird about the size of a turkey perched in the crook of a white-blossomed tree near her bedroom window. It was ugly and awkward, with a long, curved beak that gaped widely with each obnoxious squawk. She was captivated. She snapped a quick picture with her cellphone, then rummaged in her backpack for her camera.

David had given her a telephoto lens as a bon voyage gift. There was an ulterior motive. He was coming for a visit in September and wanted to get some good closeup shots on a safari. By the time she had the lens connected and the camera poised for the shot, the bird had flown away.

So much for nature photography. Time to go to the hospital and meet with her supervisor.

She followed a red dirt path to the hospital, between fields of corn, beans, and sunflowers. The ground was peppered with little holes, as though some madman with a drill had declared war on the baked earth. The openings were portals to an underground termite network that periodically erupted into phallic mounds, five to seven feet high.

A tunnel of jacaranda trees led to the back of the hospital. There were two rear entrances. One was marked *Mortuary*. Not *Morgue*. A small group of people loaded a coffin into a pick-up truck festooned with purple ribbons and a wreath. The truck pulled slowly away, followed by a procession of mourners, singing a melancholy chant.

She took the other entrance and headed for the maternity clinic.

CHAPTER FIVE

ORIENTATION

The OB clinic waiting room was hot and stuffy, saturated with baby and body odors, even though the outer wall was a latticework of brick that should have allowed ample circulation. The crowd of patients far exceeded seating capacity, with most of the women and their children resting on the floor or leaning against the walls.

A receptionist led Sarah down a dark hallway to the office of Dr. Obaye, the chairman of the OB Department. A portrait of the Tanzanian president hung on the wall behind a large mahogany desk cluttered with stacks of papers and journals. The stern-faced man glanced up but did not rise from his seat. He just waved a large hand toward an empty chair. "Karibu, Doctor Sarah. Please be seated. You must be tired from your journey." He launched into a description of the maternity service. "Our facilities are not as modern as what you have in the states. But we work hard. We do much with little." He leaned forward, folded his hands. "You will see patients in the clinic and take call in labor and delivery."

"Uh . . . what about your research program?" Her position description included "some clinical activity," but she hadn't signed on for a full burden of direct patient care. She had expected the year to be a respite from such stress.

He raised his eyebrows. "Research?"

"Yes, I have a grant to complete a research project."

"What do you propose to study?"

She squirmed, recalled ideas she had listed in her application. "I'm interested in prenatal nutrition. Maybe looking at pre-conception weight, vitamins . . ."

He smiled thinly, and his eyes glazed over. "You are trained as a surgeon, not an obstetrician. You need some experience first. Then some good research question may come to you. Meanwhile, you can work with our chief resident, Dr. Ameera Zaheer." He cleared his throat. "A few years ago, we developed protocols for managing the three main causes of obstetrical death: infection, bleeding, and eclampsia. Dr. Ameera is reviewing our results." He stood up, tapped softly on his desk. "Let me show you the clinic."

It should not have been a shock. After all, this was a third-world country. But she wasn't expecting the peeling paint and the cracked concrete floor. The long narrow room was divided by curtains into six exam cubicles. Not a single computer in sight. Patient records were sheafs of pastel-colored papers, with dog eared corners and hand-written notes, laid out on a chipped Formica covered desk.

Dr. Ameera Zaheer was slender and petite, of Indian descent, her head was covered with a scarf. She bowed slightly. "Karibu. We have a busy clinic today."

The first patient was accompanied by a toddler in a pink organdy dress and sparkly blue plastic shoes. The child fixed her huge brown eyes on Sarah's smile for a millisecond, then ducked her head and covered her face. Ameera crouched over the mother's bulging abdomen with a fetal stethoscope, searching for the heartbeat. She found the sweet spot and handed the scope to Sarah. The fluttering heart sounds were so different from the whooshes of a doppler, the electronic sensor they always used back in Philadelphia. A small hand touched Sarah's arm and she looked down at the sparkly plastic shoes next to her own sandals. She put the earpieces in the little girl's ears. The child gasped softly and reached up to touch her mother's belly.

The next patient handed her two-week-old infant to Sarah before climbing onto the exam table. Ameera smiled as she read from the chart. "This baby is sero-negative."

"You mean, she doesn't have HIV? Does her mother have AIDS?"

"Yes, but she received medication during pregnancy. So she didn't pass it to the baby."

Sarah admired the perfect tiny fingernails and rosebud lips, hoping the mother would survive to care for this baby. Her cell phone went off—David's signature alert—but she couldn't answer, not with the baby in her arms. She tried to call him back later, but only heard his voice mail message.

THE GARDENER WAS attacking the lawn when she returned to her house. He made it look easy, one arm casually on his hip, right arm wielding a curved machete like a pendulum, back and forth, precisely decapitating weeds at an inch above the ground. He bundled a huge mass of the cuttings, four feet tall and at least six feet wide, onto the back of his bicycle. He waved and smiled at Sarah, then pointed to his cargo. "Foodie for my goat."

He hopped on the bike and wobbled off, with Sarah wondering how on earth he managed to keep his balance.

Tea would have been nice, if the cord on the kettle had not been frayed. And she couldn't boil water on the stove because she still had no gas canister. A hot shower sounded good, but when she switched on the hot water heater, she realized there was no power. A neighbor said it was not unusual. Power routinely went out one or two times a week, rarely more than a couple of hours. Maintenance work. Good thing her laptop was charged up. She decided to conserve that battery and settled down on the sofa to read a book. Soon she was fast asleep.

HER PHONE RANG several times before she found it under a cushion.

"Hey, Sam. I was afraid you weren't going to answer. Again."

David always called her Sam. Family nickname. Allegedly, her little sister could not pronounce "Sarah."

"Sorry. I'm really zonked out."

"You should stay up until at least ten tonight. That's the best way to change time zones. Just like jumping into a cold swimming pool."

"I thought I'd never hear from you. Didn't you get my text messages?"

"I did."

"I thought they didn't go through. I was afraid you'd be worried about me."

"I knew you had to be alright. If your plane had crashed, it would've been in the news."

"What if I got abducted from the airport?"

"Uh . . . well . . . sorry. Really sorry. I should have called sooner."

"That's okay." Sarah's constant refrain of conflict avoidance. Never admit annoyance. "It's nice to hear your voice. But hang up, and I'll call you back on Skype. Then we can see each other, too."

"So your house has internet?"

"No, but I got a wireless hot spot. They sell them at a tent in front of the hospital. And I got a neat little cellphone for local calls. I can even use it to pay for stuff. They have this system called m-pesa."

David appeared on her computer screen, with his dark brown eyes and pouty smile. "There you are," she gushed. "Across an ocean, a continent, and the equator."

"Yeah, thanks to true love and technology. But we're not really gazing into each other's eyes. We're both looking into a camera, so on the screen it looks like we're looking somewhere else."

"Let's take turns looking at the camera. First you." She watched as his eyes rotated. "Now me."

David laughed. "We just had fake eye contact. What's next?"

"You can let me know if a cheetah is sneaking up on me."

"Cheetahs don't sneak! They're the fastest mammals. A leopard would be more likely to stalk you. I have a wild animal here who wants to see you." He scooped up Sarah's cat, Whiskers, and raised one of his paws in a kitty wave. "Say hi to Mommy."

"He looks well."

"That's because I took him off wet food. He's on the wagon. Dry food only."

"The vet says wet food is good for him!"

"I don't buy that. More importantly, wet food stinks. What about Kilimanjaro? Is it as beautiful as the pictures?"

"I haven't seen it yet. The weather's not cooperating. How are things going for you?"

"The usual. Rounds every morning at seven, then clinic. Call every fourth night. The lab takes up most nights and weekends." He droned on about his experiments in great technical detail. Sarah was fading and had trouble concentrating on his tales of gels and primers.

David shouted, "Hey, wake up!"

Sarah yawned and stretched, struggling to keep her eyes open. "Sorry."

"I'm boring you."

"No, no, it's just—"

"I understand. Jet lag." He made his puppy dog face. "I miss you way too much. I think I'm gonna go nuts while you're gone."

It was going to be a long year.

CHAPTER SIX

FORKS IN THE ROADS

Mothers normally do all the real work in childbirth. After successive contractions, the baby suddenly pops out, slithering and slimy. All that remains is to cut the cord and deliver the placenta. Simple and natural. As long as nothing goes wrong.

Sarah examined the young woman one last time, and then nodded at the medical student. "Okay, tell her to push."

George barked a command in Swahili, a bit too loudly. He was certainly enthusiastic, but his bedside manner left something to be desired. This was his first delivery and his eyes glowed with wonder as the baby slipped into his waiting hands. Sarah handed him the clamps and scissors. "Tell me how long we should wait before cutting the cord."

"I know this. I read my assignment. We wait three minutes so that the baby can get more blood."

Sarah reminded him that this third stage of labor, after the baby was out, was a critical period when dangerous bleeding could occur. And bleeding was the single-most common cause of maternal death.

He nodded. "And that is why we should now give oxytocin now. To stop bleeding."

"You did great job." She patted him on the shoulder. "Shall we go to the café for some tea?"

"I prefer coffee."

George stirred four spoonfuls of sugar into his cup. "Doctor Sarah, you do not like coffee?"

"I like espresso from freshly ground coffee beans. It seems odd that in the middle of all these coffee plantations, everyone drinks instant coffee."

"The best coffee gets exported. This instant stuff, it's all I've ever had."

"What kind of doctor do you want to be?"

"A good one." They both laughed. "But seriously, I want to be a surgeon."

"Not a baby catcher?"

He pointed his spoon at her. "What do you think is more important?"

"They're both important. Not enough of either. OBGYN is more basic and would directly affect more people's lives. Just think about it. Around here, childbirth is one of the deadliest experiences a woman can encounter."

"So, you think I should deliver babies?"

"You should do whatever you feel called to do. Your country needs surgeons, too." She took a sip of tea. "What's on the schedule for the rest of the day?"

"Dr. Obaye is lecturing to the students this afternoon."

"Where will that be?"

"In the main floor conference room. But OB fellows never go to the lectures."

"I guess it's pointless if you don't understand Swahili."

George shook his head. "The teaching is always in English."

"Really?"

"Tanzania was a British protectorate for many years. We all learn English in primary school. From secondary school on, all classes are in English."

THE CROWDED CLASSROOM buzzed with chatter. Many students sat two to a chair. All fell silent when Dr. Obaye strode in, a tall and imposing man with a booming voice. "Today, we discuss the unacceptably high maternal mortality in our country." He glanced around the room and did a double take when he saw Sarah in the back corner. He nodded at her before continuing. "I repeat. The mortality rate is unacceptable. We must work hard to change this. Someone tell me the commonest causes of death in childbirth."

A young woman raised her hand. "Bleeding is first, and eclampsia is second."

Dr. Obaye nodded, slowly. "Correct. Who can tell me what eclampsia is?"

George raised his hand. "Convulsions, high blood pressure, and protein in the urine, usually in late pregnancy. But it can also start just after delivery."

"Good. Have any of you ever seen a patient with eclampsia? Yes, Daniele."

"Sybil, in *Downton Abbey*."

The students tittered, muttering behind their hands. Daniele explained that Sybil was a character on TV.

Dr. Obaye stroked his chin. "Was it an accurate depiction of the problem?"

Most of the female students nodded their heads vigorously. "Well, then, let's hope it did a good job of raising awareness." He went on to talk about the causes of eclampsia and presented the protocol they had instituted for treating this problem at NTMC.

Then he asked the class, "What is the number one priority once a pregnant woman has a seizure due to eclampsia?"

Several answers were called out: "Lower the blood pressure." "Give diazepam." "Treat with magnesium-sulfate."

"You are talking about controlling the blood pressure and suppressing the seizures. But are these the things that cause death? No. It is the swelling of the brain."

Finally, Daniele gave the correct answer, "Deliver the baby as soon as possible."

"Correct."

Daniele beamed, very glad to have redeemed herself.

After the lecture, Dr. Obaye asked Sarah to meet with him briefly in his office.

"How are things going so far?"

"It's all very interesting," she replied. "And I'm learning a lot."

"Do you sometimes wonder why you were chosen for this fellowship when are not trained in obstetrics?"

"Actually, yes."

"It was your essay. Mrs. Stanford, the benefactor of the foundation, was impressed by your grasp of the key role that women's health plays in the welfare of the entire country— of any country for that matter. You seem to have a passion for women's rights in general." He smiled and leaned forward with his arms on the desk. "She believes that progress requires thinking outside the box. And you are definitely outside the box." He settled back into his chair and frowned. "As for me, I was not so convinced. Perhaps I am cynical, but we have had many fellows who did not have a sincere interest; they merely wanted to spend some time in

Africa. They all write impassioned essays to get the position. Not one of them has ever completed a successful research project."

She tried not to squirm in her seat. She had included all the stuff about women's rights because she didn't know much about maternal mortality.

"So far, I think Mrs. Stanford was right. You did not object when I pointed out that you needed to do some clinical work. The students say that you are a good teacher. And you came to my lecture today."

"I have a lot to learn."

"Mortality is too high here. We are improving, slowly. But in your country, the United States, maternal mortality is increasing."

"I wasn't aware of that. Why is it going up?"

"I am not an expert on health care in your country. But from my reading, I have seen two factors cited. There are too many caesarian sections, possibly due to malpractice fears. The other reason is poor access to care. How is this possible? The richest country on earth does not have enough doctors and nurses?"

"Doctors tend to cluster in urban areas. Also, many women don't have health insurance."

"We have similar issues in Tanzania. Perhaps what you learn here will be relevant when you go home."

DINNER WAS A tuna sandwich on her sofa, while surfing the internet for articles about eclampsia. Her cellphone pinged with a message from her sister, Allison: *Help! I'm puking my guts out. I don't think this baby is worth it.*

It's normal. It's called morning sickness.

Well I'm sick all the time. And you're not very sympathetic.

Sarah logged onto Skype and called her sister's cell-phone.

"Hi, Al. Sorry you're feeling sick."

"Thanks. Isn't this an expensive call?"

"Nope, I'm on Skype."

"Oh. Good. I need your advice. I think I'm going to stop looking for a job. Do you think that's bad?"

"It depends on your reasons."

"Well, for one thing, I haven't been able to find a job."

"You're discouraged."

"And now I'm feeling sick all the time. Not really in shape for an interview."

"Good point."

"Michael makes enough money for us both. But I would barely make enough to cover childcare."

"So not working makes sense economically?"

"And I don't really want to work. I want to stay home with the baby."

"Well that's the best reason of all."

"You think so? But I feel like a wimp. Look at you."

"Don't be silly. I would not wish my lifestyle on anyone. My plan was to have a baby by now."

"Seriously, Sam? You've had trouble getting pregnant?"

"It's not that. We want to get married first. But David says we'll pay more in taxes, so we can't afford parenthood until we finish training. Of course, if he hadn't taken time out to get a PhD, he'd be out in practice by now. And now he wants to do a fellowship, so . . ."

"Sorry." Allison cleared her throat. "How is Africa otherwise?"

"In two words? Very interesting. Listen, it's great to talk

to you, but I need to finish reading a couple of articles and get to bed."

It was impossible concentrate on her reading. Allison had not asked the big question. It was the one she kept asking herself.

Did I come to Africa because I'm angry with David?

CHAPTER SEVEN

BAPTISM BY FIRE

A nurse led Sarah to a cubicle in the corner of the bustling emergency room. The thin curtain provided meager refuge from the tumult of moaning patients and clattering gurneys. A young woman lay on the stretcher, her ebony face studded with beads of sweat that gleamed like diamonds. Her mother sat beside her, clad in a royal blue shuka and a broad collar of beads, her earlobes stretched into long dangly loops.

Sarah tried to introduce herself, using her limited Swahili. "*Habari. Jina langu ni* Daktari Sarah."

No response. Just blank stares.

The nurse shook her head. "They don't know Swahili. They are Massai."

"I'll start an IV. Bring me some mag sulfate."

The needle was poised above a very promising vein when the young woman's eyes rolled back, and a massive convulsion wracked her body. Her mother let out a blood curdling, ululating wail. The nurse came running with a syringe, and Sarah unloaded the entire contents into the patient's hip. But the seizure continued unabated and the young woman's lips went from dusky to black.

A tall blond man in scrubs threw back the curtain at the

head of the stretcher, a bouquet of loaded syringes in his hand. He frowned at Sarah. "Didn't you start an IV?"

"I can't—not when she's jerking around like that."

He muttered under his breath and injected something under the woman's jaw. Within seconds, the patient was totally limp.

Sarah resumed her quest for a vein. "What did you give her?"

"Succinylcholine. Gets absorbed really fast when you shoot it into tongue muscle." He put an endotracheal tube into the woman's throat and connected an oxygen tank. "It paralyzed her. Brain is still seizing, though."

She had heard about this man. Pieter Meijer. Visiting anesthesiologist from Holland. She threaded a catheter into a large vein and attached an IV line. Dr. Meijer tossed three syringes to Sarah. "Push these."

"What's this stuff?"

"Diazepam, mannitol, steroids. They're waiting for us upstairs. Let's go!"

He released the brake on the stretcher, and they raced into the elevator. The door closed. For a brief moment, it was an oasis of calm. The only sound was the rhythmic whooshing of the Ambu bag. "Your name is Sarah, right?"

"Yes."

"Margo said she met you on the plane."

"Do you carry those drugs around all the time?"

"Not all the time." He adjusted the flow of the IV. "I keep an eclampsia stash on hand."

"That's a little less regulated than what I'm was used to. At my hospital, the drugs are locked up in a computerized box. We have to log and request meds, even in middle of an arrest. It's kind of insane."

"Two ends of the health care spectrum. Each with its own problems."

The elevator door opened, and they bolted out.

Ameera and the scrub nurse stood ready, gowned and gloved. As soon as the patient was moved to the operating table, someone doused her bulging abdomen with orange betadine. Sarah went out to scrub and cursed herself for using too much soap, because the trickle of water from the tap was maddeningly weak and it took forever to rinse her hands. She walked back into a room abuzz with frantic Swahili chatter that she could not understand. Ameera had not made a cosmetic incision below the bikini line. It was a straight-down-the-middle-get-this-baby-out-now slash. Sarah struggled to pull gloves onto her soap-sticky fingers and then took her place across from Ameera. Suddenly the table abruptly tilted as Dr. Meigher cranked the head of the bed down, lower than the feet.

"Hypotension?" Sarah queried.

Ameera nodded, "She's crashing." She sliced into the womb, releasing a flood of greenish sour smelling fluid, extracted a purplish mass which was the baby, and cut the cord.

Sarah placed the floppy infant on the back table and suctioned the mouth. He was blue and motionless, but his heart was racing. "AGAR 4," she called out.

Please God, save this little baby.

She ventilated him with a mask and after a few breaths of oxygen, he wailed loudly, flailing four perfect limbs. Sarah counted ten fingers and ten toes and announced, "It's a boy. He's okay."

No one cheered. The beeping of the monitor ominously decelerated, then flatlined. Dr. Meigher threw back the drapes and started chest compressions.

Per protocol, Ameera took over compressions after a few minutes, and then it was Sarah's turn. She stacked her hands between the breasts that were supposed to feed this little baby and called upon the technique she had honed on a Rus-suci-Annie mannequin with a light that flashed when you pressed quickly and firmly enough. In her CPR class, the instructor had set the tempo by playing "Stayin' Alive" on a boom box, so, Sarah worked to the rhythm of the Bee Gees in her head, desperate to keep this young mother's soul on earth.

But it was futile. After thirty minutes, there was no heartbeat, no breathing. The pupils were fixed and dilated.

Ameera sat down heavily on a stool. "Doctor Meigher, you are the only one of us who speaks Massai. Will you talk to the family?"

Sarah followed him into the hallway, where the patient's mother and a young man sat on a bench. Dr. Meigher squatted on the floor in front of them and spoke softly. Before he finished his sentence, the woman collapsed on the floor, beads and fists clanking and pummeling the worn terrazzo. The young man hunched over, kneading his scalp, shaking his head. Then he sat up slowly, squared his shoulders. "I want to see my son."

THE NEXT DAY was a welcome change of pace: getting involved in research. Sarah and Ameera met in the library, one of the few air-conditioned spaces in the hospital. The musty smell of the old books summoned pleasant memories Sarah's childhood: hours spent with her nose in a book in the public library. The hospital library in Philadelphia smelled of plastic and disinfectant. It had been pillaged, books destroyed and replaced by computers.

Ameera lifted two large bound volumes from a trolley and heaved them onto the table, "Obstetrical Unit logs— lists of all deliveries." She tapped on the newer book. "This one is last year—the other one is from 2008, the year before they initiated the protocols." She waved at the piles of papers remaining in the cart. "Those are the medical records of the maternal deaths from those years."

"Okay. You know how many deliveries, and you know how many deaths . . . you know the maternal mortality for those years. So that's the answer to your question, right? The hospital began following the protocols and mortality either got better or it did not. End of story?"

Ameera shook her head. "We deliver about 3,500 babies a year in this hospital. Last year, we had eighteen maternal deaths. In 2008, there were twenty."

"If it's not getting better with the new protocols, the next question is . . . why not?"

"Exactly. Either the protocols are not effective, not likely, or we are not complying. So we need to review each one of these deaths and find out what happened."

Sarah stared at the stacks of papers in the trolley. Each chart contained the stories of suffering and motherless children, every tale as heart-wrenching as the events of the night before. Multi-colored, dog-eared pages, hand-written in variable legibility.

"We are beginning to use electronic records," said Ameera. "But we only have hard copy charts for the years we are reviewing."

They pored through the records, checking for compliance with protocols and entering data into an Excel spread sheet. Around noon, Sarah's phone pinged with a text from Margo.

Just finished surgery. Can you guys meet me for lunch?

✕

THE HOSPITAL CAFÉ was an open-air space with a corrugated metal roof, its perimeters bound by privet hedges. A
large plastic container full of water by the entrance had a
spigot on the side for hand washing, and food was served
from a glass encased steam table.

They selected their food and settled around one of the
square red plastic tables emblazoned with Coca-Cola logos.
There were also a few round Pepsi tables, but Coke was
definitely the dominant theme.

Sarah poked at some white, sticky stuff on her plate.
"What's this?"

"Ugali," said Margo. "It's made from corn."

She sampled a bit. "Tastes like grits."

Ameera tilted her head. "What is a grit?"

"Kind of like polenta. Have you ever eaten that?"

Ameera and Margo shook their heads.

"Do you miss surgery?" Margo asked. "You must be getting twitchy to operate. You can scrub in with me any time."

"I'd really like that. Don't want my skills to get rusty
this year."

Ameera looked hurt. "We do surgery in Ob-Gyn."

Margo said it wasn't real surgery. "Not like hernias and
gall bladders."

"No fighting, ladies." Dr. Meigher set his lunch tray on
the table and kissed Margo on the cheek.

She smiled and squeezed his hand. "Pieter, this is Sarah,
the one I met on the plane."

"I have already had the pleasure to meet her. How do
you like African food?"

"I really like the chapati."

"Everyone likes chapati. What about the ugali?"

Sarah hesitated a moment, pursed her lips until she thought of a diplomatic answer. "It has an interesting texture."

Pieter laughed. "We are not offended if you don't like it. In fact, I can't stand ugali."

"Hmph!" Margo retorted. "You do not know good food, you *mzungu*. Sarah, we should take you to the barbecue place Saturday night. I think you'll like it. All kinds of grilled meat."

"What kinds of meat? I mean . . . you don't eat monkeys, do you?" Sarah recalled that chimpanzees had been the source of the AIDS virus.

"Where do you think you are? In the Congo? We don't eat bush meat in East Africa. Ameera, you and Rasheed should come too."

"Sounds like fun. I'll check with him."

"I could use a night out," said Sarah. "That case yesterday was rough."

"Why? What happened?" Margo asked.

"Eclampsia. The mother died. Not something I've ever seen before."

Ameera sighed. "It happens too often around here. That woman was doomed before she got to the hospital. Too late for us to make any difference. Once they start seizing, they never make it."

CHAPTER EIGHT

DAMSELS AND DISTRESS

Saturday morning. Sarah had survived her first week. She yawned, stretched, and contemplated going back to sleep. But she heard that bird squawking. The green one. He flew away before she could aim her camera, and her eyes followed him up to the sky.

There it was. Kilimanjaro, finally emerging from its veil of clouds. She couldn't see the whole mountain, just the main peak, projecting above the trees. The sky was perfectly clear, and the snow atop the mountain gleamed golden in the morning sun.

The field outside the compound provided an unobstructed view. She was totally unprepared for the enormity and grandeur of this mountain, far too vast be encompassed in a single camera shot. The main peak, Kibo, immediately commanded attention, a treeless lavender cone iced with a few patches of shimmering white near the top. Off to the right, the jagged secondary peak, Mawenzie, looked like something between a sea urchin and rooster's comb. She had to look both east and west, nearly 180 degrees, to take in the totality of this massive dormant volcano with long shoulders sloping down to the horizon. No way could her camera do justice to the splendor of this view.

David would have to come and see it for himself.

AFTER A LIGHT breakfast of bread and jam, she took a taxi into town, where commerce was bustling under a blazing equatorial sun. The sidewalks were crowded with vendors. Hundreds of used shoes were carefully laid out on blankets. Shirts, trousers, and backpacks hung from hedges. Fragrant ears of corn roasted on charcoal braziers. Ladies carried impossibly large loads of bananas on their heads. Women constructed dresses and shirts on sewing machines beneath awnings in front of their shops. Bright sparks tumbled into the red dust from a bicycle-pedal-powered knife sharpener.

Shopping was like a scavenger hunt. Iron? Check. Hot water kettle? Check. Canned tuna? Check? Gas tank? She arranged for a shop to deliver one to her house. The mosquito net was the most important item on the list, protection from the nocturnal mosquitoes that spread malaria. A huge variety was available, including pink ones with ruffled canopies. She showed a picture of the hooks on her ceiling to a shopkeeper who recommended a spacious, cuboidal net.

She browsed a souvenir shop—not too early to think about Christmas gifts for folks back home. Shelves were laden with carved wooden animals, T-shirts, and brightly colored placemats.

A grizzled old man called out from the back of the shop. "I have what you need." He waved his arm over a glass case. "Tanzanite. A rare gem found nowhere else in the world." He pulled out a tray laden with a rainbow of glittering stones—mostly varied shades of blue, but also a few pink, green, and even yellow stones. "This one looks like your eyes." He placed an aquamarine sliver in the palm of Sarah's hand. "In the ground, they are just gray pebbles. They only show their true color when exposed to intense heat."

"It's lovely." She handed it back. "But I'm not in the market for jewelry."

"What a pity."

KNOCKING DOWN THE old mosquito net was easy. Just a few strategic pokes with a mop handle. But hanging the new net was a different matter entirely. She didn't have a ladder, so she dragged a desk next to the bed and piled a stack of books on it. Teetering on tiptoe atop the books, leaning, reaching, and biting her lip, she nearly reached the first hook. Nearly. Startled by a beeping cell phone, she tumbled onto the bed, banging her arm against the desk.

It was a text message from David, summoning her to Skype.

There was so much to tell him. The mountain, the babies, the intimidating task of reviewing charts, and of course, her battle with the mosquito net. She carried her laptop from room to room on a virtual tour a tour of her house, ending at the scene of her failed attempt to deploy the new mosquito net.

"Sam, that was stupid. You're lucky you didn't break your neck."

"I know."

"You need a big strong guy to come and fix it for you."

"Hop on the next plane."

"I wish I could. I'll be there in September."

"Just in time for your birthday."

"Turning thirty on top of Kilimanjaro. That will be so cool."

For a few moments, the silence was deafening. Then she said, "I'm trying to think of something else to say. I don't want to hang up."

"You don't need to talk all the time. It's nice just looking at you." He frowned. "But your arm's bleeding."

She grabbed a tissue to wipe the rivulet of blood. "It's just a scrape."

"You should go clean it up."

"Right. And I need to get ready to go out. I'm having dinner with some friends."

"You're not going out on me yet, are you?"

"Nope. I'm the fifth wheel tonight."

IT WASN'T BAD. Just a scrape. She was washing her wound in the kitchen sink when she spotted the headlights of a Land Cruiser pulling into the driveway. Margo hopped out before the car came to a complete stop and rapped on the door.

Sarah called out, "Come on in."

Margo stared at her arm. "What happened?"

"I tried to hang a mosquito net, but I didn't have a ladder. The housekeeper will be here on Monday. I'm hoping she'll take care of it."

"Nonsense. Pieter can do that right now."

He did not need a ladder, just pulled off his shoes and stepped up onto the bed and touched his palms to the ceiling. "Good thing you didn't break your neck." In less than a minute, the net was in place. He leapt onto the floor and took a sweeping bow. "Voila."

Margo adjusted the net to form a diaphanous cube enclosing the bed. "This is how you keep the bugs out. And in the daytime, you can pull it up, like this." She poked the corners of the net through some loops on its side.

"It's an elegant canopy," said Sarah. "I feel like a princess."

Pieter snorted. "What do you know about princesses? You have no royalty in your country."

"Yes, we do." She counted on her fingers, "Sleeping Beauty, Snow White, Pocahontas . . ."

"Cartoons."

"My dad always called me his little princess."

Pieter shrugged. "Perhaps it suits you."

A FULL MOON shone through the jacaranda leaves, casting dappled patterns on the white tablecloths. The scent of gardenias blended with the aroma of roasting meat.

Ameera was already seated at a table with her fiancé, Rasheed, an engineer who worked at his family construction firm.

Sarah shook his hand. "It's nice to have one non-doctor in the group. The conversation won't be doomed to medical stuff."

"I don't mind if you talk about medicine." He beamed at Ameera. "I like hearing about her work. What about your fiancé? Is he a doctor?"

"Yeah. He was supposed to come over here, too, but his funding fell through."

Margo nodded toward Sarah's left hand. "He gave you a beautiful ring."

"It belonged to his grandmother. I think it's a little over the top, but he says he wants me to be well marked."

Margo explained the service at the restaurant. "They'll bring around all kinds of meat and slice it right onto your plate. When you can't eat another bite, you raise this little white flag."

A waiter plopped a sausage onto Sarah's plate.

Pieter chuckled. "They bring the cheaper cuts first—so you'll be full when they bring the tenderloin."

Ameera, not surprisingly, was the first one to raise the flag of surrender. Pieter was the last, after tucking in massive quantities of meat.

Over coffee, Sarah asked for advice on buying a car. "I found a couple of possibilities on the internet."

Rasheed shook his head. "You should look for a car in Arusha. Something with four-wheel drive. But not too big. A Rav4 would be perfect."

"With air-conditioning and automatic transmission," Margo added.

Pieter rolled his eyes. "She is obviously hoping you will let her drive it sometimes." He winked at Sarah.

Margo scowled at Pieter. "My father can help. He has a friend who is a dealer."

Sarah asked Margo what her father did for a living.

"He owns a furniture store. Started out as a carpenter, but now has his own company, ships carved furniture all over the world. He was the first person in our family to go to secondary school. The rest of his family still lives out in the Serengeti. We're Massai."

"Massai?" Sarah had read about the iconic nomadic cattle herders. "Did your father go through warrior training? Killing a lion and all that."

"Killed a lion, got circumcised . . . no anesthesia."

Both men winced.

"You gotta be tough," said Pieter.

"Yes," Margo laughed. "It takes balls to get circumcised."

Ameera gasped, and Sarah choked on her beer.

Pieter chuckled and patted Margo on the back. "Well said, my lady."

Sarah decided to change the subject. "I'd like to go for a hike tomorrow. Can you recommend a trail? Nothing as extreme as Kilimanjaro."

Margo turned to Pieter. "Can we take her up to Marangu? I think she would like the waterfalls."

THE ROAD WOUND its way up the mountain through a lush forest. Marangu was an intersection of two minor roads, with two small shops and a bar, with tables and chairs scattered out front under a yellow and black Tusker Beer pavilion. Road signs painted in crude letters pointed to three different waterfalls. Sarah pointed at a sign that proclaimed in big letters, *This way to the BIG waterfall.* "Is that where we're going?"

Margo scoffed. "That waterfall is dinky. We're going to the one with the lady and the leopard."

Trees and shrubs scraped the sides of the Land Cruiser as they bounced down the deeply rutted road. Sarah kept her jaw slack, so her teeth wouldn't chatter. "Off the beaten path, are we?"

"This is not exactly a major tourist attraction," said Pieter. "Nothing like Victoria Falls or Niagara."

The road ended near a small reception kiosk that flanked the entrance to a steep trail. Margo bounded out and raced down the steps. An attendant rushed out of the kiosk and shouted after her. Pieter spoke to the man in

Swahili and reached into his pocket. Sarah opened her fanny pack. "How much do we pay?"

Pieter waved his hand. "I have this."

The trail dropped precipitously, with multiple switchbacks. Sarah asked Pieter how long it took for him learn Swahili.

"I don't remember. I was only four when we moved here."

"I thought your family lived in Holland."

"They do now." He pointed through the trees. "There. You can see the top of the falls . . . and lady and the leopard."

The wooden statue of a woman was dotted with patches of faded pink and blue paint.

"I don't see a leopard."

"Look to your right."

The large cat was bright yellow with black spots, and big white teeth in a gaping red mouth. Not at all realistic, but the eyes were piercing. "If there's a story that goes with these statues, I need to hear it."

Pieter scratched his head. "As I recall, this young woman was pregnant and unmarried. The punishment would have been severe, so her mother encouraged her to jump off the waterfall."

"How severe?"

"Pretty bad. I think they would run a spear through both her and her lover and leave them staked out in the sun."

"I can see how jumping off a waterfall would be preferable."

"When she got to the top, she was too afraid to jump."

"And the leopard?"

"The leopard crept up on her. When she saw him, she turned to run, but fell over the falls."

"And died?"

"Yes."

"That's not exactly a pleasant little story. Why would they put up anything to commemorate it?"

Pieter shrugged. "Cautionary tale?"

Margo called out, "I'm already down at the falls!"

A narrow waterfall cascaded down a rocky cliff to feed a shallow pool. Margo tried to shove Pieter into the water. He caught his balance, but she fell in, laughing.

He reached down to help her up. "You are such a witch!"

"Who's calling who a witch?" She jerked his arm and he tumbled into the pool.

He stretched out on his back, hands clasped behind his neck "Sarah, you should really join us. The water is nice."

She laid her pack on a flat dry rock and lay down in the cool water, looking up at the walls of the narrow gorge, sheer cliffs densely covered in vegetation. Above was a narrow strip of brilliantly blue sky.

A group of small children descended the cliff effortlessly, like spiders, and jumped into the pool, giggling and sloshing. Pieter slapped the water and sent a huge wave crashing over the children. They screamed and ran away but returned quickly for more. Sarah gazed at the waterfall, the sky, and the pink lady, wondering if she had ever felt happier.

CHAPTER NINE

FRIENDS IN NEED

Ameera felt Sarah's forehead. "You're hot and you look awful. Are you having diarrhea?"

"It's coming out both ends." She had made five trips to the restroom during clinic.

"You should lie down in the back cubicle, where I can keep an eye on you."

Sarah insisted on walking home. Sick as a dog, she intermittently hugged or sat on the toilet until she finally passed out on the bathroom floor. Her cellphone rang, somewhere in the distance.

Ameera's voice woke her up. "You are so sick! Let's get you to bed."

Pieter scooped her up and carried her across the hall. "I'm going to start an IV. Okay?"

She had not felt this sick in a long time, not since she was a little girl. She recalled her bedroom, pale blue with white organdy curtains and a pony-shaped clock with a pendulum for a tail tick-tocked on the wall. She begged for water because her mouth was so dry, but her mother said her tummy was too sick. She wiped Sarah's face and put a damp cloth on her forehead. "Watch the clock. When the big hand is at the top, I will bring you a drink." As soon as her mother left the room, Sarah pulled the cloth from her forehead and sucked out the cool water.

IT WAS DARK outside when she awoke. Pieter was fiddling with her IV.

"Where's Ameera?"

"Rasheed fetched her. Are you feeling better?"

"Yes, but I need to go to the bathroom."

"More diarrhea?"

"No, thank heaven."

"Don't get up too quickly." He held her arm and carried the bag of IV fluid as she walked across the hall. "Do you need me to stay in here with you?"

She would have blushed if she had not been so dehydrated. "I'm okay, thanks. Close the door, please"

A few minutes later, he called out, "I'm not listening."

"Yes, you are, you liar."

"I am only listening for a loud crash in case you fall."

"Then how do you know I haven't peed yet?"

No answer.

"I thought so."

"Maybe you should turn on the tap."

That worked.

Once she was back in bed, he hung another bag of fluid. "You didn't pee much."

"I thought you weren't listening."

"How's your stomach?"

"Still queasy."

"I'll give you some more Zofran."

"That's what zonked me out, eh?"

"Yep. Settles your stomach, helps you sleep." He patted her shoulder. "Sweet dreams."

SHE AWOKE TO sunshine, the smell of coffee, and enough strength to get out of bed.

Pieter sat at the dining table with his laptop. "Good morning. You look much better."

"Thanks."

He pulled out a chair for her. "I made you some tea and soup. I hope you don't mind that I slept on your sofa."

"Not at all. Thanks so much for taking care of me. Maybe it was something I ate."

Pieter bit his lip, trying not to laugh. "It's the *mzungu* scourge. You'll adapt in time."

CHAPTER TEN

SURGERY: A TEAM SPORT

A ribbon of yellow fat billowed in the wake of Ruben's knife as he sliced through the skin, carefully following the line that Margo had etched with the tip of a blade. Sarah followed close behind the scalpel, dabbing up blood and cauterizing oozing vessels. The intern paused to admire his work. Then Margo took over the quest to remove a diseased gall bladder. Ruben's role was reduced to tying off blood vessels. He was not very good yet. An artery squirted his face and Margo chided him. "You should have worn safety glasses. It's lucky the blood didn't get into your eyes."

Sarah showed him a better way to tie. "Loop the suture around twice on the first throw. We call this a surgeon's knot. See? Right over left. The second throw has to be in the opposite direction, left over right, so the knot lies flat and tight. Otherwise, you have a granny knot that won't hold."

Abdominal surgery back home tended to be endoscopic: operations almost became video games. Sarah had not often seen the belly so widely split open and was not accustomed to the work of tugging on retractors, as she and Ruben struggled to keep the liver out of the way. The human liver is much like that of a chicken—albeit much larger—slippery, soft, mottled red-brown. Sarah peered into the wound, trying to see what was going on. "Do you have a self-retaining retractor?"

Margo shook her head.

Sarah turned to the scrub nurse. "Hold my retractor. I want to see what's on the back table."

"Just hold what I gave you," Margo snapped.

Ruben's eyebrows disappeared up under his scrub cap. His lips, behind his surgical mask, were probably pursed into a tight, "Oooh!"

After an awkward silence, Sarah decided to fill the void with some teaching. "This part is very tedious. Margo has to has to seal off the stalk of the gall bladder, without damaging the common bile duct. If that gets obstructed, it's a very bad complication. The liver won't be able to drain." She offered advice to Margo. "You could use a fine right-angle clamp—"

"I am doing this operation, and you are assisting. When you do an operation, I will be happy to help you."

Suddenly the wound filled with blood. After a few tense moments of suctioning and searching, Margo clamped off the bleeding vessel. "Sarah, you should tie this."

It was a narrow space, only wide enough for one hand. Sarah kept tension on the suture with her left hand while the fingers of right created the knot.

Ruben was impressed, "One-handed tie. Very cool."

Margo removed the gall bladder, which looked something like a gray poached egg. Or maybe a testicle. Sarah retired to the doctor's lounge, leaving Margo and Ruben to close the wound.

Pieter poured Sarah a cup of Masala tea, with hot milk and spices. "Today we have a treat: mandazis!"

"What?"

"Mandazis. African doughnuts."

Irregular blobs of dough, no holes in the center, sort of like New Orleans beignets, but without powdered sugar. She took a nibble. "Delicious. Did you sense the tension in the operating room?"

"Dueling alpha females."

"Thanks for not calling it a cat fight."

"I saw no claws."

"I didn't mean to offend her. Guess I got off on the wrong foot."

"It will be fine. She knows she can learn from you."

She took a sip of tea. "How did you wind up here, anyway?"

"I could ask the same thing of you."

She explained how she had gotten a grant to do research in obstetrical mortality, but didn't share her disappointment in the position, or her struggles to get data from medical records. She didn't tell him how foolish she felt, in retrospect, responding to a notice on the internet, accepting a position at this hospital, sight unseen.

He tilted his head. "Research, eh? Me too. I came to study altitude physiology. We compare Kilimanjaro guides to the poor souls that get admitted to the ICU with mountain sickness. Two-year furlough from my university. I've trained technicians to do the testing, so I have time on my hands. I volunteered to help supervise the anesthesia residents."

"So, you're here because of the mountain."

"More accurately, the mountain gave me an excuse to be here. I was homesick for Tanzania."

Margo flopped into a chair. "Ruben's almost finished."

Pieter set down his teacup. "I'll go wake up the patient."

"Will I have to make my own tea?" Margo whined. "I am so disrespected."

Sarah handed her a mandazi. "That was a tough case. Lots of scar tissue."

Margo pulled some leftover sutures from her pocket. "Can you teach me the one-handed tie?"

"Sure."

Pieter winked at Sarah, handed Margo a cup of tea, and left.

Sarah looped the thread around the arm of her chair. "It's sort of second nature now. I'll have to tie one myself first to remember exactly how to do it." She tied one knot very quickly, and then another in slow motion. "You should practice this about a jillion times, until it just flows. My father showed me how to do this when I was a little girl."

"Your father was a surgeon? So, what does he think of you following in his footsteps?"

"He died a few years ago."

"Oh, I'm sorry." Margo practiced a tying a few knots. "I think I have it now."

"Yeah, looks like you've got it. You know, back home we have a surgical skills lab where we practice on models or animals. We should set one up here."

"Great idea. Oh, and I can't believe I almost forgot to tell you this. My father called this morning. He found the perfect car for you. Let's ask Pieter to take us to pick it up."

He was stooped over a patient in the recovery room. Margo pulled his stethoscope from one ear. "My father found a car for Sarah. Can you take us to Arusha on Saturday?"

"Sorry, this is the weekend for my clinic in the mountains."

"Darn it. I forgot. We'll have to take the bus."

"Don't take the bus. Not a good idea for the two of you to drive back by yourselves. Sarah hasn't driven in Tanzania before, and you don't drive much yourself. We can go next week."

Margo pouted. "We'll have to find some other entertainment for the weekend."

Sarah smiled. "I have an idea."

CHAPTER ELEVEN

MOVIE NIGHT

Sarah set her laptop on the coffee table. "I can't believe you guys have never seen *Titanic*! I've lost track of how many times I've seen it."

Margo was skeptical. "What's so great about a shipwreck movie?"

"It's a great love story, too. Fictional, of course."

Ameera called out from the kitchen, "Is it a tragic love story?"

"If I answer that question, I give away the ending."

Margo laughed. "But we already know the ship sank. Besides, you said you kept watching it over and over, and unless you have a very bad memory, you knew the ending after the first time."

"True, but you know how little girls love to keep hearing the same stories again and again."

Ameera sat down between them with a bowl of popcorn. "Fairy tales. Not all of them have happy endings."

They huddled together on the sofa, focused on the small screen. When Leonardo de Caprio's character showed up in a borrowed tuxedo, Margo though he had "cleaned up well."

Ameera said, "All men look lovely in formal wear."

At the movie's end, Margo was perplexed. "Why did she throw away the necklace?"

Ameera had tears in her eyes. "She found her one true love and lost him."

Margo pointed out that Rose had a granddaughter in this movie. "Obviously, she got on pretty well with someone else."

Sarah refilled Margo's wine glass. "You're not very romantic. Don't you believe in one true love?"

"How can there be just one person for each of us? Look at how many people there are in the world. What kind of magic would it take for each of us to find that one person?"

"What if we're hard-wired to expect 'one true love'?" Sarah mused. "And once we fill that slot, we can't feel the same about someone else?"

Margo stared at her wine glass. "Maybe we don't want to feel so strongly about another one because that would make the first one less special."

"I think my mother felt that way about my father," said Sarah. "Since he died, she's had no interest in any other man."

Ameera asked, "How did your father die?"

"Pancreatic cancer. Kind of ironic. He was a big Whipple surgeon. You know what that is, right?"

Margo nodded. "Big operation to take out the pancreas."

"Many of his patients died anyway after suffering for months. So he refused any treatment. He and my mom went on a trip around the world while he still felt good."

Ameera pointed at the computer. "Back to this movie. Why didn't Rose want to marry the man her mother picked out?"

Sarah shook her head. "Duh! Because she didn't love him."

"Arranged marriages can be very successful."

"But would you want to marry someone your parents picked? Instead of marrying Rasheed?"

Ameera pursed her lips.

Margo laughed. "Sarah, how do you think she met Rasheed?"

"It's an arranged marriage?"

"I don't have to marry Rasheed. Our parents arranged for us to meet, and we liked each other. Actually, there are fewer divorces with arranged marriages than with love marriages."

"What about your people, Margo? Do the Massai have arranged marriages?"

"In the past, fathers sold their daughters. Got paid in cows! Not so much now."

"So, you could marry Pieter?"

"Ha! Pieter is just a friend. Like a brother. Besides, my father would never let me marry a *mzungu*."

"Mah-zoon-ga?"

"It is a term for a white person," said Ameera. "Not a very polite term, I'm sad to say. Tell us about your fiancée. What is he like?"

"David? I can show you some pictures." Sarah pulled up photos on her laptop. "Here we are at medical school graduation. And here he is holding my cat." She enlarged the image for a close-up view of his face.

Ameera touched Sarah's shoulder. "You miss him very much."

"Yes, I do."

"Is he your one and only?"

"I've never had another boyfriend."

Margo said, "Then he is, by definition."

THERE HAD NEVER been a romantic proposal from David, simply a tacit understanding, evolved over time, that they would eventually marry. The wedding was always a mirage sparkling on a desert highway, continually evaporating and then reappearing in the distance.

Shortly before Sarah left for Africa, David's parents came for a visit. As they were leaving, his mother slipped a small box into David's pocket. He showed the box to Sarah later, as she was brushing her teeth. "What do you think this is?"

"Maybe cuff-winks?" Her voice was muffled by tooth-paste foam.

He opened the box. "Oh . . . shit . . . I don't believe this."

Sarah rinsed out her mouth, tapped her toothbrush on the sink.

He pulled a ring from the box. "This was my grand-mother's. I guess, um, I'm supposed to give this to you." He smiled and slipped the ring onto her finger. "Do you like it?"

"It's beautiful," she whispered.

"We should get married when you come home."

"Next July."

"That would be cool. This is actually great timing. With this ring, you'll be well marked when you go to Africa."

CHAPTER TWELVE

FACING FEAR

Margo was oblivious to the hair-raising traffic, sitting sideways in the front seat and chattering non-stop. The painted line was a mere suggestion for cars, motorcycles, bicycles, mini-buses, huge transport trucks, large motor coaches, safari vehicles, and donkey carts. Sarah covered her eyes in terror as an oncoming minibus overtaking a tractor trailer swerved into their path. Pieter braked sharply to avert a collision.

Sarah uncovered her eyes. "Pieter, you have nerves of steel."

Margo punched his shoulder. "Macho man. Fears nothing."

He jerked his shoulder. "Do not assault the driver."

Sarah sighed. "I hope the traffic isn't this bad tomorrow."

Pieter glanced in the mirror. "Sundays are much quieter. And we'll leave early."

"Most of the casualties happen late at night." Margo stated this with great authority. "Drunk, crazy drivers who can't see where they are going in the dark. A few months ago, there was a terrible crash. So many bad fractures that we used up every single bone plate and screw in the hospital."

The landscape was flat and arid, the air hot and dusty, and the distant mountains were barely visible through the haze. Traffic halted for a herd of livestock crossing the road. Two little boys with their plaid shukas flapping in the wind waved their staffs at forty or so perky brown goats and five scrawny Brahma cows. Three donkeys brought up the rear.

"Those boys look young to be herding," said Sarah. "It must be dangerous."

Margo nodded. "It is. My mother knew a boy who was nearly crushed by a snake. It was after one of his goats. He grabbed the goat and climbed a tree, but the snake still got him." She made two fists and twisted them together to demonstrate.

"Did the little boy die?"

"No. He was sitting in a tree, so the branches kept him from being squished."

"We'll show you some of those snakes," said Pieter. "At the snake park."

Sarah shivered, "I kind of hate snakes."

The last donkey crossed the road, and they continued their journey until a policeman stepped into the road and raised a big stick. He looked something like an ice cream man, in a spotless white short-sleeved uniform and a white cap with a black bill.

"What's wrong?" Sarah asked.

"Random stops," said Margo. "They check for driving license and required equipment."

Pieter opened his window and greeted the officer pleasantly. "*Shikamo*, Papa."

The policeman studied the windshield of the car for a moment. Then he raised his stick and waved them on.

"Why did he let us go?"

"Doctor sticker." Pieter pointed to a decal on the windshield.

"What equipment are you supposed to have?"

Margo counted items on her fingers. "A first aid kit, a fire extinguisher, and a hazard symbol to put out on the road if you break down. Don't worry. They will already be in your car."

Pieter tapped on the windshield. "We have one of these stickers for you."

MARGO'S FATHER WAITED in front of the car dealership, stone-faced. He had the tall, lean physique of a Massai warrior, but instead of shuka, he wore a plaid Ralph Lauren sport shirt and beige linen pants. When he spotted Pieter's car, his face cracked into a broad smile and he waved both hands in the air. Margo leapt out before the car came to full stop and ran to hug her father.

Pieter switched off the ignition. "What is the name of that toy with a crank that you turn until the funny guy pops out?"

"You mean a Jack-in-the-box?"

"Yes, that's it. She is a Jack-in-the-box."

The eight-year-old Rav4 gleamed with a fresh coat of metallic blue-green paint. Mr. Ledama had taken the car on a test drive and pronounced the vehicle to be in fine shape. He started the engine while Pieter peered under the hood and gave his approval.

MARGO RODE WITH her father in his Lexus SUV, Sarah followed in the Rav, and Pieter brought up the rear. Mr.

Ledama honked his horn at a red metal gate and a shuka clad guard let them in. A tree tree-lined driveway ended at a rambling cream-colored house with a red tile roof. Margo's mother stood in the driveway, wiping her hands on her apron. Her broad face beamed as Margo bounded out of the car.

As they walked toward the house, Pieter winked at Sarah. "What did I tell you? Jack-in-the-Box."

Mrs. Ledama smothered Pieter in a bear hug, then clasped Sarah's hands. "Thank you for buying this car, so that my children come to see me. Lunch is ready. You girls go freshen up."

In Margo's room, Sarah said "Your parents really seemed to like Pieter. I thought your father didn't like *mzungus*."

"I didn't say he doesn't like *mzungus*. He just doesn't want me to marry one. I'm supposed to marry a Massai." She frowned. "Why should I have to get married anyway? Why should I let some guy always tell me what to do?"

"Good question."

"Does your fiancée tell you what to do?"

"David? All the time. But I don't always listen to him. He didn't want me to come here."

"You came here anyway? Seriously, you are some strong woman." Margo sat down on the bed and stared out the window. "The funny thing is . . . no real Massai man would have me."

"Why not?"

"I did not get cut."

"You mean . . . circumcised?"

"They cut you when you are about eleven or twelve years old. But my mother would not let them do it to me."

"I thought it was illegal."

"It is. But they do it secretly. And . . . " Margo paused, raised her eyebrows for dramatic effect and whispered, "They do this to babies."

"Why would anyone do something so horrible?"

"They say it makes us better wives. What they really mean is that if we don't enjoy sex, we won't fool around."

LUNCH WAS SERVED in the garden among bougainvillea and hummingbirds. Monkeys scampered along the top of the brick wall. Sarah had heard that Massai only ate things that came from cows—meat, blood mixed into milk. But Mrs. Ledama had prepared a bountiful feast of typical Tanzanian fare: pilau rice with goat meat, chapatis, and bananas.

When she couldn't eat another bite, Sarah leaned back in her chair and patted her belly. "That was wonderful. I could use a siesta."

"Maybe a short one," said Margo. "Then we go to the snake park."

"WAKE UP. SARAH! Time to go."

Sarah kept her eyes tightly shut and tried to breathe slowly and deeply.

Margo pounced on the bed. "I know you're awake."

"I don't like snakes."

"Ha! I thought you were a strong woman. You have to face your fears."

×

PIETER PLUNKED DOWN on a bench beside an attractive young lady in a snake park uniform. "Go on the tour without me. June and I have something to discuss."

June punched him playfully in the shoulder. "Yeah, he already knows all that snake stuff."

Margo rolled her eyes. "You and your snakes." Then she murmured to Sarah, "And his ladies." She explained to Sarah that Pieter had always liked to hang out at the snake park when he was a boy. "He was a volunteer snake handler."

The first glass case housed a huge python, its head hidden somewhere deep within its coils. A photograph displayed on the glass showed a similar large snake slashed open, with a dead man inside.

Sarah shuddered. "I hope I never run into a snake like that."

"Don't worry," said the guide. "This man was asleep—probably drunk."

His explanation provided meager comfort. Snakes in the next few cages seemed less threatening, even beautiful. One case seemed vacant at first glance. The bright green snake was nearly invisible, coiled up in a corner beneath some leaves.

Margo tapped lightly on the glass. "Green mamba. I found one like this in our bathroom, once, hiding behind the toilet."

"I wish you hadn't told me that."

"That was a long time ago. We haven't had a snake in our house in years."

A long black snake dangled from a tree branch in the next cage. "This is black mamba," said the guide. "Deadliest snake in Africa. Green mamba is bad, but he is shy. Black mamba is not shy. He will chase you. And he can jump very far, very fast."

Two men in Massai garb peered into the case. Sarah observed, quietly, that they did not look like tourists.

"They look for a snake like the one that bit their brother," said the guide. "Then our clinic will know what antivenom he needs."

There was a Massai cultural museum on the park grounds: a series of life-sized tableaux that coiled its way through a long, lumpy, dark, low-ceilinged building. The first room showed how Massai built their cow dung houses and used thorns bushes to build fences.

Sarah pointed at an exhibit of bloodletting from a cow. "That's what I was afraid your mother would feed me."

"Ha! She has lived in the city too long for that."

In another scene, a woman was seated on the ground with legs spread apart, two women kneeling on either side.

"Are they delivering a baby?"

"No, this is the cutting ceremony. Mom says the worst pain was afterwards. They kept pouring alcohol on her. It was Pieter's mother who saved me from this. She convinced my mother not to let them cut me."

"Pieter's mother? Sounds like you've known Pieter a long time."

"As long as I can remember."

Outside, the sunlight was blinding. Margo pointed to some camels near the museum exit. "Want to go for a ride?"

"No, I'd rather see the clinic."

It was just a tiny office with two small exam rooms. June, the young woman in the snake park uniform, was helping Pieter change the dressing on a little boy with a grossly swollen leg.

Margo peered over Pieter's shoulder. "So, this is the real reason you wanted to come to here."

"They called early this morning. Bad infection. I think he will need a skin graft."

"Can they transport him to NTMC?" asked Margo

"I'll take him myself. He's too sick to wait. June will come with me. I called your father to come and pick you up."

As Pieter's car pulled away, Sarah felt a twinge of anxiety, facing the prospect of driving home without an escort.

SHE NEED NOT have worried. In the morning, Pieter strolled into the Ledama kitchen.

Margo looked up from toast and marmalade. "You must have gotten up pretty early."

"How's the little boy?" Sarah asked.

"In the ICU. He's stable."

In the hall outside the kitchen, Sarah noticed an old photograph on the wall. It was a group shot, in the same garden where they had lunched the day before. Younger versions of Margo's parents stood next to a white couple, and three children sat on the lawn in front of them. One of them was a little boy with white hair and an impish grin. "That has to be Pieter." Sarah pointed to the little girl. "Is that you?"

"Yes, I was three years old."

"What brought them to Tanzania?"

"Pieter's father was a banking consultant. Tanzania was moving from communism to an open economy. Our mothers were best friends."

Mrs. Ledama looked out from the kitchen. "And we still are. We met when my husband built them a dining table. They must have loved the table, because Pieter's father helped get a loan to start his business."

"Who's the other boy?"

"My son." Mrs. Ledama sighed deeply and turned back into the kitchen.

Margo murmured, "He . . . passed away. Road accident."

It was a beautiful day for Sarah's first drive in Africa: bright blue skies with occasional puffy white clouds. Margo was in charge of the radio and found a channel with African pop. Automotive traffic was light. Most people were on foot, on their way to church, men and boys in white starched shirts, ladies in multi-colored kitangas, and little girls in pastel organdy.

Halfway home, Pieter passed them and motioned for Sarah to turn off at the next gas station.

He had noticed that her left rear tire was low. "I'll put in some air. When we get home, I'll take it over to the Oryx station to check for a leak."

Sarah watched him in the rearview mirror. "He's such a nice guy."

"Yes indeed," said Margo. "Eva doesn't deserve him."

CHAPTER THIRTEEN

FATE AND FATALITY

The clinic nurse greeted Sarah. "*Shikamo*, Mama."

"*Jambo*, Teddy." Sarah knew that "jambo" meant "hi," while "mambo" meant "What's up?"

Teddy peered over the top of her glasses. "When I say '*Shikamo*, Mama,' it shows I respect you. You should say '*mara habba*.' Did you forget?"

"Yes, I forgot."

"Then say it. Say *mara habba*."

"*Mara habba*."

"Very good, *mzuri*."

"I'm trying to learn Swahili. I know that *pole* means slow."

"No. *Pole* means sorry."

"But doesn't *pole, pole* mean go slowly?"

"Aahh." Teddy lifted her chin and raised her eyebrows. "*Pole, pole* means slow, but *pole* means sorry." She raised both hands with her palms facing Sarah. "*Shikamo*, Mama."

"*Mara habba*."

"Good, good. It is important for you to learn this. Mothers teach their children to be polite, to say *shikamo* to elders. If elders do not respond, what does this say to the children?"

"I see your point."

The first patient of the day had dangerously high blood pressure. And her tendon reflexes were super brisk. One finger tapped oh-so-gently under the kneecap sent the woman's foot slamming into Sarah's chest. A quick dipstick test of the patient's urine was positive for protein. Toxemia.

Sarah asked Teddy to explain the plan to the patient. "Tell her we need to keep her in the hospital. We'll induce labor."

"She knows this. A midwife in her village checked her blood pressure and told her to come to the hospital."

Ameera peered in from the next cubicle. "You mean a tribal midwife? It's quite unusual that a TBA would take blood pressure."

Teddy nodded. "This is what she said."

"Don't they learn it in school?" asked Sarah.

"They don't go to school," said Ameera. "They learn traditional methods from other midwives. We call them TBA's—traditional birth attendants. They probably deliver half the babies in Tanzania, especially in rural areas. This woman is very fortunate that someone checked her blood pressure. It probably saved her life."

A less fortunate woman was brought to the emergency room later that day, feverish and in a coma. She had an abortion by a tribal healer after her husband was killed in a road accident. She had two young daughters and could not cope with the prospect of another baby. When the local healer's treatment failed, and she was brought to the hospital.

She died two days later, despite intensive medical and surgical treatment. Sarah was charged with the sad task of speaking to the family. The sister was waiting in the courtyard, sitting on the grass, her own infant strapped to her back and her two nieces huddled against her. She did not look up when she heard the news—just stared into space and wailed.

SARAH COULD NOT sleep that night, haunted by the vision of the newly orphaned girls. Shortly before dawn, she called David.

A woman answered. "Dr. Segal's phone."

Sarah was silent. The woman spoke again. "Dr. Segal's phone. Who's calling please?"

"Dr. Whitaker—Sarah Whitaker."

"Dave, I think it's your girlfriend."

Sarah could hear his footsteps, and then his voice. "Sam, what's up? Are you okay?"

"Yes. I mean . . . not really. I just feel like—I don't know what I'm doing here. I should never have come."

"You're homesick?"

"No. I mean, yeah, I am, but . . . it's more than that."

"So, tell me."

"I shouldn't be bothering you. You're probably busy. Are you at the hospital?"

"I'm in the lab. But I'm here for you."

She pictured him in his long white lab coat and safety glasses, perhaps clutching a flask full of some cloudy fluid. "I'm just wasting my time here," she said. "I'll never get any research done."

"You're only there for a year. And it's a training position, right? Sounds like you're learning a lot."

"So many patients are already doomed before they get to the hospital. Even if we do everything right once they are here. Like the woman who died today from sepsis."

"You lost a patient? That's tough."

"What's tough is that it's not at all unusual for a patient to die. I don't know what's harder. Seeing a baby die, or seeing children left without a mother."

"You can always come home."

It was true. She had not let herself acknowledge this until she heard him speak the words.

"Sam, did you hear me?"

"Yes." She wished she could beam herself across the lands and ocean, like a signal bouncing off a satellite to land safely in his arms and never ever leave again.

"We can talk about it when I come over. It won't be long, now."

A voice in the background called out, "Dave, the timer just went off. Time to neutralize the slides."

"Gotta go now. Do you want me to call you later?"

"No. It's okay. I'm better now. It really helped to hear your voice."

CHAPTER FOURTEEN

EQUANIMITAS

P rincess, your patient awaits." Pieter took a deep bow, sweeping his arm toward the door of operating room number one. "And should her highness require any further assistance, I will be in the next room."

"What's going on in there?"

"Ruben is doing a tracheotomy."

"Alone? Is he ready for that?"

"I think so. He's done two with Margo. This one seems rather straightforward."

Sarah's patient had an umbilical hernia: an extreme "outie" belly button, everted and pooched out, like a little water balloon. It looked cute, but if not repaired, the bowel could become trapped in it. Worst case scenario, the little boy would die. A simple operation would prevent that from ever happening.

The surgery went smoothly, and Sarah was just beginning to close the wound, when someone opened the door. "Dr. Pieter say you come. STAT!"

She told the anesthetist to keep the child asleep. "I'll be back as soon as I can."

The room next door was in chaos, everyone was yelling and flailing about. Except Pieter, sitting at the head of the bed. He glanced at Sarah. "Chest tubes, please. Now."

Ruben was paralyzed, eyes bulging.

She snapped on sterile gloves. "Which side?"

"Both."

"Check. I'll start on the right."

She scrubbed the skin on the upper chest and threw some towels around the site, then probed to count the ribs.

Ruben looked over her shoulder as she popped the tube into the chest. "Is pneumothorax a complication of a tracheotomy?"

She snorted. "Hmmph. Ya think?"

Pieter cleared his throat loudly. His eyebrows knotted together above his face mask in disapproval. She should be teaching Ruben, not mocking him.

She sighed. "Let me show you how to secure this." She put a heavy suture in the skin and wrapped it around the tube several times. "We call this a Roman sandal tie. If you pull on the tube, the stitch holds even tighter—kind of like Chinese handcuffs."

Pieter gave a thumbs up. "O2 sat is better already."

She told Ruben that he would be putting in the tube on the other side and grilled him, "What is a pneumothorax?"

"Air in the space around the lung."

"And why is that bad?"

"Because the lung collapses."

She tapped on the man's chest. "We'll place the tube up here, because air rises and collects above the lung."

Ruben nodded and cut through the skin.

"Now feel with your finger to find the space between the ribs."

Ruben poked the tube through the chest wall and tied it into place.

"Tell me why we would ever want to put a tube down here." She pointed to a spot on the on the lower rib cage.

"If there was fluid in the chest—like blood or pus."

"Right." She patted him on the back. "Let's go next door. You can close up the skin on my hernia case."

SARAH HAD A cup of tea and mandazi waiting for Pieter in the lounge. "I was mean to Ruben. Thank you for reminding me to teach."

"It's understandable. His question irritated you."

"They say there's no such thing as a stupid question. But when you have the privilege of doing an operation, you have a responsibility to know the potential complications. Ruben wasn't prepared."

"But there are so few doctors here. And so much need. We are obliged to do our best with what we have to offer."

"I guess being a coach to surgeons is part of the anesthesiologist's job description?"

He chuckled. "Yes, and I must say it is very challenging."

"What made you decide to go into anesthesia?"

"At first, I wanted to be a surgeon. I even took one year of surgery training."

"And you changed because?"

"I learned that even if you do a great job, it's no good if the patient does not wake up."

"Good point. 'The operation was a success, but the patient died.' That's an old cliché."

"Exactly."

"I guess if I weren't here, you could have put the tubes in."

"Not as nicely and quickly as you did. You're a good surgeon. You're efficient and you don't waste motion. You decide quickly what needs to be done and take control of the situation."

"Thanks."

"By the way, Margo tells me I am invited to see a movie at your house tonight."

"Yeah, we need someone to bring a pizza."

"I am honored by such a gracious invitation."

"Ameera heads to Arusha tomorrow to get ready for her wedding. So, it's kind of like a bachelorette party. We'll pretend that you're one of the girls."

CHAPTER FIFTEEN

AMEERA'S WEDDING

Margo sifted through Sarah's DVD's of classic movies. "Okay ladies, shall we watch *Dirty Dancing*?" Ameera raised her chin and sat up primly. "That doesn't sound appropriate for a pre-wedding party. How about *Pretty Woman*?"

Sarah chuckled, "That one is about a prostitute."

Ameera frowned.

Margo picked up another disc. "*The Hangover*?"

"Definitely not that one," said Sarah.

Ameera leaned back on the sofa. "We could always watch *Titanic* again."

Margo shook her head. "Not a chance. I want to see something I haven't seen before. How about *Ghost*?"

"Oh, I love that movie!" Sarah exclaimed. "But it's sad."

Ameera sighed. "Another tragic love story."

"But it has a hopeful message."

The movie began sweetly: a happy couple deeply in love. But the man could not bring himself to say, "I love you." He just said "ditto" whenever the woman said that she loved him.

Ameera thought it was sad and stupid, but Sarah told her

it was important to the story line. "It'll become obvious later."

A record player started playing "Unchained Melody." The ballad about being far away from home brought tears to Sarah's eyes.

Margo guffawed out loud. "An old-fashioned record player with a needle. How old is this movie?"

Ameera shrieked when the man in the movie was shot. Pieter was just coming through the door and almost dropped the pizzas. Margo rescued the boxes and set them on the table. "Which one is pepperoni?" she asked.

Ameera was nearly sobbing. "I thought you said there was a hopeful message in this movie. Why couldn't he tell her he loved her?"

Pieter chuckled, "Because she would insist on getting married. Maybe he just wanted to have a little fun."

Margo grabbed a pillow from the sofa and began to beat Pieter around the head.

AMEERA'S WEDDING CEREMONY was held at a private club just outside of Arusha, under a large tent with a partition down the middle, creating separate seating spaces for men and women. The platform where the wedding would take place was visible from both sides. Rasheed and some other men took positions on the dais, and the ceremony began. Ameera was nowhere in sight.

A little girl, one of Ameera's cousins, found Sarah and Margo and beckoned them to follow her to a room inside the clubhouse. The bride, resplendent in a beautiful gown and headdress, sat between her mother and future mother-in-law, watching the ceremony through a large window. Sound was piped into a speaker.

After a number of speeches and readings, Ameera's mother announced, "Now she is married!"

AS THEY HEADED back from Arusha, Sarah asked if that had been a fairly typical Tanzanian wedding.

"No such thing," said Margo. "There are so many different religions and tribes and traditions in this country."

Pieter glanced in the rearview mirror. "For example, that was a Muslim Indian wedding. If it had been a Hindu Indian wedding, there would have been dancing, and we would have terrible hangovers this morning."

"Hangovers?" Margo shook her head. "I've never seen you that drunk."

"Have you ever seen me at a Hindu wedding?"

"No. Have you ever been to one?"

"Yes," he said. "When I was thirteen. And yes, I got a terrible hangover."

"I guess that's why you got shipped off to school in Amsterdam."

"It may have been a factor."

Sarah asked Margo what a typical Massai wedding would be like.

"Remember what I told you about the cows?"

"Oh, yeah."

"But my parents got married in a church. They met in a Christian mission school."

"So, no cows involved?"

"Cows were involved, but it was complicated. They wanted to get married, but her father had promised her to someone else, had already been paid in cows. She ran away to the mission, and they protected her until she could marry my dad."

"What happened to the cows?"

"Somehow cattle changed hands. I'm fuzzy on the details, but my father claims he had to pay a lot for my mom."

"So, you would get married in a church?"

"*If* I ever got married, which I am not going to do."

"I've seen a lot of wedding parades around town," said Sarah. "Decorated cars and pickup trucks carrying brass bands. We don't have that in the States. Is it a tribal custom?"

"Those bands are stupid." Margo folded her arms. "I would never have one at my wedding."

"Let me get this straight," said Pieter. "You are never going to get married, and yet you feel compelled to harangue us with your disgust for the type of wedding you would not have."

"I'm just expressing my opinion." She tugged on Pieter's earlobe.

"Don't assault the driver. Do you want us all to wind up in the Casualty Department? Or the morgue?"

"Wouldn't that be embarrassing?"

"Yes, we would be mortified."

Margo poked Pieter in the shoulder. "So, when are *you* getting married? You and Eva?"

"You're tormenting the driver again."

"And you are not answering me."

Pieter did not smile. "We have no plans."

Margo leaned over the back seat and said, in a stage whisper, "I think he has some commitment issues."

CHAPTER SIXTEEN

URGENCY TRUMPS IMPORTANCE

R ain. Not the gentle rain that Shakespeare compared to the "quality of mercy." This was an unrelenting deluge—as if someone dumped a big tub of water over the side of a roof.

It had been bright and sunny when Sarah walked out of the hospital. Then the skies opened, and she sought cover in the bus stop shelter. On most days, this was a popular refuge from the equatorial sun. In this downpour, it was definitely oversubscribed—damp smelly bodies huddled together and small children overshadowed by adults looming over them. No one tried to speak above the deafening din of rain on the metal roof.

After a while, it was clear that the rain was not going to let up any time soon, and Sarah gently elbowed her way out of the crowd. No one objected to letting her pass by, but they all looked at her as if she were crazy to be going out in that rain.

In an instant, she was completely soaked, and her sandals sloshed all the way home. The air in the house was heavy and the oppressive rain intensified the loneliness and isolation that had eaten at her spirits all day. Ameera was still on her honeymoon, so Sarah was alone in clinic all day, every day. Plus, Margo was away at a conference in Dar es Salaam.

She sat down with her laptop to check her email. She missed her cat, even though he had an annoying habit of plopping down on top of her keyboard, shedding his fur among the keys. Sometimes, she could almost hear Whiskers calling to her. In fact, she heard some muffled meows right then, coming from her porch. When she opened the door a flash of wet, spiky, orange and white fur streaked past her.

In that same moment, her cellphone rang. Not a text— an actual phone call.

David blurted out, "Incoming Skype." Then he hung up. He believed that if you ended the call in less than five seconds, there would be no charge. Sarah did not think this was true, but it was not worth arguing.

The cat was not in sight, but a trail of muddy footprints led into the kitchen, up onto the counter, and then down the hall toward her bedroom. There was no time to go searching for the cat, what with the incoming Skype and all. She opened a can of tuna and put it on the floor of the kitchen. If the cat were lured into the kitchen, then she could close the door and trap him.

Why would call David now?

They usually spoke on Saturday afternoon, and this was Thursday.

The bubbling booping of Skype on her computer commanded her to sit.

"Hey, Sam."

"Nice to see you. Not our usual time."

"I know, but . . ." A puzzled look flashed across his face. "Was that a cat I just saw?"

The cat was back in the kitchen, chowing down on tuna. She slammed the door. "I don't know where this cat came from. He just showed up about the same time you called. He disappeared somewhere inside the house, so I laid a tuna trap to lure him into the kitchen."

"You know you shouldn't feed stray cats. You'll never get rid of 'em."

"I know, but I wanted to get him cornered. Besides, I like the idea of having him around. It gets lonely at night. Anyway, what's up?"

"Well . . . umm . . . " He shifted uncomfortably in his seat.

"Remember what we decided? Look at the camera while talking, and at the screen when listening."

He looked toward the general vicinity of the camera. "Sam, I can't come."

"Can't come? Why not?"

"Well, you know, Dr. Cook is submitting a renewal application for his grant."

"Umm-hmm." She did not know that, but she was not surprised. Researchers continually struggle for funding.

"He needs me to finish my paper, so he can submit it with the application. The paper's essentially done, but we need to duplicate the results. You know, in molecular work they always want all the tests run twice."

"I didn't know that."

"Well, they do. Anyway, I needed to run those gels and blots today, but we don't have the kits. Carla forgot to re-order them."

"Carla?"

"The lab tech."

A woman with auburn curls leaned in front of David's face. "I'm Carla. And I am *so* sorry."

"Why can't someone else run the tests?"

"I'm the first author. It's my paper. Besides, I ran all the others tests and we need to have everything exactly the same."

"I see." Her stony face clearly said that she did not understand.

"Sarah, this is my career. It's a really important paper."

He never calls me Sarah. I'm always Sam.

"So just change your flight. Come a few days later."

"I tried that, and wow, the price really jumps up when you change a ticket, especially this close to departure."

"But you will come, right? In a few more weeks?"

"I'll take a look at the call schedule. But it's a very busy year . . ."

She stared out the window.

"Sam, are you okay?"

"I'll survive."

"Okay, then here's what I need you to do." He waggled his index finger, as if commanding a dog to sit. "You need to contact the safari company and the mountain guide and see about getting our money back. I know there were some cancellation policies on the reservations, but I can't quite remember."

"Can't you do that online? That's where you booked the tours."

He waved toward the flasks and beakers on the lab bench behind him. "I'm swamped right now."

She wanted to run out of the house and scream, but she

knew she would just get soaked again. It was too dark to see the rain, but she could feel the sound of the monsoon on the roof.

"Sam, did you hear me?"

She was tempted to shut off the computer and text him to say that the connection failed. That would be immature and spiteful.

"I heard you. I'll take care of things."

"Great. And I'm really sorry. Gotta go right now. Skype again on Saturday?"

"Okay."

"I love you, Sam."

Sarah forced a smile and shut down the computer. Then she went into the kitchen to check on this cat.

CHAPTER SEVENTEEN

ANTIDOTE FOR SORROW

The sky was cloudless. The air was cool, and the rain had settled the dust. A fresh blanket of snow atop Kilimanjaro sparkled in the morning light. Sarah resolved to stop feeling sorry for herself and focus on this lovely day. David didn't cancel his visit, it was just postponed.

The clinic waiting room was overflowing, but most of the women were healthy, just here for routine checks. Only one patient was worrisome. Her belly was huge, as if she could deliver twins at any minute. But Sarah heard only one fetal heartbeat and an ultrasound confirmed only one fetus. The womb was massively distended by way too much fluid. "Polyhydramnios," Sarah said, almost to herself.

"What is that?" asked Teddy.

"The baby isn't swallowing any of the fluid. There's a blockage somewhere."

Dr. Obaye frowned when Sarah showed him the ultrasound. "There is a large mass on his neck. We need to do a caesarian section now, before she goes into labor."

"You mean, an EXIT procedure."

"Exactly."

The small thin woman lay on the operating table, struggling to breathe under the weight of her distended abdomen. Pieter explained the EXIT procedure to the two anesthesia residents, Ben and Stephen. "She has to be deeply anesthetized, so that the surgery won't induce labor. The baby needs oxygen through the umbilical cord until we make sure he has an airway."

As Sarah slathered orange-brown antiseptic solution over the belly, Dr. Obaye said, "Better go scrub. You're doing this case."

She paused for a moment, sponge stick poised in midair. "I've never done a C-section before. Only assisted."

Pieter chuckled through his mask. "Don't be ridiculous. You cut into the belly all the time—gall bladders and whatnot."

A gush of sour smelling fluid erupted from the womb as Sara sliced into it and extracted the tiny boy, still attached to the spirally lilac/gray umbilical cord, like an astronaut doing a spacewalk. But the baby was hideously deformed. There was a huge purplish blob where the head should have been. A shocked silence fell over the room. It was a hemangioma, essentially a birthmark on steroids, totally covering the scalp and face. A pediatrician tried to pass a breathing tube through the baby's mouth, but only succeeded in stirring up brisk bleeding. Pieter could not get a tube in either.

Time for a tracheotomy. All eyes turned to Sarah.

Fortunately, the skin on the neck was normal. There was a sudden rushing sound as she opened the windpipe and the baby drew his first breath. She slipped in a tube. The pediatrician listened to the baby's chest and gave a "thumbs up" sign.

Sarah packed gauze into the baby's mouth to staunch

the bleeding. To her amazement, he began sucking on her finger. Just like a normal baby.

The pediatrician said, "He's neurologically normal, but he won't survive. There's so much blood flowing through the malformation—too much for his little heart to handle. He'll be dead by morning."

Even in the most advanced medical center in the world, there was nothing that could be done for a problem like this.

Sarah assumed that the patients in the clinic would have given up and gone home. But everyone was still there, and no one complained about the wait. It was long after dark by the time she finished seeing the last patient and went to the nursery to check on the baby with the hemangioma. But he was nowhere in sight. The desk clerk waved her arm toward a dark corner of the room. "He is behind that screen,"

"Are the parents with him?"

The clerk shook her head. "They do not want to see him."

The infant was alone in his agony, kicking his legs and waving his arms. His whole body contorted with his voiceless sobs—wails that no one could hear because the air was escaping from the tube in his neck, rather than flowing through his voice box. Sarah picked him up and held him close. He stopped crying and turned his head toward her breast. Rooting reflex. He was hungry.

She carefully removed the packing from his mouth The bleeding had stopped. She sat down with the baby in a vacant rocking chair and called for one of the nurses to bring her a bottle of sugar water. The baby fed hungrily, and when had his fill, he fell asleep.

So did Sarah.

✕

SHE WAS STARTLED awake by Pieter's hand on her shoulder. "I'm afraid the baby has passed away." He picked up the infant gently and handed him to a nurse. "It's late, Sarah. Did you bring your car to the hospital?"

"No, I walked."

"You shouldn't walk home in the dark. I'll drive you home." He pulled out his cell phone and looked at an incoming text. "I have to go and check on a patient, but it won't take me long. Just wait here."

The nurse wrapped the infant's body in a green cloth and took it to the morgue. Sarah rocked in silence, until tears threatened to well up in her eyes and she could no longer stand to stay in the room. In the cool dark hallway, she tried to breathe normally.

Pieter found her. "I was afraid you'd left without me."

"No." She sniffed. "It was just too warm in the nursery."

She bowed her head to hide her tears as they walked out to the parking lot.

After a few steps, he draped an arm around her shoulders. "It's okay to cry."

She collapsed onto his chest, her sobs soaking the front of his shirt.

She gradually regained her composure and stepped back. Pieter wiped her face with his shirt tail. "Sorry. I don't have a handkerchief."

"No one," her voice was interrupted by two agonal sobs, "carries a handkerchief anymore."

He laughed softly, "Well, maybe I am old fashioned. I usually do. I just gave it away."

"To whom?"

"The mother of that baby. Think about it. If you give a paper tissue to someone who's crying, they blow their noses and toss the tissue. But if you give them a handkerchief . . . they might keep it. Maybe remember someone cared."

"Do you go through a lot of handkerchiefs?"

"My mother keeps me well supplied—every birthday and Christmas."

"Monogrammed?"

"Sometimes. One time, she gave me some with little leopards on them."

Sarah laughed. "You have a thing about leopards?"

"I used to have one as a pet."

"What? You had a—"

"Don't ever walk home alone at night. You and Margo. You're just alike. Think you're indestructible. Anytime you need a ride home, you should call me. I just live two doors down from you."

When they reached Sarah's house, he reached for her cellphone. He typed a short message and handed it back to her. "I just texted you, so now you have my number. No excuse not to call."

As she opened her door, the cat dashed between her legs and her cell phone pinged with an incoming text.

"Hi. This is Pieter."

CHAPTER EIGHTEEN

THE SAFARI

Saturday morning at last. Sarah would have slept in, if that orange cat hadn't worked his way under the mosquito net to lick her face, begging for breakfast.

She needed a treat. Like breakfast on the veranda of the Coffee Hut. There was free wi-fi, so she could take care of the travel agent duties that David had assigned. As she pulled out of the driveway, she got a call from Margo.

"Good morning, *mzungu* Princess. I am back in town. What are you doing?"

"On my way to the Coffee Hut for breakfast. Shall I come by and pick you up?"

"Absolutely!"

Margo climbed into the car, announcing that her week in Dar had been great: informative lectures and fun-filled evenings. "I met some very cool guys at the conference and there are some great clubs in Dar. You should come with me some time. We could have a blast."

"I'm engaged to be married—not interested in clubbing."

"But he's over there, and you're over here. If he's not here to claim his conjugal rights, the engagement is not completely enforceable, is it?"

"It's not about rules, it's about trusting." Then she sighed deeply. "David canceled his visit."

Margo's eyes grew wide. "Nooo! Why?"

"Some glitches in his research. He needed to finish some important experiments."

"Couldn't he just come a little later?"

"Changing the ticket would cost a lot."

"*Pole sana.*"

"Adding insult to injury, he put me in charge of canceling the climb and the safari and getting our money back."

"Good luck with that."

They ordered American breakfasts, and Sarah attacked her travel agent duties. First, she called about the Kilimanjaro climb. No cancelation penalty. Unfortunately, the company would keep the deposit, to be applied toward a future assault on the mountain.

News was worse for the safari. They had already paid in full, and according to the website, they could only get a 50 percent refund.

"So, take me." Margo stated this as the obviously best solution.

Sarah thought she was kidding "Yeah, right."

"I'm serious. You can only get half your money back if you cancel and don't go. But if I pay you for my half, then it's the same as if they refunded you 50 percent. Plus, you still get to go on safari."

A DUST-COLORED Land Cruiser pulled into Sarah's driveway and a muscular young African man stepped out, wearing pressed khaki pants and a shirt embroidered with the Rainbow Safari logo.

Margo did a double take. "Israel, is that you?"

"Margo? This is a surprise. It's been so long."

"I haven't seen you since graduation." Margo hugged him, then stepped back and looked him over. "So this is what you're up to. I thought you went to university to study history."

"You have to know a lot of history to be a guide."

Margo turned to Sarah. "We were classmates in secondary school."

Israel pointed at Sarah. "You cannot wear that shirt."

It was a Houston Astros T-shirt. David's favorite team. Wearing it made her fell closer to him. "Why? You don't like the 'Stros?"

He shook his head. "Blue colors attract tsetse flies. Black clothes are bad, too."

"Tsetse flies?" She had learned about those exotic bugs in tropical disease class. "The ones that carry sleeping sickness?" She went back into the house to change into a white shirt, wondering what other hazards lay in store.

THE SIGN AT the Lake Manyara National Park entrance proclaimed it "The Home of Tree Climbing Lions." Israel raised the top of the SUV, so that Sarah and Margo could stand up and look over the side, in the shade. The forest teemed with baboons, monkeys, impala, giraffes, and elephants. Sarah especially liked the dik-diks, antelopes as tiny as chihuahuas. Israel kept up a running dialogue with other guides over a radio, sharing information about the locations of interesting wildlife.

The road emerged from the forest into a savanna, bordered on the right by the tall rocky cliffs of a fault line. The top of the ridge was dotted with baobab trees. One the left was Lake Manyara, with a pink monolayer of thousands of flamingos. The array of wildlife was mind-boggling, but after three hours, they had still not seen a single lion.

They paused to watch a mother warthog and two babies forage for bugs in a dry river bed. Suddenly, the mother startled. She and her babies took flight into the forest, tails straight in the air, and a herd of impalas galloped into the woods behind them. Baboons took to the treetops and a papa baboon bellowed a warning that could have been heard for miles. The radio squawked with excited voices. Israel smiled. "Lion."

He put the car into gear, and left the road, heading into thick bushes. Branches tore at the windows as they lumbered over uneven terrain, finally coming to rest under a giant acacia tree, surrounded by four other safari vehicles.

A lioness lounged above in the branches, her tail hanging down, like a bell pull, almost within reach.

"Wow!" Sarah was awestruck. But a little nervous. "You're sure she won't jump in with us?"

He shook his head. "They are used to safaris. In this car, we are safe."

After a while, the big cat yawned, stretched, and lumbered down the tree and off into the underbrush. The photo op party broke up, each vehicle picking its way back to the one-lane road, creating quite a traffic jam. After several minutes without forward movement, Sarah asked, "What are we waiting for?"

Israel listened to the Swahili feed from his radio before answering. "There is a bridge ahead. We're waiting to cross."

Margo settled back and rested her feet on the opposite seat. "Boorrring."

They moved ahead one car length, then stopped again. For fifteen minutes it was stop-start, until they emerged from the trees. There the road dipped down to a bridge over a dry river bed. As they crossed, the reason for the traffic jam became clear. A pride of nine lionesses lay nearby, in the shade of a tree, huddled together like a litter of oversize kittens. Israel stopped the car and switched off the engine. David's zoom lens came in handy, as Sarah snapped some amazing shots of the tawny cats, some lying on their backs with bulging bellies, some grooming each other. The truck behind honked its horn. Time to move on. But when Israel turned the key, a strange clicking noise came from under the hood, instead of the roar of an engine. A warning on the dashboard read: *Check Engine*.

Sarah waved her water bottle. "We can hold out for a while. Plenty of water. We haven't even eaten our lunches yet."

Israel chatted calmly on his radio as the curious eyes of every lioness stared at them. One cat stood up, yawned and stretched. They could all be up on the bridge in a heartbeat, if they so chose.

Another car emerged from the brush and drove slowly toward them onto the narrow one-lane bridge. No room for the rescue vehicle to pull up beside them.

Margo grabbed Sarah's arm, "Surely they don't expect us to get out of the car."

The other SUV rolled onto the bridge until the front bumpers kissed.

Sarah whispered. "Battery's dead. Guess they're gonna give us a jump."

Two more lionesses stood up and one strolled towards them.

"Israel," Margo cried. "Don't get out!"

Their car jolted and began to roll slowly backwards, as the rescue truck pushed it off the bridge and up the slope. Israel put on his brake until the other truck retreated. Then he let the car roll down the slope and popped the clutch. The engine roared to a start, and they were off again, waving goodbye to the lady lions.

Israel grinned in the mirror. "I won't be switching off the engine again today. I'll put in a new battery at the lodge tonight."

ON DAY TWO, they visited Ngorongoro Crater, a geological wonder that boasts a concentration and diversity of wildlife unequaled anywhere else on the planet. Israel stopped outside the park gate and said that he had to go pay the entry fees. He waved toward some baboons lurking around the perimeter of the parking lot. "Watch out for these guys. They are out to get lunches and know how to open car doors."

Sarah and Margo browsed through the visitor center, and then sat down outside, under a tree. Margo was just about to peel a banana, when Sarah spied a mammoth baboon galloping toward them, huge teeth bared.

"Uh . . . there's a great big baboon—"

"I know. There are baboons all over the friggin parking lot." Margo glanced over her shoulder, then screamed and tossed her banana into the air. Israel was returning, just in the nick of time, and pretended to aim an imaginary slingshot at the animal. The baboon halted, hands raised in surrender. Then he grabbed the banana and took off.

Israel laid an arm across Margo's shoulders. "Are you okay?"

She shook her head, fuming. "That monkey got my banana."

The narrow red dirt road wound back and forth, through jungle, up a precipitous slope. The scenic overlook at the crater rim was already crowded with tourists. Israel explained the geology. "Millions of years ago, this was a gigantic volcano, nearly as tall as Kilimanjaro. It exploded and collapsed, leaving this gaping hole in the earth. It's the world's largest volcanic caldera—20 kilometers across and 2000 feet deep."

A young woman spoke to Israel in German, asking him to take a picture of her with her friend. Sarah asked him, "How many languages do you speak?"

"Let me think, European languages—French, English, Italian, German, Spanish, and a little Portuguese."

Margo teased him. "What, no Russian?"

"Only a few words of Russian. I know more Japanese than Russian. Japanese grammar is pretty simple."

"How did you learn all that?"

"Mostly picking things up on the job. We have clients from all over the world."

THEY CRISSCROSSED THE floor of the crater, through herds of zebras, wildebeest, and elephants grazing on the savanna. They forded a river full of buffalo and saw crowned cranes, Egyptian geese, secretary birds, and ostriches. For the first few hours, Sarah clicked her camera continuously, trying to capture every creature they encountered. Eventually she put the camera away and just enjoyed the experience. Lunchtime entertainment was provided by dozens of hippos splashing in a pool next to the picnic area.

By late afternoon, they had succeeded in viewing four of the Big Five: lion, elephant, rhino, cape buffalo. Admittedly, their view of the rhinoceros required binoculars. But hey, who really wants to get that close to a rhino? They also saw two cheetahs. But no leopards. Israel told them, "To see a leopard, you must be very lucky."

The sun was setting when they reached their lodge, a rambling chain of buildings that clung to the edge of the crater. Dinner was a bountiful buffet of colorful salads, a carvery station, and steaming tureens of fragrant curry. As they filled their plates, Margo whispered, "Don't look now, but we have some fans."

Sarah glanced over her shoulder. Two young men were close behind—one in a black silk shirt and a shorter one in tight leather pants. They weren't bad looking but were acting sleezy, snickering and elbowing each other and wiggling their eyebrows. The tall one literally breathed down Sarah's neck at the salad bar and brushed against her shoulder as he reached in front of her to scoop up some croutons. "Ah, pardon," he said, putting heavy emphasis on that last syllable, then leaned in to wink and flash an impudent grin. Sarah snorted and walked away, hoping the creeps would not be seated near them.

Unfortunately, the guys sat down at the next table. Sarah tried to concentrate on eating, but the snarky chuckles were driving her nuts. She couldn't understand what they were saying. It sounded like Italian.

The one in the silk shirt reached over and patted Sarah's arm. "Mademoiselle, *parlais vous Francais?*"

She shrugged his hand away, eyes glued to her plate.

The short one said, "Hey, baby, do you speak English?"

Sarah flung her fork onto the table. "Don't call me baby."

"Ah! She speaks English."

Margo's chair clattered to the floor as she stood up and shook her finger at the men. "*Lasciaci da solicer! Chiamo di mangiare in pace.*"

A waiter rushed to pick up the chair. Margo sat down, arranged her napkin neatly in her lap, and proceeded to cut up her roast beef.

Sarah chuckled. "You sure took care of them. Where did you learn Italian?"

"I was an exchange student. Three months in Italy."

"You learned a language in only three months?"

"It gets easier to pick up successive languages—especially if you start early. I grew up speaking both Massai and Swahili. Then I learned English in school, a little Dutch from Pieter's family."

"What language do you dream in?"

"Good question. I don't know."

A CROWD GATHERED in the lobby after dinner for a Massai performance. Wiry men in plaid shukas brandished carved wooden clubs, chanting and wailing as they sprang high in the air to the rhythm of drums. A chorus of women chimed in, clad in royal blue shukas and headdresses that looked like something out of *The Handmaids Tale*. The women jumped too, but not quite as high, their wide beaded collars flopping up and down with each bounce.

Margo began swaying with the beat. "I can jump higher than any of those women."

Sarah sighed. "Please don't."

But she had already joined the show, her blue jeans and yellow sweater contrasting nicely with the Massai garb. She bounded into the air five times, higher with each jump, the last bounce nearly as high as the best male performer. The crowd clapped and whistled and the Massai hooted their approval. The two Italian men cheered louder than anyone.

The guys apologized profusely for their bad manners during dinner and invited the ladies to share a drink out on the terrace. They sat on rocking chairs, looking out over the crater, dimly lit by more stars than Sarah had ever seen in her life. Margo chattered on, trying to keep the conversation in English, but the men kept switching back into Italian. Maybe they were uncomfortable with English. More likely, they were fascinated by hearing a beautiful woman speaking their language with an African accent. Sarah's eyelids grew heavy and after dozing off a couple of times, she announced that she was ready to turn in. She reminded Margo to ask a guard to walk her back to the room. "They said there could be wild animals wandering around after dark."

SARAH WAS AWAKENED by a jolt that felt like an earthquake. She heard crunching and snorting noises outside and went out on the balcony to investigate. A huge buffalo grazing below rubbed his shoulder against a support post and the floor shuddered violently beneath her feet. She had a sudden vision of a balcony collapse, dropping her down onto the horns of the beast. She scurried back to bed, pulling the covers over her head, hoping Margo had not run into any animals like that.

Margo tiptoed in just before sunrise.

"Where've you been?" Sarah scolded.

"We were just talking, and it got so late." She tried to stifle a giggle. "I didn't want to bother the guards."

"I was really worried."

"*Pole sana*. Sorry."

"Guess I shouldn't be such a nag. I'm not your mother."

"I'm sorry I scared you."

"We don't leave for the Serengeti for another couple of hours. You should skip breakfast, lie down and try to get a little sleep."

"I thought you said you weren't my mother!" Margo snuggled under the covers, snickering.

"If I didn't know you better, I'd say, maybe you just met the man of your dreams."

"Mmmmm. Maybe I have."

CHAPTER NINETEEN

ADVERSE EVENT

Sooo, finally coming back to work, are we?" Pieter didn't look up from the chart on his lap. "About time, now that you have exhausted all the major tourist activities around here."

Sarah poured a cup of tea. "It's nice to see you, too."

"Your poor fiancée. When he finally comes for a visit, there will be nothing left for you to do with him."

"Busy day today?"

He put his face in his hands. "Do you ever feel that the world is against you?"

"Oh, yes. Digging through old charts and—"

"Like this morning. Two very tough cases at the same time. Neither Ben nor Stephen is ready to manage either one alone, and I can't be in two places at once. One patient is grossly obese, with severe sleep apnea, and Margo seems to think he can't live another day with his gall bladder."

"And the other case?"

"Your patient."

"My patient?"

"Yes, the one with the huge thyroid. Did you not notice that he has a little trouble breathing?"

"Haven't seen him yet. Ruben scheduled the case while I was gone."

"Well, I suggest you take a look at him. First, check out his chest X ray."

She held the film over the window, so the sunlight could shine through. "Wow, the trachea's really squished!"

"Can you get it out without cracking his chest?"

"Probably. I'll examine him to be sure."

"In terms of which patient is more likely to die before we even start, I would say that Margo's patient wins that contest. So why don't you go see your patient and babysit Ben until I get there." He rubbed his temples. "Make sure he does NOT put the patient to sleep until I'm in the room."

Sarah's patient was already on the operating table. She put a rolled-up blanket under his shoulders. When she tilted his head back, the large mass bulged out above his collar bones. "Good. It's not stuck in his chest. We can get this out through his neck." She turned to face the team. "The riskiest part of this procedure will be putting him to sleep. His airway could collapse under the weight of this gland. We need to have a rigid bronchoscope in the room. Size six. If he stops breathing, that's our only hope."

Ben raised his hand. "You could do a tracheotomy."

She pulled Ben into the hallway and said, in a coarse whisper, "He has a huge mass on his neck. Can you imagine the bleeding if I had to cut through it? And what are the chances I would even find his airway before he croaked?"

"Umm . . . bad?"

"Dr. Pieter wants be here when you put him to sleep. So, wait for him. Understand?"

They returned to the room where everyone sat silently,

listening to the constant beep-beep-beep of the monitor. Sarah scrolled through text messages on her little African cell phone. Nothing new. She looked at pictures: Ameera's wedding, the waterfall—and of course, Spike, the cat. She had settled on the name Spike because his fur was so spikey.

The patient grew restless. He had to be uncomfortable, lying flat on his back with the weight of the gland on his throat. Sarah tipped up the head of the bed up so that he could breathe more easily, then returned to her pictures. From the corner of her eye, she saw Ben inject something into the patient's IV line.

"Hey, I thought we were waiting 'til Dr. Pieter gets here!"

"It's just something to help him relax."

"If you relax him, he may stop breathing."

Her remarks were sort of prophetic. Except that prophets predict things that you don't expect. What happened next was totally predictable.

The patient snored loudly, then stopped breathing altogether. Ben could not intubate him. "You need to do a trach, Dr. Sarah!"

"No can do, remember? Someone go get Pieter. STAT." She moved to the head of the table and demanded the bronchoscope. *Stay calm*, she thought. *Don't panic. Hands, do not shake.*

After a brief struggle, she managed to push the bronchoscope through the slit-like windpipe. On the clock, only three minutes had passed. It had seemed like an eternity.

WHEN THE CASE was finished, Sarah apologized to Pieter. "I should have specifically told Ben not to even sedate the patient until you got there."

"Even if I had been there, you would have had to use the bronchoscope. If you had not been there, then the patient would probably not be alive."

Sarah thought for a minute. "No, I think you would have handled it. You would have induced the patient very slowly, and—"

"You're not good at taking compliments."

Sarah looked at the floor. "I've heard that before."

"Some very bright and capable people are learning a lot from you—and they will teach others. Your influence will be here long after you leave."

"Thanks. I was needing some encouragement."

"Glad to provide that. But there's one other thing you should learn."

"What's that?"

"You need to learn to encourage yourself. You cannot always expect to have someone around to praise you."

CHAPTER TWENTY

FAVORABLE BIRD TO STONE RATIO

Now that's something you don't see every day." Sarah nodded toward a man standing against the wall among the recent and soon-to-be mothers and crying babies.

Ameera glanced over her shoulder. "Yes, men don't usually come with to clinic with their wives."

"I was talking about the surgical mask on his face."

"Oh, I see. Perhaps he is sick and does not want to spread germs."

"But he's wearing it wrong—tilted over one eye. And it doesn't cover his mouth."

Halfway through clinic, Ameera peeked into Sarah's cubicle. "Remember the masked man?"

"How could I forget?"

"He is here with his wife. Come and take a look. He says he was robbed—attacked with a machete."

The face had an eerie skeletal quality. Most of the nose had been chopped off. Part of the right cheek was gone, along with the lower eyelid and that eye was red and swollen.

Sarah examined his eye. "Exposure keratitis. He needs surgery to repair that eyelid or the eye will go blind. Eyelid repair is tricky. But rebuilding the nose is next to impossible. Can your plastic surgeons deal with this?"

"They mainly treat burns and skin cancer."

"Perhaps he could go to India?"

"He couldn't afford that."

Sarah snapped several images with her phone. "I'll send these pictures to a surgeon back home, Dr. Wallace, and ask him for advice. He goes on mission trips to Honduras every year, fixing cleft lips. I went with him one summer. I'm sure he'll be interested. I could Skype him into the OR, and he could direct the surgery."

AN AWFUL STENCH floated in with the next patient as she shuffled in with her head bowed. The chart said she was twenty years old, but she looked ancient. Her name was Charmaine. She was a victim of genital mutilation and a pregnancy gone wrong. The baby was trapped by scarring and after four days of labor, a dead infant was delivered in pieces. Charmaine was left with holes in her bowel and bladder and continually leaked urine and feces.

Ameera had seen her a few months before. "She had a bad kidney infection, and we had to treat that before we could operate. Then there was a big road accident, and the operating rooms were tied up with trauma patients. By the time we could do her surgery, she had another infection."

"She's febrile again today." Sarah sighed. "Kind of a vicious cycle, isn't it? I mean, we can't repair her while she has an infection, and if we can't close the fistulae . . ."

Ameera took a deep breath. "She needs a colostomy."

A stone-faced Charmaine accepted the plan. She had no choice. She was an outcast.

"So sad," said Sarah. "Even her husband has rejected her."

Ameera didn't look up from writing in the chart. "She should be glad to be rid of him. No more getting ripped open every time he feels like fucking." She snapped the chart closed, fire in her eyes. "That poor woman has never had an orgasm. And she never will."

Charmaine lay on a stretcher, just outside the operating room, eyes closed. Sarah spoke in broken Swahili, wanting to be certain that her patient understood what was about to happen to her. A part of her bowel would be opened through her skin. All feces would empty into a bag attached to her belly.

Without opening her eyes, Charmaine grabbed Sarah's hand. "I am grateful for your help. I pray that you will heal me."

Sarah felt foolish. "I didn't know you spoke English."

"I was a very good student." She opened her eyes, gazed at the ceiling. "I wanted to be a nurse."

"Maybe, someday . . ."

Her eyes closed again.

PIETER WATCHED FROM the head of the table as Sarah and Margo worked wordlessly and efficiently. "You ladies make a great team. Almost like you have telepathy."

"It's nice to have a cheering section," said Margo. "What is your ulterior motive in such flattery?"

"I am wounded."

"I think he wants us to stay late," said Sarah. "He wants us to do that tracheotomy after this case."

Margo sighed. "There will be a price. You will have to take us to dinner afterwards."

"Cruel punishment, but if you insist."

"Why are you so anxious for us to do the trach today?"

Margo pointed a pair of scissors at Pieter. "Because he's going back to Amsterdam for the weekend. He doesn't want us to do a trach when he's not around."

"You can understand my concern. Not good to have a fresh trach in the house when we're not fully staffed."

"You're going all the way to Amsterdam for a weekend?" asked Sarah.

"My mother's birthday A big one. She'll be sixty."

"Will you see Eva?" asked Margo.

"Of course. The party was her idea."

"A plan to get you home." Margo chuckled.

"Yes, she is a bit clever that way."

Sarah attached a colostomy bag to Charmaine's belly. "I hope they can fix these fistulae. Otherwise, she'll be stuck with this colostomy for life. Ameera says this is the worst case she's ever seen."

"She should go to Dar es Salaam," said Margo. "There's a surgeon there who is a fistula expert. Dr. Mbala—he doesn't do anything else. If anyone can fix it, he can."

"Ameera already called. The wait list is months long."

Pieter chimed in, "I could probably get her an appointment more quickly. I have a friend at that foundation—not in fistula repair—he does cleft lips and palates. He also volunteers at that mountain clinic. He's going to fix lips on a couple of boys from that village, and I'll be taking them to Dar. If he can talk Dr. Mbao into scheduling your patient at the same time, then she can ride with us."

"I thought the foundation provided transportation for

patients," said Margo. "Why do you need to take those boys?'

"Their mother cannot go with them. She has other children and a sick father. She was afraid to send them until I promised to be with them. Sarah, you should come along. It would be good for you to visit this foundation And I think you would be fascinated by the village."

Sarah hesitated. *What would David think of a road trip with Pieter?* "Can we all fit in your Land Cruiser?"

"We'll go in a hospital van. Tumaini will drive us. It could be a great adventure."

CHAPTER TWENTY-ONE

ROAD TRIP

Charmaine's stench permeated the entire van. Sarah breathed shallowly and slowly, avoiding any sniff that would carry a blast of the putrid molecules to the smell area in the top of her nose. Over time, her brain would adapt, and the smell would cease to torture her. But it seemed like forever. She stared at the backs of Pieter's and Tumaini's heads, atop ramrod stiff necks. They were suffering, too.

Kilimanjaro was shrouded in clouds, despite the brilliant blue sky everywhere else. Off to the right was a boring landscape: miles and miles of flat brown fields. "What are those plants?" she asked.

"Sisal," Pieter answered.

"Like . . . what they use to make rugs?"

"Yep."

Are there enough floors in the universe to use all that straw? Sarah leaned forward. "Tumaini, don't you have any music to play?"

"Why yes, good idea." He dug through his backpack while Pieter grasped the wheel to keep the van on the road. "Any requests?"

"Hymns please," said a small voice from the back seat. The first words Charmaine had uttered that day.

Tumaini popped a cassette into the player and the strains of "Praise the Lord," filled the vehicle. Charmaine sang along lustily, clapping and singing, and dancing in place, and urged the others to join in.

At midmorning, Tumaini pulled off the road into the parking lot of the Elephant Hotel. Pieter said, "This is an important stop for you, Princess."

"Why?"

"Last sit-down toilet until we get to Dar es Salaam."

When Sarah exited the washroom, Pieter was deep in conversation with a giggling young waitress. "Sarah, you must meet my friend Amaya."

Amaya held out her hand. "Karibu. Do you want something to drink?"

"Coke Zero, please."

"We'll have the drinks to go," said Pieter. "Still a long drive ahead."

THEY TURNED OFF the highway, wending their way along a winding road up mountain, through a dense forest that disappeared at the crest. On the other side of the ridge was a bucolic panorama: heavily cultivated terraces cascading down into deep valleys, the mountainsides covered with green and gold patchworks of crops. Water falls tumbled down to streams that ran along the valley floor. The scenery was breathtaking, but the route was terrifying, hugging the edges of precipitous cliffs. With each fork, the road became narrower and there were multiple hairpin switchbacks.

The road ended abruptly at the village of Kandu, a

hodgepodge collection of mudbrick buildings distributed randomly over the uneven terrain, as though someone had tossed a handful of small stones. Pieter pointed to a dominant structure, the building closest to the road. "That's the dispensary." It was also the only building with screened windows. "Volunteer doctors have a weekly clinic. I'm here once a month. It's supposed to be temporary, until a full-time medical officer can be assigned, but they're not having much luck. That unfinished building was supposed to be a delivery room, but they gave up working on it."

Charmaine would not exit the van, but the others walked up the hill toward the village, with a gaggle of giggling children close behind. Pieter suddenly spun around, crouching, grimacing, growling, deploying fingers like claws. The children shrieked and scattered, and Sarah could not help screaming, herself. Pieter shrugged his shoulders and started back up the path. Slowly, the children gathered behind him, and Pieter repeated the monster performance.

Sarah laughed. "Do you always play this game with them?"

"Ah, this is not just a game. It is a sacred ritual."

A little boy ran toward them. "There is Hamid." The child grinned broadly, exaggerating the split in his upper lip.

The younger brother clung shyly to his mother's leg. She had a baby on her back. A little girl peered shyly around her hip. The woman grasped Sarah's hand. "Karibu to my house. My name is Keisha. I cook foodie for you."

Several steaming pots of rice, bananas, greens, and a little chicken were set out on a straw mat that on the ground. Keisha filled plates for her guests, bending over at the hips, in that graceful jackknife posture unique to African women. No stooping or squatting.

Keisha hugged each of the boys as they climbed into the van, sitting in the middle seat with Pieter between them. Sarah claimed the front passenger seat, and Keisha handed her a bulging burlap sack filled with bananas and some other unidentifiable snacks. "I wish you good safari," she said. "Keep my boys safe."

Sarah smiled and nodded. "We'll take good care of them. As if they were our own."

CHARMAINE RETIRED TO her room at the hotel. Everyone else had supper in the courtyard, by the swimming pool. Pieter cut pizza into small bites for the boys and used a knife and fork to feed himself.

Sarah scoffed, "That's not the way to eat pizza. Pick up a slice and bite into it."

"How often do you burn your mouth on hot cheese?"

"Once in a while."

"Never happens with my technique. I can blow on each piece before I bite."

Without warning, Hamid jumped into the pool. He couldn't swim, so he splashed and screamed and bobbed below the surface a couple of times.

Sarah jumped up, ready to plunge in after him. But Pieter just sighed, stepped into the pool and grabbed the boy by the arm. "You can stand up, you know."

Hamid was tall enough for his head to be well above the surface. Pieter showed the boy how to blow bubbles, then pushed him around the pool, like a toy boat.

Sarah entertained Jamal by showing him some pictures and videos on her cell phone. He giggled especially loudly at one clip.

Pieter looked up. "What's so funny?"

"Just something I recorded one night, after a couple of beers and nothing better to do. Ants crawling over a slice of banana. Who knew it would be so entertaining?"

Hamid graduated into jumping into the pool and dog paddling to Pieter, over and over. Every time he climbed out of the pool, he would cry out, "Again!" Pieter would move backward, a little more each time, until Hamid swam all the way across the pool.

Sarah's father had used a similar technique to teach her to swim. He would stand not far from the edge of the pool and coax her to jump in. But he didn't stay in that spot. He was a moving target, kept moving backwards as she swam. The deception angered her at the time. But in retrospect, she had to concede the efficacy of the method.

Jamal climbed into Sarah's lap and tapped on her cell phone. "Again."

Sarah replayed the ant video and Jamal cackled with glee. "Again."

The cycle repeated over and over until Jamal slipped from her lap, jumped into the pool, and disappeared below the surface. Pieter grabbed him. "I could use some help in here, Princess. He's too short to stand up."

"In my clothes?"

"Why not?"

"But . . . shouldn't they go to bed soon?"

"Maybe they'll never have another chance to swim in a pool like this."

Sarah waded into the water lifted Jamal onto the side of the pool. "Jump," she commanded. He splashed down into her arms and cried, "Again!"

CHAPTER TWENTY-TWO

A DAY IN DAR

The clerk at the reception desk held up her hand. "Wait." After a phone call, she looked at Pieter. "Dr. Mercier say you doctors come back to his office." She pointed at Charmaine and the two little boys. "Not them, just you." Charmaine nodded and ushered the boys to a waiting room bench.

Dr. Jean Mercier was a dark and slender Frenchman, with long tapered fingers. "Pieter, it is so good to see you! And who is your lovely colleague?"

"May I present Dr. Sarah Whitaker, an outstanding surgeon from the US."

"*Enchante, mademoiselle docteur.*" He bowed, lifted her left hand to his lips, and noted the diamond ring. "Ah, you are spoken for. *Quel dommage!* You are a surgeon? I thought you were in obstetrics."

Sarah explained how a surgery resident had come to be working in the OB department. "I've never seen a fistula repair before."

"You are welcome to watch Dr. Mbala do that surgery. He does nearly ten repairs each week, so he is quite an expert. My specialty is cleft lip and palate. Do you have any experience with such cases?"

Sarah nodded. "I went on a mission trip to Honduras for a couple of weeks. We repaired thirty-five lips."

"Then you can scrub in with me."

ONCE THE PATIENTS were settled on the hospital ward, Pieter suggested to Sarah that they go out for lunch. "Lots of options, here in the big city. What kind of food strikes your fancy?"

"Any chance of a hamburger?"

"I know just the place."

The trendy café had brightly painted walls, tall chrome barstools, the luscious aroma of French fries.

"I didn't expect to get food like this in Tanzania. I thought the hamburger at McDonald's in the Amsterdam Airport would be my last one for a while." She grabbed the burger with both hands and took a big bite. Then she frowned. Pieter was using a knife and fork. "That's not how you're supposed to eat it."

"Your technique does not look sanitary to me."

She swallowed and wiped a bit of mustard from her lip. "But I washed my hands!"

Pieter laughed when a slice of pickle fell into her lap. "I will continue to eat my food in a civil manner."

"Suit yourself. Be uncool."

"Want to see something of the city? There's a big market nearby. Right on the harbor."

Standard Dar es Salaam weather. Hot and sunny and muggy with the salt smell of the sea in the air. Initially Pieter led the way, but then he lagged behind. Sarah glanced back at his reflection in a shop window.

"Are you looking at my butt?"

He sped up and fell in step beside her, suppressing a chuckle.

"You were looking. I saw you."

Striving to look innocent, he pointed down the road. "The market is just ahead."

"So . . . do I have a nice butt?"

"Why would I look at a not nice butt?" Sarah scowled.

He wiggled his eyebrows. "Can I just, grab it?"

"What? Nooo!"

He jogged ahead for a few steps, then turned around, shuffling backwards, arms spread out, like a guard on a basketball team. "Like they always say, no harm in asking."

"They also say there's no such thing as a stupid question. But we both know that's not true."

"What about, 'Better to beg for forgiveness than to ask for permission'?" He reached behind her, snatched the cell phone from her back pocket, and waved it aloft.

Sarah gasped.

"It was hanging out, like an advertisement for pickpockets. Let me carry it for you."

The market was huge. Multiple concrete stalls topped by tile roofs, aisles filled with bountiful displays of fruits, vegetables, fabrics, crafts, and spices. A man in a white peaked cap stood proudly in front of his display of beautiful seashells.

Wide counters near the water's edge displayed a rainbow of fish, octopus, sea turtles, conchs, and shrimp. Fishermen sorted and cleaned their catch on a slab of concrete that sloped down into the harbor. The scene was icky, smelly, slimy, and fascinating.

Pieter pointed to a few small boats resting on the shore. "Want to go for a ride?"

"Is it safe? They look kind of small and rickety."

"I haven't drowned yet."

"That's comforting."

"These boats are called dhows. They've been sailing around the Indian Ocean for two thousand years." Pieter selected a boat, negotiated a price with a man in a caftan, and they climbed aboard. The canoe-like craft had an outrigger on each side, and single sail with no boom. The hull was narrow, and they perched on the edge with their feet inside the boat. Sarah held her breath as the man pushed the boat into the water and then jumped aboard. The water was a little murky, at first, but as they moved out of the harbor, they were surrounded by sparkling turquoise water and fresh air, far from the smells of the market. Gliding over the sea was like flying. Sarah leaned out and trailed her fingers in the water.

The boat tilted sharply when they headed back to shore. Sarah gasped and grabbed at the sides of the boat. "This boat is so skinny—not much to sit on!"

"Then it is fortunate that your butt is little and cute."

She glared at him. "Where I come from, that comment would be considered harassment." She tried to scowl at him, but his grin was too charming.

"With all due respect, doctor, you specifically requested my assessment of your butt."

Funny, she hadn't noticed before, his eyes were bluer than the sea.

CHARMAINE STOOD AT the hospital entrance, wringing her hands and sobbing. "The boys . . . they run away!"

"Why?" Pieter was stunned. "Did you see them leave?"

"That man came back."

Sarah shuddered. "What man?"

"He talked to them this morning. When you were not there." Charmaine covered her face with her hands and sobbed. "I told them, no, that is a bad man. Don't believe him."

Sarah put her arm around Charmaine. "What did he tell them?"

Her nostrils flared, and her eyes bulged. "He tell them —when you are asleep, they will cut out your heart . . . and other things."

Pieter shook his head. "How could they believe something like this?"

"I think so that he followed us into hospital. I go to toilet. When I come back, they are leaving with him. I say 'Stop' but they run away."

Sarah asked "How long ago?

"Maybe two hours. I can show you where they went. I followed them."

A faded sign proclaimed the "Precious Heart Orphanage." Beneath a pink heart that radiated yellow sunbeams, these words were painted, in crude letters: *Taking Care of God's Precious Children.*

"Is this one of those bogus orphanages?"

Pieter nodded. "They use pictures of the children to bilk money from well-meaning people, particularly from overseas. Sometimes, they abduct children who are not orphans."

"Should we call the police?"

"We can't wait to act. They may not keep the boys here —maybe they deal in trafficking."

"But if we just go in and ask for them, they could hide

them or something. They certainly wouldn't admit to kidnapping them."

He draped an arm across her shoulders. "Well, darling, weren't we wanting to adopt a child?"

A middle-aged woman answered their knock at the door. "Karibu. What can I do for you?"

"My wife and I are interested in adopting a child."

"These children here cannot be adopted. They all have AIDS. We take good care of them." She handed them each a glossy tri-fold brochure with pictures of happy children on a playground—a far cry from the dirty establishment in front of them.

Sarah tried to look through the door. "But surely at least one of these children might benefit from a good home. Especially with parents who could afford to provide the best medical care—even if they have AIDS."

"I think so, maybe. It would be expensive."

Pieter stepped closer and peered around the woman. "May we come in and meet some of the children?'

"Will you make a donation?"

Sarah nodded vigorously, "Of course."

A short hallway led to a musty room where several hollow-eyed waifs sat on the floor. Jamal and Hamid were not among them.

Pieter whispered into Sarah's ear, "I saw Hamid in the next room."

Sarah turned to the woman, "I'd love to tour the place. Can you show me the kitchen?"

Pieter sat down on a chair. "I don't need to see the kitchen. That's for women."

The "kitchen" was a courtyard behind the house with a bare earth floor. No refrigerator, not even a sink—just a charcoal brazier. Sarah glanced around. "You could really use a stove and some plumbing, couldn't you?"

"It would be very generous of you to provide this."

Sarah looked past the woman, into the house, and caught a glimpse of Pieter dashing out the front door, with Hamid in tow and Jamal in his arms.

She smiled and extended her hand to the woman. "Well, thank you very much for your time. We will be in touch."

The woman looked puzzled as Sarah walked briskly back into the building. "Aren't you going to make a donation?"

"Yes, I can do that online."

"Wait! Let me give you more information."

For some reason, Sarah thought it would be rude to leave abruptly, so she followed the woman into an office.

A man seated at the desk gazed at Sarah for a moment. Then he stood up and lunged at her. "What are you doing here?"

The woman looked confused. "She wants to make a donation."

Sarah turned to leave, but the man grabbed her arm. "Why are you leaving? You said you wanted to make a donation."

"Yes, but I don't have money with me."

"I saw you at the hospital. You are looking for those boys." He tightened his grip on her arm. "I could find them for you . . . for a price."

He murmured something to the woman, and she ran from the room. Sarah understood enough Swahili to know that he had ordered her to hide the boys.

He jerked roughly on Sarah's arm. "There is an ATM nearby. You can get plenty of money there."

"How do I know you still have them? I want to see them before I agree to pay you anything."

The woman appeared in the doorway. "The boys are not here."

He laughed. "Of course not. She won't see them until she pays."

The woman spoke more loudly, desperately. "No, they are gone. I think her husband took them."

His eyes bulged. "You took my children!"

Sarah started to point out that they were not his children, but he grabbed Sarah's other arm and pulled her so close that their faces almost touched. His breath reeked of alcohol. "You will not leave until we have been paid for our trouble. Call your husband from your cell phone and tell him—"

"I don't have a phone." It was true. Her cellphone was still in Pieter's pocket.

"I saw it this morning, hanging out of your back pocket."

He tried to spin her around, and Sarah grabbed the opportunity to break free, jamming her knee into his crotch. He screamed and collapsed onto the floor as she sprinted from the building. Just outside the door, she nearly collided with Pieter.

"What took you so long?"

"I was . . . detained." Sarah saw the van waiting at the corner, with the motor running and good old Tumaini at the wheel. "Let's go."

In the van, Pieter asked, "Did they see me take the kids?"

"No, but they noticed they were gone. And a man in the office recognized me from the hospital. Boy, was he mad!"

"I tried to call your cell phone—but then it rang in my pocket. I forgot to give it back to you. Here it is."

Jamal nestled against her and cried, "Again!"

Sarah scrolled to the video clip of the ants on the banana. Hamid climbed into Pieter's lap. "I sorry."

Pieter hugged the boy. "I would never let anyone do anything bad to you."

Sarah said, "I can understand why they freaked out. For them, coming into this city must have been like being abducted onto a flying saucer. They might have believed anything." Then she had another thought. "What about the other children?"

"Tumaini called the police."

The nurses at the hospital fussed over the boys, relieved to see that they had been rescued. Once they were tucked into bed and asleep, Pieter did not want to leave them unguarded. "I'll stay at the hospital tonight."

"Good plan. Tumaini can take me back to the hotel."

Pieter noticed bruises on Sarah's arm. "What happened?"

"Oh, remember? I told you I was detained?"

"I should never have left you there."

"What else could we do? And everything turned out fine. Really."

"How did you get away from him?"

"I, uh, sort of . . . got him with my knee . . . where it hurt."

"You are a formidable woman."

"Just applying what I learned in a self-defense class. If I had car keys, I could have gouged his eyes out."

"Remind me never to assault you."

CHAPTER TWENTY-THREE

PUTTING THE PIECES TOGETHER

J amal shrieked, clung to Pieter's neck, and refused to let go. Pieter looked at the nurse apologetically. "I'm usually the one ripping the child from his mother's arms."

Sarah had already changed into her scrubs. "We should wait a bit. The sedative hasn't kicked in yet."

The nurse frowned. "We must go now."

Then Sarah had an idea. She pulled out her cellphone. "Jamal, would you like to see the ants?"

Jamal stopped sobbing. He took the phone into his little hands and watched Sarah's video clip of the ants attacking the banana slice—again and again.

In the operating room, Dr. Mercier waved his marking pen like a magic wand. "Repairing a cleft lip is like mending a broken teacup."

Sarah nodded. "Except you don't just pick up the pieces. You have to create the right fragments."

"*Vraiment*! You speak the truth."

He began sketching incision lines on Jamal's face, predicting where pieces of tissue would line up to create a complete smile. Then he began slicing the skin. "I prefer to use a number eleven blade for this. And you?'

"*Le meme chose. Onze.*"

"Ah, *vous parlais Francais! Tres bien!*"

"Actually, that's about the extent of my French."

"*Quel dommage.*"

Sarah blotted the oozing incision. "Too bad that we can't completely avoid a scar. I wish all tissue could heal like a fetus."

"Ah, you have touched upon my area of research."

"Fetal surgery?"

"No. Stem cells."

"You mean, tissue from human embryos?"

"No. You can get plenty of stem cells from adults, in fat, bone marrow, skin. But I am no longer doing such research." He handed the scalpel back to the scrub nurse. "So, Dr. Sarah, are you ready to sew?"

"*Mais oui!*"

She handled the tissue delicately and tied the knots with just the right amount of tension.

"Why did you stop doing research?" she asked.

"I don't have a lab here. Still, I am doing clinical research."

"David doesn't have a high regard for clinical research. He calls my project a fishing expedition."

"Ah yes. Your fiancée. So what type of research does he do?"

"He's working on a vaccine for malaria."

"Old fashioned!"

"No, he's on the cutting edge—you know, molecular stuff."

"Surely vaccination is a very old concept. You just force the immune system to do its work."

"But if we did have an effective vaccine, just think how many lives could be saved."

"Perhaps there will be some molecular solution," he suggested. "Some gene that we can patch into our own DNA."

"That would be pretty transformative."

"Most major medical advances are transformational—and often the result of looking for something else. Like penicillin coming from mold that contaminated an experiment."

Sarah tied the last knot. Jamal had a new lip!

"*Tres bon!*" Jean ripped off his gown and gloves. "You have been very well trained."

Sarah carried drowsy Jamal out to the holding area and laid him on a stretcher. Hamid let out a joyful whoop when he saw his little brother's new face. Then he gave Pieter a hug and skipped into the operating room.

Sarah took a deep breath as she picked up the marking pen and sketched out the incisions on Hamid's face.

Jean made a slight correction and the scrub nurse slapped a scalpel into Sarah's hand.

Forty minutes later, Hamid awoke with a new face.

CHARMAINE LAY ON a stretcher in the recovery room, moaning softly, her eyes screwed shut and her brows furrowed. She startled when Sarah touched her shoulder, and struggled to focus her eyes. "Daktari. It is you, is it?"

Sarah leaned over. "Yes, it's me. Your surgery is over. Are you in pain?"

Charmaine clasped Sarah's hand. "I hurt . . . very bad . . . but I am happy. So happy."

"After a couple of weeks, you'll need a second operation, to take down your colostomy. I have to leave tomorrow, so I can't be with you for that."

"I thank you for all your help. *Asante sana*. I wish you safe safari, and I hope I see you again someday."

"What are your plans? What will you do when you're well?"

"I want to go to school, to be a nurse. But I must find a sponsor to pay the tuition."

Tears welled up in Sarah's eyes. "I will be your sponsor. And I promise, we will always be friends."

As Sarah left the room, she realized Charmaine wasn't moaning in agony. She was singing hymns.

CHAPTER TWENTY-FOUR

NIGHTLIFE

Jean insisted that Sarah and Pieter sample the night life in Dar. He picked them up at their hotel in his red two-seater Porsche. Pieter whispered to Sarah, "I think he likes you."

"That's obvious. But I'm already taken."

"Flash that diamond at him."

Sarah offered to get into the small space behind the seats, but Pieter insisted on being a gentleman. It was a bit comical—the site of him folding himself into the car like a pretzel.

The club was chic and lively, with a retro look: Disco ball, lighted dance floor, and Lucite lounge chairs, trans illuminated by constantly color-changing LED lights. The music was an eclectic mix of techno, electro soul, African pop, and an occasional oldie.

They were putting in their drink orders at the bar when an inebriated man grabbed Sarah by the arm and tried to drag her onto the dance floor.

Jean shoved the man away. "Pieter, you wait for the drinks. Sarah and I will find a table."

They found a comfortable spot, not too close to the speakers, and Jean asked if she would like to dance.

"We should wait for Pieter."

"Right. It would be rude to desert him."

A waitress brought a bowl of peanuts as Pieter returned with the drinks. He winked at Sarah, "I think your blonde hair attracts too much attention."

"You're blond, too."

"But he is neither beautiful nor a lady," said Jean. "Perhaps a gentleman, but who can say for sure?"

Pieter rolled his eyes and popped a few peanuts into his mouth.

Sarah asked Jean what had brought him to Africa.

"It was after a nasty divorce. I heard of an opportunity to come here for a year, and I thought, 'Why not?'"

"For a year? So, you'll be going back to France soon?"

He laughed and shook his head. "That was five years ago."

Sarah smiled. "The place does grow on you."

Jean wanted to know more about Sarah, so she gave him the elevator speech about how she had come to be in Africa, pretending to be an obstetrician. "I'm supposed to be doing research, but it's not going so well."

He leaned forward. "You are a very talented surgeon, Sarah. You should come to Dar again, often. I can teach you so much. You don't have to wait to come with this guy." He jerked his head toward Pieter.

Pieter cleared his throat softly and pointed to his own left ring finger.

Sarah reached into the peanut bowl, positioning her hand so that her diamond reflected lights from the disco ball into Jean's face.

Pieter tried to stifle a chortle.

Jean turned abruptly to look at him. "What's so funny?"

"Oh nothing. I was just thinking about how Sarah handled that man at the orphanage—when he grabbed her arm."

"I hadn't heard that part of the story." Jean raised a glass to his lips.

Pieter cocked his head sideways and waited until Jean had a mouthful of wine before answering. "She kicked him in the nuts."

Jean choked, and wine spurted out his nose.

Sarah grabbed a paper napkin and sprung forward to wipe Jean's face. "Oh, I'm so sorry."

Pieter lips flashed a nano-smirk as he glanced at his watch. "It's getting late, and we have an early rise. How about one more round of drinks?"

Sarah excused herself to the ladies' room. It was directly across the dance floor, but she slunk around the side of the room, hoping to be inconspicuous in the relative darkness.

Heading back to the table, she heard the opening strains of one of her father's favorite songs: "My Girl." It took her back to Saturday mornings in his convertible with the top down. The Motown beat was catchy, and she was feeling the wine, so she bounced a bit with the beat as she strode across the floor. The drunk who had accosted her before came back again and grabbed her arm. "Looks like you want to dance."

Pieter sprinted onto the dance floor and tapped the man on the shoulder, "May I cut in?"

At first, they were stiffly formal, as if in a ballroom dance class. Pieter placed one hand on her waist and held her right hand gracefully aloft. Then he wiggled a finger in the air. "We should do some twirly things, okay?"

As the violins kicked in, he spun Sarah around, under his arm and back again, over and over again, finally tipping her back into a dramatic dip. Then he pulled her in close, and she felt his chest resonating with his voice as he sang along softly. She surrendered control of her body as they swayed rather than stepped to the beat.

The Motown music faded into the next song, African pop with a rapid techno beat. Sarah realized, with some embarrassment, that they clung together after everyone else had disengaged for the fast dance.

Jean, at the edge of the dance floor, rattled his car keys. "Time to go, *n'est pas?*"

PIETER ANNOUNCED THAT he wanted to spend the night at the hospital with the boys.

"*Certainment*," said Jean. "I will take you there, and then Sarah and I can share another drink at her hotel."

"No way. The hotel is just a few blocks away from here."

JEAN LEAPT OUT to bid Sarah adieu at the hotel, kissing her hand. "You really must visit again."

Pieter unfolded himself from the back seat. "Wait here, Jean. I'll see her safely to her room."

She had drunk more than usual, and she hoped it wasn't obvious. Her spine tingled when Pieter placed his hand on her lower back to guide her across the courtyard. As she stepped inside her room, she gazed at Pieter, wondering what it would be like to kiss him.

He tapped on the door jamb. "I'm not leaving until you close the door and lock it."

She complied, turning the dead bolt with a loud "clunk."

"And put the chain on, too."

CHAPTER TWENTY-FIVE

HEADING FOR HOME

S arah shivered, staring down at the blue water of the hotel swimming pool. She had always been a good swimmer—fastest girl on her team. Once in the water, she was a fish. But she hated the chilling shock of the first dive. David would always say, "Why don't you just jump in and get it over with?"

She dangled a foot in the water, then inched down the steps, bouncing a few times at each level. Finally, the water was up to her chin. She did a surface dive, kicked off the side, and shot across the pool underwater, like a torpedo, all the way to the other end of the pool. Her signature race had been the individual medley. *Butterfly, breaststroke, backstroke, crawl. Or was it butterfly, backstroke?*

She charged back down the pool, her arms sweeping over the water in broad arcs, legs locked tandem in a dolphin kick. Tom, the captain of her swim team, did a powerfully mean butterfly—his torso thrusting up out of the water with each breath, displaying his impressive lattisimus dorsi muscles. She hadn't known the name of those muscles then —she was only thirteen. But she had been very impressed with his physique. And she had a secret crush on him. At the end of the pool, she remembered what to do in the next lap. *Backstroke.*

She pulled her knees up under her chin and pushed backwards off the side of the pool. Three kicks for each stroke, arms reaching back toward the other end of the pool.

One two three, one two three . . .

As she pushed off for the breaststroke lap, there was a huge splash beside her. It was Pieter, forging ahead with a butterfly stroke every bit as awesome as the old swim team captain's style. But there was something odd about his left shoulder. Was it scarred? It would be rude to ask.

Pieter lazed against the edge of the pool. "Good morning. What took you so long?"

"I didn't know it was a race."

"It wasn't. Just friendly swimming, right?"

Sarah touched the wall, executed a racer's turn, and took off on her final lap. It was her best stroke: freestyle. AKA, crawl.

She swam as fast as she could, concentrating on her technique: One-two-three-one-two-three-one-two-three, BREATHE; one-two-three-one-two-three-one-two-three, BREATHE.

When she popped up at the other end of the pool, Pieter was sitting up on the edge. "You know, you're not a bad swimmer. For a girl."

"Hmmph. Out of shape. No place to swim near the hospital."

"You mean you haven't joined the health club at Kibo View Lodge?"

"Didn't know about it."

"You should join. Nice pool, nice gym. They even have

some of those Zumba classes—you know, like you . . . girls like."

"Thanks. I'll check it out."

Sarah pulled herself out and sat beside him. "Where are the boys?"

"In the room."

"I'm surprised they didn't follow you out here."

"Room service breakfast for them. And video games. I wasn't planning to go for a swim, until I looked out the window and saw you tiptoeing into the water."

Sarah blushed. "I didn't think anyone saw me. I know I should just jump into the water and get it over with, but I really don't like to do that."

"If you don't like jumping in, why should you?"

"You don't think I looked silly? Creeping into the water like that?"

"Actually, you did look quite silly." He hugged himself and pretended to shiver. "Oooh! I'm so cold!"

Sarah jumped back into the pool and began sloshing water onto Pieter.

"Careful now. You don't really want to start a war with me. Besides, you shouldn't feel so insulted. What's wrong with looking silly sometimes?"

She glanced at the clock on the wall. "I'd better go get ready."

SARAH AND PIETER took the back seat in the van with a large well-stocked cooler between them, including ice packs for the boys' lips. The rush hour had abated but traffic was still crazy. Vendors walked up and down the street along the traffic jam, hawking a variety of goods: peanuts, shoes, candy, pots and pans. One enterprising young man sold tropical fish from a plexiglass tank balanced on the top of his head.

Finally, they were out on the open road.

"So, tell me, Pieter, exactly what brought you to Kandu?"

"It is a bit of a long story."

"It's a long drive."

"Okay, I told you I was a small child when my family came to this country."

"Mmm, hmm."

"Our housekeeper was Mohammedi. I called her Mo Mo. She was like another mother. I didn't see her much after I went to boarding school, and then my parents moved back to the Netherlands. When I was a medical student, I came here to study for two months, and I wanted to see her. But my mother told me that she had died."

"And no one had told you before that?"

Pieter shook his head. "She had moved back to her family's village, which is Kandu."

"And Hamid and Jamal are—"

"Her sister's grandchildren."

Sarah gazed at the two boys. "How did she die?"

He shrugged. "Fever"

"Typhoid?" *Preventable,* she thought, *vaccinations, sanitation . . .*

"No, something else—not clear what. It was a sudden outbreak that flared up and died out quickly. Some kind of hemorrhagic fever. About two hundred people died."

Sarah's pulse quickened. "Like, Ebola?"

"No, no, no. We don't get that around here. When Robert and I went to visit Mo Mo's family, they called it red eye fever."

"Robert. Margo's brother? She told me he died in a road accident."

"He was on a motorcycle, struck by a minibus. They took him to surgery to repair a leg fracture. But he never woke up."

"Operation was a success, but . . ."

"Exactly. They did not recognize his head injury. Epidural hematoma."

Sarah knew all about epidural blood clots. A ruptured artery in the lining of his brain. Patients are briefly unconscious after a severe blow to the head. Then they are fully conscious during a "lucid interval," followed by sudden death. If Robert had not been put to sleep for the leg surgery, someone would have checked his eyes and noticed a dilated pupil—a sign that an expanding blood clot was pushing his brain down toward that opening in the skull where the spinal cord exits. Like squeezing toothpaste from a tube.

If he had been awake, someone would have noticed the telltale change in his eyes. Someone could have drilled a hole into his skull to relieve the pressure. Sarah had done that once before—made a life-saving burr hole in a child with a head injury. If she had been there, she could have done that for Robert. And if Pieter had been there . . .

He stared silently out the window. Then he opened the cooler. "I need some water. Anyone else?"

"Any Coke Lite?" Sarah asked.

"Coke Zero." Pieter pulled out a bottle and handed it to her. "Here is your poison."

Sarah touched his arm, tentatively. "It's still hard, isn't it?"

"Robert was a great fellow. We were best friends, as long as I can remember—like a brother. I would go with him to visit his grandparents, out in the Serengeti. And he came to Amsterdam with me for the first year of boarding school. It was culture shock for both of us. I would have been miserable if I had gone there alone. But he was this Massai warrior, and all the boys were fascinated by his tales."

Hamid twisted around to look at Pieter. "Robert was warrior?"

"Yes. I was invited to his circumcision ceremony."

Hamid's eyes grew wide. "Did he kill lion?"

Pieter nodded. "He was in a group that killed a lion."

The two little boys wriggled from their lap belts and kneeled to peer over the seat. "Did you see Robert kill lion?"

Tumaini called out to them to sit down and buckle up.

"I didn't see the lion kill. But he told me how they did it."

There was no way the little boys were going to keep their seats now.

"It took five of them. First, the shield man jumped in front of the lion." Pieter held up his hand to show how the man would hold the shield. "Then a man in back would grab the lion by the tail."

Jamal gasped and put a hand over his mouth.

"Then the spear man stabbed the lion."

Hamid thought it was too bad that Pieter did not get to see this. Tumaini again ordered the boys to sit down.

"I'm glad I didn't see it," said Pieter. "Lions are beautiful creatures." He rubbed his chin thoughtfully. "But I did kill a leopard."

The two boys popped back up and Jamal bumped his lip on the seat, and it started bleeding. Pieter pulled an ice pack from the cooler, and Sarah gently scolded the boy. "This is why you need to sit still." She pressed the ice against the wound and glanced at Pieter. "You're kidding about the leopard, right?"

He shook his head. "She would have killed Robert."

Tumaini called out, "I want to hear this story!"

Pieter clambered over the seat and settled between the boys.

"We were visiting Robert's grandmother and went out walking outside the manyatta."

Sarah asked, "What's a manyatta?"

"Sort of like a camp. A temporary enclosure for animals and sleeping huts. When you take the animals somewhere else to graze, you go to another manyatta, or build a new one."

Hamid was getting impatient. "Where was leopard?"

"I am getting to that. We were just wandering around, pretending to hunt. Actually, looking for hyrax. You know those little furry creatures?"

Both boys nodded.

"The leopard jumped out of a tree and knocked Robert to the ground—like this." Pieter locked an arm around each boy and jerked them forward.

As they erupted into shrieks and giggles, Sarah scolded, "Hey, they're supposed to be quiet. Not jumping around."

"Sorry." He buckled both boys into their seats before continuing the story. "Robert was helpless—pinned down on his stomach. My rifle was small, so I had to get close. And I had to be careful not to hit Robert. So, I crouched down and shot the leopard in the eye. It didn't kill her, but she was stunned and rolled off him. Then I grabbed his spear and . . . that's how I killed her. But she got me here." He opened his shirt, so the boys could see the scars on his shoulder. The marks Sarah had seen during their morning swim.

"You were a warrior," said Tumaini. "They should have let you keep the skin."

"They did. And I kept the cub as a pet for a few years. That's why she attacked us—she was protecting her baby."

The boys giggled and squirmed and tried to keep Pieter from buttoning up his shirt. He told them to settle down and climbed back next to Sarah. She said, "So you're a real Massai warrior?"

"Honorary. There was a special ceremony. My parents were invited. And Robert's cousin offered to share his wife with me for the night."

"You mean, sleep with her?"

"Yes—traditional Massai hospitality."

"Did you?"

"Of course not. I was only twelve. I thought my mother would faint. My father was much calmer. He made a nice speech thanking them for the honor, but he explained that a white man should only sleep with his own wife. On the way home, in our car, he gave me quite a long lecture about the dangers of sex: horrible incurable diseases, girls getting pregnant . . . He said if I was not careful, I might wind up having to get married and live in one of those huts. And that is when my mother decided that I should go to boarding school in Amsterdam."

"That was the reason? Nearly being killed by a leopard had nothing to do with the decision?"

"Well, I am certain many factors were involved. But that was another piece of hay."

"Hay?"

"You know, the hay that was too heavy . . ." Pieter tapped an index finger against his chin, trying to recall the phrase.

"You mean the straw that broke the camel's back."

"Yes, that's it."

"I'm charmed by the way you almost get these old sayings right."

"Thank you for your feedback. My charm requires continual maintenance."

CHAPTER TWENTY-SIX

THAT SPACE BETWEEN LIFE AND DEATH

W e need an exit strategy." Pieter gazed out at the throng of village children that surrounded the van, hands and noses pressed against the windows. "I'll carry Hamid. Sarah, you take Jamal. Tumaini, open the door for us."

"And run interference," said Sarah.

Tumaini looked confused. "You wish me to interfere?"

"It's a term in American football." Sarah raised her forearms in a feeble imitation of a linebacker. "It means you block for us, get between us and the kids."

"This is something I can do." Tumaini imitated her arm posture. "I am very wide."

Tumaini tried his best to be a human bulldozer, but the children swarmed like bees. Sarah held on tightly to Jamal, making sure that his freshly repaired face remained above the reach of curious little hands.

"Maybe you should try your boogie man shtick," said Sarah.

"Can't do that. My arms are full, and I don't think it would work right now, anyway."

Sarah and Pieter managed to keep the wriggling Hamid and Jamal under control and delivered them safely to their mother. Keisha fell on her knees, laughing and weeping, embracing her sons and staring at their faces. Then she grasped Pieter's hands. "*Asante sana.* We have prepared food."

The aroma of roasted goat wafted over the village, and pots of rice, greens, and yams simmered over charcoal braziers.

Sarah shot a worried glance at Pieter. "It's really nice of them to do this. But we need to get going soon. We don't want to be heading down the mountain in the dark."

"We can stay overnight. There's a lodge nearby."

So, they relaxed, enjoyed the feast, and watched the children sing and dance.

THE SUN WAS setting as they pulled up in front of the lodge. Pieter asked the woman at the desk if she had any rooms available. "We were delayed by the celebration in the village, and it's too late to drive home."

"There's always room for you." She reached for Sarah's hand. "I'm Betje. You must be the doctor from America. If you had a celebration, then I guess the boys' surgeries went well."

Sarah showed her some pictures on her cell phone.

Betje pointed toward the dining room. "You're just in time for dinner."

Sarah patted her tummy. "We were well fed in the village. I couldn't eat another bite."

"Then Yusef will show you to your rooms and you can rest a while. See you later for drinks?"

It was a steep walk down to Sarah's "room," a mini-villa

built into the side of the cliff, with a terrace that offered a sweeping view of the plains below. Yusef pointed into the distance. "There is Kilimanjaro." From this distance, the tallest mountain in Africa looked like a tiny pimple.

After a nap, Sarah showered and changed and headed back to the main building. Pieter was in the lobby, conversing with a woman who was clearly upset. He switched to English when Sarah approached. "This is Balinda, the midwife from Kandu."

Balinda bowed. "Karibu, Dr. Sarah. A woman has been in labor two days. I cannot turn the baby. Can you come and help?"

BALINDA LIT A kerosene lantern and led them into the dark dispensary where a young woman crouched in the corner.

Balinda coaxed the woman onto the exam table.

Sarah examined the woman and felt a small hand in the birth canal. "It's not breech. It's a transverse lie. And not coming out anytime soon. She needs a C-section. We have to get her to a hospital."

Pieter had already started an IV. "You'll have to do it here. She's bleeding, won't survive a long drive." He rolled the woman onto her side and began prepping her back for a spinal anesthetic. "Balinda will show you where to find the instruments and suture. Equipment is basic, but sterile. I'll scrub in and assist you."

Sarah took a deep breath before slicing into the skin. She and Pieter worked methodically in the eerie amber light of the lantern, rarely speaking, each anticipating the other's steps.

Sarah handed the tiny boy to Balinda. The infant was limp and covered with patches of white cheesy vernix. Balinda gently cleaned out his mouth, and he began to wail.

Sarah tied the last knot in the skin closure and looked at Pieter. "We're not out of the woods, are we?"

"She's losing a lot of blood. We have to get her to the hospital in Lushoto."

"But driving down that winding road in the dark. It's dangerous."

"We have no choice."

THE ROAD WAS slick and deeply rutted from the recent short rains of November. Pieter had to get out of the car twice to clear the road, once for a fallen tree, and once for a herd of goats. They had removed the back seats from the van so that the woman could lie down, Balinda holding the baby and Sarah monitoring the IV drip, periodically checking pulse. Suddenly the mother sat up, clutching Sarah's arm and screaming, "Bibi! Bibi!"

Sarah tried to soothe her, "Shh, the baby is okay."

"She is not calling for the baby," said Balinda. "Bibi means grandmother. She sees her grandmother."

A chill ran up Sarah's spine. "Is her grandmother by any chance dead?"

"Yes. She died of red eye fever. The same fever that took Mohammedi. I was sick, too. My mother took care of me." Her voice choked. "She died, and I did not. When she was dying, she saw her mother in our house."

"My father saw dead people, too." Her father had dozed in and out of consciousness during his final days, loudly conversing with long-departed friends and relatives. He would call out a name, reach out to some invisible visitor. Just before his final breath, a half-smile almost fluttered across his lips. And that was it. His soul slipped out of his body before the air finished oozing from his lungs.

Sarah checked the woman's pulse again. "Pieter, will we be there soon? She's not doing so well." She decided not to mention the grandmother thing.

"About ten minutes. I called the hospital. They have one unit of O-negative blood. When we find out this patient's type, we'll see if there is any more compatible blood around."

AS THE FIRST unit of blood flowed in, the lab reported that the mother's blood type was A negative. There was no more compatible blood in the hospital.

"Not good," said Pieter. "Surely one of us could donate, but not me. I'm A positive."

"I'm A negative," said Sarah.

"One more unit," said Pieter. "Better than nothing."

Balinda's eyes grew wide. "You should not give your blood. It is your life."

THE LAB TECHNICIAN pierced Sarah's arm with a large bore needle and dark blood flowed through the tubing into a clear bag. Balinda sat nearby, slowly shaking her head and murmuring some chant. When the bag was full, Sarah put her hand over the needle. "Don't take it out. One unit won't be enough."

The technician protested but Sarah insisted.

Balinda asked "Is my blood good for this?"

"I'll check," said the lab tech.

Pieter sprang into action when the Sarah delivered her two units. He was delighted to hear that Balinda was A neg, too, and would donate another unit.

Sarah felt a bit dizzy and clutched the foot of the bed to keep her balance. Everything began to look fuzzy, sounds became fainter and fainter, and the floor got closer . . .

It was a familiar place. Beautiful music—almost too soft to hear. No words, no melody, just chords. The air was pleasant, not too hot, not too cold, and smelled of flowers. She was floating, or perhaps lying on something incredibly soft. Everything around her glowed pinkish and golden.

Then she felt the cold hard concrete hospital floor beneath her. Pieter held her wrist, looking grave until he noticed her eyes were open. Then he smiled. "I can't feel a pulse, but apparently, you're still alive. Are you pregnant?"

"Not unless there is a bright star in the east."

Balinda sobbed, "I told you. Do not give your life away."

The lab technician wrung his hands. "She gave two units. I tell her—too much."

Pieter frowned. "That was really foolish."

SARAH HUNKERED DOWN in the back of the van, shivering under a thin sheet. She thought about going back to the hospital to look for a blanket but could not bring herself to get out into the night air again. She called out to Tumaini, who was slumped in the driver seat, snoring away. "Can you start the engine? Turn on the heat?"

He didn't stir. It was going to be a long night.

The door opened, and Pieter tossed her a blanket. "Still alive in there? How are you feeling?"

Sarah grabbed the blanket, teeth chattering. "I'm f-f-f-f-fine."

"You're not fine. You're freezing." He wrapped himself around her and pulled another blanket over both of them.

She soaked up his body heat, savored his breath on the back of her neck. Her rigors gradually subsided, and she whispered her fear. "She's going to die, isn't she?"

"We don't know that. I think she'll make it. As long as she doesn't go septic or get shock lung."

"But she saw her grandmother."

"She what?"

"She was crying to her grandmother. You know, sometimes when people are dying, they see dead people. And the near-death people, the ones who see a light at the end of a tunnel, a lot of them see dead relatives."

"Brain dysfunction—maybe lack of oxygen, low blood pressure," he said. "It doesn't mean she's going to die. Try not to worry. We've done our best. Especially you."

Perhaps he was right about the near-death stuff. Poor blood flow to the brain, just like her fainting spell. She remembered the other time when she had been in that weird netherworld. Her horse had stumbled into a culvert on the way back to her grandfather's barn. Maybe she had fallen asleep, maybe she had been knocked unconscious. There had been the soft light, the music, the softness and sweet smells. And then she was lying in the tall grass, with the horse and Grandpa standing over her.

CHAPTER TWENTY-SEVEN

A PLAN EVOLVES

A note was scrawled on the label of a bottle of Gatorade. *Drink this before you get up.* Volume replacement. Good advice. It would be embarrassing to faint again. Sarah found Pieter dozing in a chair on the hospital ward. He yawned and stretched when she tapped him on the shoulder, then glanced at the new mother, who looked healthy and was feeding her baby. "Looks like all the patients survived the night." He winked at Sarah. "Even the surgeon. Time to head home."

But they had to go back to Kandu first, to retrieve the back seats of the van, not to mention their duffel bags. Balinda was happy to get a ride back home. The ladies sat cross-legged in the back of the van.

The conversation forever altered Sarah's life.

Sarah was impressed that Balinda could measure blood pressure. Pieter had taught her. She was not good with numbers, so he had modified the sphygmomanometer. Balinda pointed to the dial. "See, when the sounds start above the red line, the pressure is high. Below the blue line, the pressure is low."

"You should check blood pressure on all the pregnant women you see. Send the ones with high blood pressure to the hospital. Not long ago, a woman came to our clinic because someone checked her blood pressure. That saved her life. The baby's too."

"I know. I sent her to you." Balinda grinned with pride, cupping a hand over her mouth to hide her missing front tooth.

"You sent that woman? You're already screening for high blood pressure? Are any other midwives doing this?"

"No. You should teach them. You could teach us many things."

Something clicked. Sarah had been searching for a project. She wanted to make a difference—not just publish some data. This was it. She could train tribal midwives. Not just how to take blood pressure, she could teach them first aid, hygiene, CPR . . . The possibilities were endless.

Pieter threw a little cold water on her enthusiasm. "It's not a new idea. Other people have tried, and it's fallen out of favor."

"I've read some of those reports. But those studies gave pretty minimal training—a class or two. How much can you teach in such a short period? Look how long it takes to be a nurse or a doctor. I'd like to do something more intensive."

Balinda grasped Sarah's hands. "You stay in Kandu. You teach us. Midwives will come from other villages."

"That would be a big project," said Pieter. "You would need some funds."

"I have a budget for a research project. I just need Dr. Obaye's approval for the foundation to release the money."

"It won't be research unless we can show that the training makes a difference. Otherwise, it's just charity outreach.

Dr. Obaye will want to know what outcomes we plan to measure."

"I'm glad you said 'we'."

IT WAS IMPOSSIBLE to sneak up on Kandu. The sound of a motor could be heard from miles away and there are no trees to block the view of the road. The children mobbed Pieter as soon as he stepped out of the van. The women waited outside the dispensary with solemn faces but shouted for joy when Balinda announced that both mother and child were alive well.

Pieter directed Sarah's attention to the unfinished delivery room. "The men gave up on construction because they haven't been able to attract a full-time medical officer. But if you're going to spend a few months here, I'm sure they will finish it. They can build a house for you to live in, too."

"Do I really need to have my own house? Where do you stay when you're here for the clinic?"

"In that tent over there."

Sarah grimaced. "Maybe I could stay with one of the families."

"Trust me. You'll be more comfortable in your own place."

"I don't have a huge budget."

"I know of at least two foundations that would be interested in supporting the construction. The village men will supply the labor."

"Okay." Sarah shrugged. "You've convinced me. I need a house."

"There is one very important thing that we need to do

before we go any further. We need the permission of the village elders."

"How do we do that?"

"I'll talk with them." He glanced at his watch. "It's too late to head back this afternoon. I'll try to get the elders together right now. Tumaini can take you to the lodge. I'll come over later and let you know if they approve."

CHAPTER TWENTY-EIGHT

A COMPLICATION

Pieter was still not back. Sarah tried not to worry, focused on the star-studded velvety black sky and counted six falling stars before she heard his footsteps coming down the path.

The news was good. "The elders approved our project."

"Wonderful."

"And they are excited about finishing the delivery room and building a house. After you leave, it would be a home for a medical officer. You have to realize, though—the house will be a bit primitive. No electricity or running water."

"But much better than a tent." She took a deep breath of the night air, filled with the scents of pine trees and jasmine. "This place is so beautiful." Clouds had rolled in, covering the plains with a fluffy white blanket, as if someone had unfurled a giant roll of cotton batting that gleamed under a full moon. "It looks like the sky in *Peter Pan*, when Tinkerbell sprinkles Wendy and her brothers with pixie dust so they can fly off to Neverland."

"Neverland?"

"Yes. Did you ever see that movie?"

He shook his head. She pointed out to the horizon.

"They flew toward the second star to the right, straight on 'til morning."

"Did you want to go to Neverland when you were a little girl?"

"No, I just wanted to fly. Like Wendy." She leaned over the railing of the balcony and stretched out her arms.

"Don't jump!"

"Don't worry, I've given up my childhood dream of flying."

"What's your grown-up dream?"

"I don't think I ever really had a dream before this. I've always been a good girl, doing what I'm supposed to do." She pushed back a few strands of hair from her face. "I don't want to be melodramatic, but this project we're planning . . . for the first time in my life I feel like I really have a purpose."

Pieter leaned on the railing beside her. "If we can pull this off, it will make a huge difference for the people of this village and could be an example for programs all over Africa."

Sarah hugged herself and shivered. "I didn't know it would be so chilly up here. I should have brought a jacket."

He patted her shoulder. Twice. "You should go inside."

"Those were your dismissive pats."

"My what?"

"Whenever you want to end a conversation, you pat someone on the shoulder, twice."

"I didn't mean to be dismissive. But it's cold out here."

"I doubt that it's much warmer inside."

"There's a fireplace in your room."

"And your point is?"

"Don't you know how to build a fire? You'll have to do when you live up here. I'll teach you."

Sarah watched from the sofa, curled up under a blanket. "Did you learn this in Boy Scouts?"

"I was never a Boy Scout."

"Massai warrior training?"

"This is just common sense, Sarah. You cannot get a big log burning with just a match. You have to have kindling—stuff that catches fire very easily—and then something intermediately flammable, like sticks or wood strips to burn before the log hot is enough to catch fire."

He struck a match and lit wads of paper stuffed around the logs, then squatted down to watch the flames grow. "It can take some time for the fire to get going."

"Well don't just sit there shivering. Hop under the blanket with me."

Pieter slid under the blanket, and Sarah snuggled against him.

He put his arm around her. "You aren't worried about me, you just want me to warm you up." He rubbed her shoulder briskly. "Seems my new job is keeping you warm. Not a bad job. But the pay is lousy."

They sat in silence, watching the flames grow. Pieter's "let me warm you up" rubbing morphed into a slow and tender stroking. With some alarm, Sarah felt her breathing become slower and deeper, entranced by the motion of his hand, each breath synchronized with a caress of his fingers.

She stiffened. "It's getting late."

That should have broken the spell. Except that she tried to give him a quick thank-you-for-building-my-fire peck on the cheek as he was starting to get up. She missed her target, her lips landing on a tender spot just behind his jaw.

He seemed paralyzed for a moment before his lips brushed hers, little more than a breath. Then a real kiss, intoxicating. She was giddy and disoriented—falling through space. Not like tumbling off a cliff. More like drifting down a rabbit hole like Alice in Wonderland, awash in a slow-motion flash flood of confusion. It was like being in quicksand. His hands were wandering. She should have protested, when he reached into her pants, but it felt too nice. No longer floating, she soared through space like a comet. Or more like fireworks bursting into a fountain of sparkles that drifted slowly back down to earth.

In a fog, she was dimly aware that he was pulling off her jeans. Things were getting out of hand. She had let it go too far. She moaned softly, "Oh no."

"Did you say no?"

"No."

"No, like, you didn't say 'no'? Or like... just... 'no'?"

"I don't know." She sat up, face in her hands, knees drawn up under her chin. "I'm so sorry. I just . . ."

He rolled off the sofa and knelt on the floor.

Her breath came in little gasps. "I'm sorry. So sorry."

"I'm the one who should be sorry." He sat back on his heels, arms folded across his chest. "I guess I should go now."

She didn't look up. Just listened to the door close, staring into the fire.

THE MORNING DRIVE was incredibly awkward. Tumaini played a couple of songs on his ancient cassette player, but no one else felt like singing, so he eventually switched off the music.

They arrived at the Elephant Hotel in time for lunch. Amaya greeted them enthusiastically. "Karibu, Dr. Pieter. Do you want some foodie? Maybe chicken and chips?"

"Sounds good to me," said Pieter. "How about you, Sarah?"

She nodded and headed for the washroom.

When came out into the narrow hall, Pieter was waiting for her. "Are you okay?"

She chewed her lip, pondering what to say. Then Amaya came into the hallway and announced. "Foodie is ready!"

Sarah brushed past Pieter without saying a word. She ate her chicken and chips alone, on the front steps of the hotel.

SPIKE THE CAT was waiting at the door to her house. She fed the cat, then tumbled into bed without unpacking or even brushing her teeth. She was sound asleep when her cell phone chirped.

Text from Pieter: "*Can I C U 2 nite?*"

She took a deep breath and began typing: "*Not tonight, I'm pretty tired.*"

She studied the message, and then backspaced to revise it.

"*Not just now.*"

Perhaps she should say, "*Not ever.*"

She frowned, and then deleted all the letters, except "*No.*"

Then she pressed the send button.

CHAPTER TWENTY-NINE

PITCHING THE PLAN

D r. Obaye tapped his fingers together, slowly and precisely—each digit matching its mate on the other hand. He did this without watching, eyes glued to the sheaf of papers before him. "I presume that all of this material is in the documents that you sent me by email?"

Sarah and Ameera nodded.

He cleared his throat. "You realize of course, that this is not a new idea. It has been tried before."

Sarah and Ameera glanced at each other.

He continued. "Studies have not shown any benefit from training traditional birth attendants. This was confirmed by a Cochrane review. Many have raised the concern that 'a little knowledge is a dangerous thing.' These TBAs, to use the acronym, could become overly confident." He arched his eyebrows and dipped his head slightly to one side. "And so, the health ministry gave up on this approach. They have actually restricted the activities of TBAs."

Ameera sat up, ramrod straight, making herself as tall as she could. "Dr. Obaye, you have always said that lack of evidence is not proof. It just means that further study is needed." She pointed to the stack of papers. "Did you not read the more recent Cochrane review? A few small studies have shown such training decreases perinatal mortality. For example, in Pakistan, a very simple and short training intervention had measurable benefit."

"I did read that. It is intriguing."

"And our training will be much more intensive. Sarah will actually work directly with TBAs for four months."

"Such an intensive program would not be practical on a large scale."

"This is an exploratory project," said Sarah. "So yes, this first iteration will be time and labor intensive. Our plan is to develop a standard curriculum that could be widely used."

"How will you know if the training is effective? This could be very difficult to prove."

Ameera said they could use at maternal mortality outcome data.

"You have learned how difficult it is to get reliable data just within this hospital." He peered over his reading glasses. "Do expect it to be any easier in remote areas?"

Ameera bit her lip.

Sarah spoke up. "We could give tests before and after the training—maybe even structured hands-on assessments."

He still looked dubious, so Sarah tried a different tack, telling a story. "Recently, a woman came here in very early stages of toxemia. We followed protocol and delivered a healthy baby. The reason we were able to save her was that a tribal midwife took her blood pressure. She recognized danger and sent her to us. She knew what to do because Pieter taught her at that clinic, where he volunteers in a mountain village. That simple intervention alone—teaching TBAs to take blood pressure—could save many lives."

"Hmm. Dr. Pieter thinks this is a good idea?"

"Oh yes. He has been on board all along. He's the one who convinced the village elders to give us permission."

Dr. Obaye stroked his chin thoughtfully. "Hmm. He has much experience with his clinic in the mountains. So, yes, sure. I am happy to support your project."

The women replied in unison. "Thank you!"

"This will need to go through the Human Subjects Committee. You will need special approval for TBAs to work under your supervision. And of course, the big issue remains. How will you measure success?"

As they walked back to their clinic, Ameera fumed. "It's always this way. Only a good idea if a man thinks so. He didn't agree until he heard that Pieter was involved."

Sarah's cell phone rang. Another call from Pieter. She pressed *Ignore*. He had called multiple times since the return from Kandu and left four identical voice mail messages: "Sarah? This is Pieter. Please call me."

She couldn't bring herself to speak with him. It was just too awkward. Then she realized something disturbing. The "Masked Man" was on the surgery schedule in the morning. Dr. Marshall, an American surgeon, would be supervising the surgery via the internet. She had to be in the operating room, Pieter's domain.

At home, she sat down with her laptop, trying to compose an email to David. But an alert in her inbox announced that her sister had sent her a Facebook message. Allison had posted some pictures of baby cribs and wanted advice on which one to select. Sarah viewed the pictures and decided to call her sister.

Allison squealed with delight. "I'm so glad to hear from you! What do you think about the cribs?"

"I'm partial to the classic white one."

"Not the oak or the maple? Won't the white show dirt?"

"You don't plan to keep your baby's bed clean? It says the finish is water and stain resistant. It should be very easy to wipe down."

"If it's a girl, white would be great. But what if it's a boy? Wouldn't a brown crib be more masculine?"

"Do you expect your son to spring from the womb with a macho persona? No. He will be a sooky mama's baby."

"Good point. Thanks."

"Now I need some advice from you."

"Really?"

Sarah explained the plan to train birth attendants. "The biggest problem is documenting efficacy. Collecting data around here is not easy. Did they teach you any tricks in grad school?"

"Really, Sam? You told me you read my thesis."

"I did, but the methods kind of washed over me."

"I used qualitative research. You know, surveys, focus groups."

"Where can I learn how to do that?"

"You should to get someone else to handle that. You don't have time to learn the methods. And anyway, you shouldn't do the interviews yourself. That would bias your study."

"So, you're coming over?"

"Of course not. I'm in my nesting phase, getting ready for the baby. You should check with my friend Susie, from grad school. She's working for an NGO in Zambia."

"Do you think she'd be interested?"

"I know she would."

After the call, Sarah returned to the task of writing a message to David. But after, "Hi David, I miss you," she could not think of anything else. What could she tell him? David was not enthusiastic about her project. His exact words had been, "That's not real research. You can be a missionary or scientist. Not both."

There was a time when she thought she would never run out of things to say to David. Later, there was less need to talk. It was good enough just to be together—no need to fill a vacant space in time with words.

Isn't absence supposed to make the heart grow fonder? Maybe they had just been too far apart for too long. He should have come to visit her. The fiasco with Pieter was David's fault. If she hadn't been so lonely . . .

She came up with a few bits of news for the email and got ready for bed. As she set the alarm on her cellphone, she noticed that Pieter had left a new voice mail. She thought about deleting it without listening. But she could not. In fact, she had saved all of Pieter's messages, listening to them over and over.

The latest message was different. He waited for a couple of heart-stopping seconds before speaking. "We need to talk." That was all he said. His voice was cold and stern.

CHAPTER THIRTY

OPERATION ACROSS AN OCEAN

The Masked Man was unmasked, lying patiently on the operating table. His left eye slowly closed as the anesthetic drugs flowed into his arm. The right side stayed open, a white moon of sclera showing as the eye rolled back into his head. Once he was sound asleep and positioned for surgery, Pieter exited the room, leaving Ben in charge of anesthesia. Sarah breathed a sigh of relief.

Dr. Marshall's face appeared on the video monitor. "Good morning from the United States. Everything ready there in Tanzania?"

"All systems are Go here," said Sarah. "Thanks for getting up in the middle of the night to help us. Are you getting video feed of the patient's face?"

"Yes, it's excellent. As we discussed yesterday, we need to start by recreating the original defect. Then we'll move some tissue in to fill the space, so that he can close his eye."

Sarah sketched out her proposed incision with a marking pen, and Dr. Marshall approved. Then she sliced along the blue ink lines, peeled back the skin edges, and the wound gaped open.

"Now sew the eyelids shut. That will protect the eye

and keep the eyelid in a functional position while we reconstruct his cheek."

Sarah drew a line extending out from the eyelid. "I'm thinking the cheek advancement flap we discussed will fill in the defect and relieve the downward tension on the eyelid."

"It looks to me like you'll need a relaxing incision to get enough rotation."

"I think you're right. And we might need a skin graft to fill the defect left by the flap."

"That would leave a depression and not a good color match of skin. Use a rotation flap from the neck."

Sarah sketched a curving line. "Like this?"

"Exactly."

The flaps fit perfectly, and Margo and Ruben began suturing them into place.

"What about his nose?" asked Ruben.

Dr. Marshall said that there was no practical way to reconstruct the nose. "Too much missing tissue. He will do better with a prosthetic nose. Just remove the jagged edges. When the swelling goes down, make a cast of the hole in his face and send it to me. Then I'll have a new artificial nose made and bring it with me when I come for a visit."

Sarah clapped her gloved hands. "Yay. You've decided to come."

"Yes, and I'll bring a resident with me. I think you remember Jeff?"

"Of course, Jeff was on the Honduras mission trip. That's great. We can line up a bunch of cases for you."

Sarah was startled by Pieter's voice. "Nice work." She wondered how long he had been looking over her shoulder.

"Thanks. We should be through in about twenty minutes."

Pieter laughed. "That's what you surgeons always say, 'twenty minutes.' When we ask again an hour later, you still say 'twenty minutes.'"

He patted Sarah's shoulder—twice. Then he left the room.

ONCE DR. MARSHALL signed off, Sarah made a beeline for the dressing room. No stopping in the lounge for tea. She just wanted to get out of there as fast as possible, without running into Pieter. But when she stepped out into the hall, there he was, leaning against the wall, arms folded across his chest. He was not smiling.

"You met with Dr. Obaye. You discussed our project."

"Umm . . . yeah, he seems to think it's a good idea."

"This is my project, too."

"Of course. It—it was just easier for the three of us to get together. You're so busy. I'll set up another meeting—"

"Already done. Dr. Obaye called me yesterday. He and I both feel it's important to include the faculty of our midwife school in the project. We don't want any pushback from them. And they'd be a big help with the curriculum."

"Good point."

"We meet on Friday afternoon, three o'clock."

"Okay."

"If you don't want sex, you just have to say 'no.' You don't have to hide like a little girl."

"Sorry." She glanced nervously up and down the hall, hoping no one else heard what he said, her face on fire. She wanted to fall through the floor. She settled for leaving as fast as she could.

Dr. Obaye opened the meeting by thanking everyone for coming. Then he briefly stated the objectives of the project.

The midwives sat stony-faced. Helena, the older one, pointed out that such training had already been tried. "A little knowledge is a dangerous thing. We should follow WHO recommendations and just focus on getting women to deliver their babies in proper facilities."

Sarah switched on the projector and began her Power Point presentation. "The older studies didn't prove any harm—they just didn't prove any benefits." She reviewed recent research that showed more positive results. Then she showed a photo of Balinda. "Dr. Pieter trained her to take blood pressure, and now she screens all the pregnant women in her village. Balinda recently detected toxemia in one of them and sent her to us. That young mother is alive with a healthy baby, thanks to a little knowledge."

Helena looked at Pieter. "Do you believe in this training?"

"It's an excellent idea. I've been working with Balinda, and she has become an effective community health care provider. Sarah had the vision to train others, and I am so glad she has the courage to take this on. We hope that the school of midwifery will help us develop the curriculum. And would you allow Sarah sit in on your classes, to help her prepare?"

Helena smiled and nodded. "You have convinced me."

After the meeting, Pieter helped Sarah store the projector. "I hope you don't mind that I suggested you sit in on their classes."

"It's a very good suggestion. And thanks for making it sound like it was my idea."

"You would have thought of it yourself."

"And if I'd spoken to you sooner, you would have told me. I'm sorry for being such a baby."

"Not a problem."

"And thanks for editing the proposal. You made it much stronger."

"I've had some experience in writing grant applications."

"Yeah, I noticed that you have an NIH grant. I didn't know they funded non-US researchers."

"My collaborator is American professor. By the way, your plan to use qualitative outcome measures is excellent."

"Thanks. I got that idea from my sister." She picked up her backpack and turned toward the door. "I'm really sorry that I've been avoiding you. This project is your baby, too."

"Ah, so we're having a child together." He chuckled.

Sarah rolled her eyes and flounced out of the room.

CHAPTER THIRTY-ONE

OUTSIDE CONSULTANT

It was easy to identify Susie among the deplaning passengers. Sarah had met her at Allison's graduation ceremony: low-maintenance-curly-wash-and-wear hair. And a butterfly tattoo on her neck.

"Karibu, Susie. You're traveling pretty light. Just one little bag for a week in the mountains?"

"I lean toward lightweight trekking stuff that can dry overnight."

"We can go by my place first, so you can drop off your stuff. You have time for a shower before the meeting. I switched on the hot water heater for you."

"Wow, you have hot water? Uptown. Only cold showers at my place. You're brave to drive by yourself."

"This road is actually pretty safe in the daytime. I wouldn't drive it alone at night. Tell me more about qualitative research methods. You're using this approach in Zambia?"

"Yeah. We're studying HIV transmission. With quantitative methods, you would find out things like how many people are infected. But you don't learn what could be done to decrease the incidence. Qualitative research asks 'why,' not 'what.' We use interviews and focus groups."

"How does that work?"

"It's like, why is it that programs to distribute condoms don't have much impact? What we learned from focus groups is that women don't feel entitled to insist that their partners use protection. Now that's something we wouldn't have found out from a questionnaire or even from talking to individuals in a clinic. But get a group of women in a room, they'll start talking."

"So, the conclusion of your study is that we should empower women to demand protection?"

Susie shook her head. "Good luck with that. You know, in most African cultures, women are really fucked." She laughed hollowly. "I didn't mean that literally." Then she sighed. "But it is literally true. In some areas, like Mali, young girls have to be kind of broken in by a man, just after they start having periods." She made air quotes with her fingers around the words "broken in." Then she rolled her eyes. "Parents actually pay some older guy to essentially rape their daughter. That is the guy's job. They call them coyotes."

"Do they test them for HIV—the coyotes?"

"Are you kidding? This happens in the boonies." She ran her fingers through her curls and sighed. "It's hard to change tradition."

DR. OBAYE ROSE from his place at the head of the conference table and crossed the room to clasp Susie's hands. "Karibu. Thank you for coming to help us." He introduced her to Ameera, Margo, and the two midwife nurses, Helen and Ruth. They all helped themselves from a side table laden with mandazis, chapatis, samosas, and steaming ginger tea. When all were seated, Dr. Obaye opened the meeting. "We are very pleased that Professor Susie is here to help us with collecting the data for our project."

Pieter came through the door and grabbed a mandazi.

Susie poked Sarah in the ribs, "Who's that?"

"That's Pieter, the anesthesiologist."

"He's gorgeous."

"And he knows it," Sarah muttered. She cringed when Pieter sat down next to her.

Dr. Obaye called on Susie, and she rose to speak. "We know that education is the key to improving public health. But our opinions alone are not sufficient to garner financial support. They want data. Credible and unbiased data. Let me repeat the word, 'unbiased.' I am not here to prove that your project works. My job is to assess the effects of your program. I won't just ask: does it work? I want to find out what specific attitudes and practices are changed. And to be unbiased, I must be disconnected from the execution of the training program. I must not know which villages participate in training. Is this clear?"

She glanced around the room at nodding heads. "Over the next week, I'll meet with midwives and elders in several villages to discuss logistics for my surveys in January. Our goal is to have twenty villages in the study. It's probably not a realistic number, but that's our pie-in-the-sky goal. Frankly, I'd be happy to get useful feedback from even one village. But if you want information to influence policy makers, we need numbers."

She looked at Sarah. "I'll need at least two graduate students to help me get this done."

"We requested stipends for four grad students."

"Great. But there's another group of people who should

have stipends: the midwives in training. It will be important to motivate them to participate."

Helena, the midwife professor, agreed. "Payment would be very helpful. Not just the money per se, but the recognition of their value."

Sarah frowned. "I didn't think of that. It's not in our budget."

Pieter raised his hand. "I think my mother's foundation might fund that, WHIT—Women's Health in Tanzania." He turned to Sarah, "I'll email you the link to apply for a grant."

As the meeting broke up, Pieter reached across Sarah to shake hands with Susie. "It's great that you could work with us."

"It's a great opportunity for me," she gushed. Susie didn't release her grip on Pieter's hand as she continued to speak, leaving Sarah pinned against the back of her chair. "This is exactly the kind of project I have dreamed of. I can hardly wait to get up to the mountains."

Pieter extricated his hand. "I'm driving up to Kandu tomorrow. It's my day in the clinic. You two can ride up with me."

Susie wrinkled her nose and twiddled one of her brown curls. "That sounds like fun."

"I can bring Sarah back on Sunday. Tumaini could come to collect you later."

Sarah's chair scraped loudly against the floor as she stood up. "Actually, if Pieter's going, Susie doesn't need me. I'll just stay here. I still have a lot of things to do around here before I head home for the holidays."

CHAPTER THIRTY-TWO

A TRUCE, OF SORTS

Come onnnnn, Margo." Pieter's fingers drummed on the dashboard. "Are you sure she had the right time?"

Sarah checked the text message. "Yes, she said 'Pick me up at 6:15.'"

They leaned against respective car doors, as if a "third rail" ran between them, eyes fixed on the entry to Margo's apartment building, waiting for her to join them and puncture the oppressive pressure cooker atmosphere.

He beeped the horn. "Always late. Why am I surprised?"

"I thought you said she was like a Jack-in-the-box—always ready to pop up."

"Ah, but Jack does not pop up immediately. You have to crank and crank and crank." He demonstrated the motion, holding up his left fist and cranking with his right hand. "The timing is always the same. At the 'pop' part of the song, he jumps up."

"No. It's not always the same point in the song. The pop doesn't go with the music. It's the balance of forces. You crank and crank, and spring inside gets tighter and tighter the force overcomes the latch on the lid. That's when Jack explodes out of the box."

"I feel sorry for Jack."

"Why?"

"Always getting stuffed back into the box." He sniffed, rapped his knuckles on the steering wheel a couple of times. "You're flying home tomorrow?"

"Yep."

"So, you have a few days to recover from jet lag before Christmas."

"Mmm-hmm."

"This is torture." He started drumming on the dashboard again. "Please don't be angry with me."

"I'm not angry with you."

"Then why do you keep avoiding me?"

"It's just hard to be around you." Sarah stared out through the window, wishing she could be almost anywhere in the world than here, in a car with the living indictment of her failing fidelity. She was supposed to be pining away for David.

"I'm sorry to make you feel bad."

She did not respond.

"I just said I was sorry. I was being polite. You should also be polite." He honked the horn again. "Come on, Margo!" Then he started doing the cranking pantomime with his hand again.

"You look like you're fishing."

The door burst open and Margo dashed toward them, babbling about a big laceration in the emergency room, the hot water heater, and a few other excuses. Pieter got out of the car and opened the door for her. "Just shut up and get in."

PIETER PRAISED THE food. "Rasheed, you are lucky to be married to such a master chef!"

Ameera smiled meekly. It was her first time to entertain in their new home. The table was adorned with a beautiful silk cloth and fresh flowers, and the smell of curry spices filled the air. The meal was bountiful: crispy samosas and pakoras to start, multiple main dishes, and perfect garlic naan.

Rasheed had just returned from supervising construction in Kandu. "Your house is looking good, Sarah. I introduced a new design feature: transoms. Much better ventilation. The men in the village thought it was a wonderful idea." The men had been less impressed with Rasheed's insistence on level surfaces and right-angle corners.

Sarah said, "It's so generous of you to help with construction."

"Nonsense. It's a very good cause and important to Ameera."

"I can hardly wait to see my house."

Margo waved her fork. "Then you should have gone with Susie on her site visit."

"I didn't want to bias the process. When I took her to the airport, she seemed to be pleased with how things went."

"Pleased" was an understatement. Susie had bubbled with enthusiasm, charmed by the children of the village. And charmed by Pieter too, it seemed. She praised his work at the clinic and little thoughtful things he had done. Sarah got sick and tired of hearing Pieter this and Pieter that.

Pieter raised his glass. "A toast to Susie. She is a dynamo, and she knows what she's doing. Her Swahili is great, and she picked up the Kisambaa language very quickly. The village elders took to her immediately."

Sarah tried not to speculate on whatever might have gone on between Susie and Pieter. It was none of her business. And why should she care anyway?

Margo touched Ameera's arm. "Aren't you hungry? You cooked all this great food, but you've hardly eaten anything at all."

Ameera smiled faintly. "I'm not so hungry tonight."

Rasheed squeezed his wife's hand. "I think she had to taste too much while she was cooking." He whispered something to her, and she rose from the table and started clearing the dishes. Sarah and Margo got up to help.

In the kitchen, Ameera confessed that she had bought the Naan from a restaurant. "Don't tell Rasheed."

Margo snorted. "Why would I tell him? And why should he object? You worked so hard to prepare this wonderful meal. You look exhausted."

"Excuse me. I need to go to the restroom."

Sarah and Margo exchanged worried glances, and Sarah said, "I'll have a private word with her." Standing outside the bathroom door, she could hear the unmistakable sound of retching.

When Ameera finally emerged, Sarah observed, "You're pregnant."

"We weren't going to tell anyone for a while. Just in case something goes wrong."

The men were in the kitchen, helping Margo wash dishes. Pieter called out, "Congratulations!"

"Rasheed, did you tell him?"

"No, he just guessed it."

"It was no guess. After all, I am a doctor."

PIETER ANNOUNCED THAT he would take Sarah home first. "She has to travel tomorrow."

Margo objected. "Don't be silly! My place is on the way.

If you drop her off first, it will gain her at most, what, about five minutes?" She hugged Sarah before getting out of the car. "Have a great trip home."

He put the car in gear and drove on. "I did my best to spare you the agony of being alone with me again."

"Thanks. It's the thought that counts."

They were silent until the car pulled up to her house.

He spoke first. "I wish you a pleasant holiday."

"Thank you."

"Aren't you going to wish me a pleasant holiday?"

"Of course. And thanks for driving me tonight."

As she started to get out, Pieter reached across and pulled the door shut. "This is not a good working relationship." He shut off the engine and killed the headlights. "In fact, this is a shitty situation."

The cat sat on the doorstep, waiting for tuna.

"I've apologized, over and over," he said. "I can't take back what happened."

"I don't blame you. It's just . . . I never thought I would cheat on David."

"Oh." He scratched his head thoughtfully. "But technically, I think you're okay. I mean, we didn't actually—"

"But I wanted . . . I mean . . ." She balled her hands into fists. "I started it. I got you going and then I—" she chopped the air with her hand. "I cut you off."

Pieter clapped a hand over his mouth to stifle a laugh. "Don't worry. My manhood is intact." Then he frowned. "Look, it's your body. You can say no whenever you want. If any asshole ever tries to make you think otherwise, tell him to go fuck himself. Okay?"

She nodded but doubted she would ever use that exact language.

"Don't feel guilty, Sarah. You're a good person. These things happen. Someone just carried us off."

"You mean, we got carried away."

He nodded gravely, "Exactly. And it wasn't really like cheating. I don't think that finger thing counts as—"

"Oh-hoh, yes it does! That was definitely—"

"So, you liked it? I thought you did." He grinned.

"Hmph." She folded her arms.

"Sorry, I shouldn't have said that."

"You were trying to be funny. You think it's charming."

"I know it's not charming. Sometimes . . . things just pop out of my mouth. Look, we're working on something great. Let's please just focus on that. I'll try not to say dumb things."

"I'll try not to be so thin skinned."

"So . . . are we good now?"

"Yeah, we're good. I'm glad we talked. I'd better go. The cat's getting impatient."

He patted her on the shoulder. Twice.

She opened the car door. "Have a Merry Christmas."

"Who will feed your cat while you're gone?"

"He'll be fine. Turns out, the neighbors are feeding him, too. He's been double dipping."

"Like you."

"Pieter!"

"Sorry."

Spike rubbed against her legs as she entered the house. She watched from the kitchen window as the car backed out of her driveway. Then her phone pinged. Text from Pieter: "*C U next year.*"

CHAPTER THIRTY-THREE

BACK IN THE USA

Climate shock. Flurries of white flakes pasted themselves to the windows of the airplane as it taxied to the gate. Sarah reached into her backpack and pulled out the Falcons sweatshirt she had bought during her layover in Atlanta. After thirty hours of travel she was dead tired, semiconscious, and woefully unprepared for the winter weather in Philadelphia.

She bobbed up and down in the river of passengers flowing out of the security zone, searching for David. He had become less real to her in the past six months—a two-dimensional image on a video screen. She spotted a dark head, wasn't completely sure it was him. Then their eyes locked. He smiled, almost shyly, and waved her camel hair topcoat aloft. They elbowed their way toward each other through the throng until he wrapped her in his warm and solid arms. He was real. "Welcome home, Sam. You look great."

She knew she didn't look great. Her eyes were puffy, and her hair was stringy. But he was sweet to say so.

"Your luggage will be on carousel five."

She pointed to her roll-on bag. "This is all I brought. All my warm stuff is in our apartment."

"Then let's get going."

"Since I'm travelling light, we could take the train instead of a taxi."

"Not a chance. I booked a limo."

They settled into the back seat of the black stretch limo, and David popped the cork on a bottle of champagne.

She clicked her glass against his. "I should say, 'You shouldn't have,' but this is really cool."

"It's a special occasion."

She had forgotten how big his brown eyes were, eyes that somehow always seemed to be looking past her. Or maybe it was just that he was always focused on the future. Overly large pupils, like deep dark pools, gave no clues as to the machinations of his mind.

"I thought about booking a romantic candlelight dinner tonight, but I know you're way too tired for that."

"What about tomorrow night?"

"Lab Christmas party at Dr. Cook's house."

"Oh."

"I suppose you'll want to go shopping for something to wear."

She shook her head. "I have some nice dresses in my closet. But I do need to buy some new underwear. The African laundry process has taken its toll."

"I'd love to help you shop for lingerie."

But of course, he was way too busy to go shopping with her. Besides his usual heavy schedule, he was taking some extra call so that he could be off over Christmas.

AT THE LAB party, Sarah immediately realized that she was an outlier. "David, what did the invitation say about attire?"

"Umm . . . ugly Christmas sweaters optional."

"Why didn't you tell me?"

"Because I hate ugly Christmas sweaters?" He kissed her on the cheek. "You look beautiful."

"You just said that. When we were leaving the apartment."

"Then I'll say it one more time. You look beautiful."

David poured two glasses of wine before leading her to their host. Dr. Cook wore a red cable knit vest. His jolly green felt bowtie had scalloped edges to make it look like holly and a central cluster of red berries. David and his boss fell into a technical discussion, so Sarah excused herself to check out the food. She was just about to bite into a shrimp, when a young woman wearing a Christmas sweater that could take first prize in any ugly contest pushed her way between Sarah and the table.

"Hi. I'm Carla."

Sarah stared blankly.

Carla offered her hand to shake. "I work in the lab with David." Sarah had a drink in her right hand and a shrimp in the other, so she just shrugged her shoulders.

Carla laughed. "Oh, you have your hands full."

Sarah bit the shrimp off its tail and nodded. She shifted the wine glass to her left hand, leaving her right hand free. Carla grabbed it with both hands.

"David misses you *so* much. He talks about you all the time. He was really lonely at Thanksgiving. That's why I decided to go over and roast him a turkey. He acted like it was good, but I'll bet it wasn't as good as your turkey."

"I've never cooked a turkey."

"Really?"

"We always have Thanksgiving dinner in the hospital

cafeteria." Sarah shrugged her left shoulder. "One or the other of us is always on call."

"He was on call, but he didn't have to be in the hospital. We watched some football games."

"I'll bet he liked that." Sarah flashed a thin, tight-lipped smile. "Well I'm going to mingle—talk to some people I haven't seen for a while."

"Oh, sure, don't let me keep you."

Sarah did see one friend. Diane was an Ob-GYN resident who had been a classmate in medical school. They found a comfortable place by the fire. Diane was full of hospital gossip, and then wanted to talk about her own early pregnancy symptoms. Sarah found it hard to keep focused as jet lag closed in.

When she awoke, David was standing over her.

"How long was I out?"

"A while. We just let you sleep. I think we should head home now."

They stopped near the door to thank their hosts. Suddenly Carla appeared, and cried out, "David, you're under the mistletoe. I gotta kiss you or you'll have bad luck."

David laughed and pulled Sarah toward him for a big kiss. That drew a round of applause from the party guests. He whispered, "Let's get out of here."

IN THE UBER, Sarah remarked that Carla seemed to be quite fond of David.

"Hooh-yeah. She has quite a crush on me. It's not a comfortable situation."

"Well, if she wanted to impress you tonight, it's too bad she didn't know your opinion of Christmas sweaters."

"It was a pretty ugly sweater, wasn't it?"

"How was the turkey?"

"Did they have turkey tonight? I didn't spend much time at the food table."

"I mean the Thanksgiving turkey."

"Oh." He cleared his throat. "She told you about that?"

"Yeah."

"Well, the turkey—let's just say she got credit for trying. Her efforts were appreciated." He glanced at Sarah, concern on his face. "You're not jealous, are you?"

"Should I be?"

He squeezed her hand. "Not a chance. You're my girl."

SHE POURED A ring of pancake batter into the skillet, practicing for the family breakfast on Christmas morning. Making pancakes used to be her father's role.

David peered over her shoulder. "What is it?"

"It's supposed to be a Christmas wreath."

"Looks like a lopsided bagel."

She pointed her spatula to a piece of bacon imbedded in one side of the pancake. "This is supposed to be the bow."

"Bacon on a Christmas pancake? Wasn't Jesus Jewish?"

She snorted. "Doesn't stop you from eating it.'

"Don't tell my mother."

Perhaps the batter was too thin or maybe the skillet was not quite hot enough. And she was trying to hurry, what with David breathing down her neck. Only half of the pancake turned.

"That's okay. It'll taste just fine." He doused it with syrup. "You were so beautiful last night."

"I was overdressed."

He spoke without completely swallowing the piece of pancake in his mouth. "You weren't overdressed. You were gorgeous. I'll bet every guy there wished he was goin' home with you."

Sarah added some cornstarch to the batter to make it thicker and started on the next pancake, an angel.

David continued, "I mean, you looked so incredibly hot. I should have sent you off to Africa long ago."

She wanted to tell him he had not "sent her." But she held her tongue.

The angel pancake was not bad, although the wings were asymmetrical.

He jumped up and kissed the top of her head. "Gotta go. Rounds start at 6:30."

Sarah had plenty of time to clean up the kitchen. Her appointment with Dr. Garnett was not until that afternoon.

DR. GARNETT'S DESK was covered with stacks of paper, and she had to move a box from a chair so that Sarah could sit down.

"I've enjoyed reading your weekly reports, Sarah. It seems that the year is going very well. You seem like a different person—relaxed, happy."

"Well we can't attribute that to lack of stress or hard work."

"Those aren't the things that cause burnout. It's lack of control, no appreciation, a sense of futility."

"The challenges have been huge. But I feel like I'm making a difference. And I don't have to bother with computers and coding."

"Refreshing, eh? Will you be ready to be back in this rat race in July?"

"I'm looking forward to it. I'll be a chief, so I'll have more control. No in-hospital call."

"After that, what about joining our faculty? We discussed you at the last department meeting, and we all think you would be terrific."

"I hadn't really thought that far in advance."

Dr. Garnett leaned forward over the desk. "If you want to continue some of your work in Africa, you could do that. You could even take some classes, get a degree in global health. The school is very interested in that."

"That sounds great."

CHAPTER THIRTY-FOUR

HOME FOR CHRISTMAS

L et me have a good look at that ring."

Sarah stopped scraping plates and extended her hand to David's mother.

Christmas Eve in Houston. Also the last night of Hanukkah.

"I really wanted to have an engagement party while you were home, but that would be jumping the gun, since you haven't set a date yet. I totally understand. You still have another year of training, and he'll be doing that fellowship."

Sarah paused before speaking, taking a moment to process what she had just heard. "Thanks for thinking of it."

"Listen, whenever you do set a date, I'm happy to help with planning. You're always so busy. The ceremony would be at Palmer Episcopal, right? Where your sister got married?"

"Yeah, that's our family church."

"Episcopalians are so . . . ecumenical. Would they let us have a rabbi?"

Sarah shrugged. "Never hurts to ask."

David poked his head into the kitchen. "Better get going, Sam. Your mom expects us at 10:00."

Sarah leaned against the car door and stared out the window as they rolled past inflatable snowmen and Santas.

"You okay, Sam?"

"Not really."

"What's wrong?"

"Your mom thinks we don't have a time line. Like, she doesn't know we're getting married as soon as I get back."

David gripped the steering wheel and swallowed. "Right."

"You said we should get married when I get back from Africa. I said July, and you said that would be cool."

"But, like, we haven't made any plans."

"Getting cold feet?"

"Of course not. But we need to be practical. Talk things through."

"And when did you think we should do that?"

He parked the car in the driveway. "I guess this is not the best time."

"Sounds like you've already made up your mind." She slammed the car door and walked into the house.

THE CHURCH WAS overflowing with poinsettias and glowing in candlelight, just like so many midnight services past. How many times had she sat in this church? The last time was Allison's wedding, a slightly hungover bride struggling up the steep steps to the altar. Their father's funeral had been a more somber affair. She sniffed back a tear and David squeezed her hand.

CHRISTMAS MORNING PANCAKES were a resounding success. Even the failed reindeer that Allison's husband Mike requested. The antlers fell off, but Allison said it was okay because it could be a donkey. And Mary rode a donkey, right?

Sarah announced the offer of a faculty position in Philadelphia. "After I finish my chief year. They'll let me continue to work on my project in Africa. And I could get a master's degree in global health."

David set his hand on Sarah's shoulder. "She hasn't made up her mind yet. As a surgeon, she'd make a lot more money in private practice."

Barbara gazed at her elder daughter. "What would make you happy?"

Sarah shrugged her shoulders and took a sip of orange juice.

After the traditional gift exchange, the two sisters retreated to Sarah's old room, lounging on the bed. Allison scanned through photos of Africa on Sarah's laptop. "It really sucks that David's getting cold feet."

"It's not cold feet. It's a communication error. Like, I said, let's get married in July, and he said 'Cool,' but he didn't really think I was serious. I feel kind of stupid, actually. Haven't really thought of planning. But who wants one of those big wedding extravaganzas anyway?"

"You didn't like my wedding?"

"It was great. It's just . . . David and I have been together so long it seems silly to make a big deal out of the wedding."

Allison sniffed and continued perusing the pictures. "All these shots of birds. What's this weird one? The picture is kind of blurry."

"That's a green ibis."

"Doesn't look green to me."

"It's the lighting. And I was shooting through a dirty

window with a cell phone. He flew off before I could get the telephoto lens on my camera."

Sarah picked up an old high school yearbook. She had dog-eared the pages with pictures of herself or Allison. She and her little sister looked so much alike that they had often been mistaken for twins. But they were totally different. Allison was the popular party girl/cheerleader/prom queen. Sarah had been the serious and obedient overachiever.

"You should tell David to shit or get off the pot."

"Don't say that. It's a gross saying."

"If he won't set a date, you should break the engagement."

"We're almost common law. It would be more like a divorce."

"You're *not* married yet. And you never dated anyone else."

"Yes, I did. I went to prom with Eddie Barton. Here's the picture for proof." Sarah tapped on the yearbook page.

"But Eddie's gay."

"I didn't know that at the time."

"Did he kiss you?"

"No, we were just friends."

"Just friends. See? I rest my case. You never dated anyone else. So how do you know that David's the one?"

"The one? Get serious, Al. There's no such thing as 'the one.'"

"Mike is the one for me. We fit together perfectly. Just like jigsaw-puzzle pieces."

"People aren't rigid, like cardboard cut-outs. We're more like amoebas." She flapped her arms in a poor imitation of floppy pseudopods. "We adapt. You commit to someone and build a relationship. Did you know that divorce rates are lower for arranged marriages?"

"Makes sense. Lower expectations mean less disappointment. But you can't change someone. That's what all the marriage advice books say."

The room was full of mementos: photos, volleyball and debate trophies, programs from school musicals. "We do change." Sarah fingered the ribbons of a withered prom corsage, pinned to the curtain. "All of us."

Allison was focused on the laptop. "I love the pictures in the village. Beautiful scenery. And look at these precious little boys." It was a group shot, taken after the boys' successful lip surgery. "Who's this cutie?" She pointed to Pieter. "Is he the dreamy doctor that Susie told me about?"

"I guess so."

"Susie thought he was gorgeous! And so nice. He built a fire for her when she stayed up in the mountains."

"Hmm." Sarah thumbed through the yearbook.

"She really tried to come on to him, but he wasn't into her. She figures he must have a girlfriend." Allison studied the photo. "Looks like he likes you, though."

Allison was right. In the picture, Pieter's eyes were fixed on Sarah. He had that slightly lopsided smile, unilateral dimple.

Sarah cleared her throat and furiously flipped pages.

"I think you like him."

"Hmph." She slammed the yearbook shut as a rosy blush spread from her neck up to her face and down onto her chest.

Allison smirked. "Oooohhh, Sarah! Did you?"

Sarah shoved the back into the book shelf.

"I think you did!"

"I kissed him, once." Sarah chewed her lip for a moment. Then she corrected herself. "I mean, one night, but that's all. I feel terrible about it."

"Oh, Sarah!" Allison couldn't stop giggling. "You? Miss Perfect!"

"Shhh!" Sarah plopped back on the bed. She closed her laptop and stowed it away.

"A kiss is no big deal. And you've never had a fling, have you? Besides, you were lonely. David should have come over to see you. He wimped out on you."

"That's no excuse. I think Pieter is a player."

Allison wiggled her eyebrows. "You're acting too guilty. I think it was more than just a kiss. Did you give him a blow job?"

"What? No!!" Sarah picked up a pillow and smacked her sister with it. Soon they were tumbling all over the bed, squealing, reenacting childhood pillow fights.

The door popped open and Mike came in. "Allison, what are you doing? Are you trying to kill our baby?"

"We're fine," Allison laughed.

Sarah said, "Actually, exercise during pregnancy is healthy."

NEW YEAR'S EVE found Sarah and David back in their Philadelphia apartment, watching TV: Anderson Cooper in Times Square. David was on back-up call—not required to stay in the hospital, just had to be prepared to go in if needed. They dined on take-out Chinese, toasted each other with ginger ale, and both dozed off long before midnight. Around 11:30, they awoke and decided to call it a night.

He was still brushing his teeth when Sarah got into bed. She pulled the covers up around her neck and faced the wall and did not stir when he climbed in beside her and tentatively touched her shoulder. It was not an imploring caress—more of a polite inquiry. She pretended to be asleep. His fingers trailed lightly down her arm.

She focused on breathing rhythmically and deeply.

If I just lie still, he'll eventually give up.

CHAPTER THIRTY-FIVE

COMING HOME FROM HOME

The ghost of most recent Christmas past haunted the Amsterdam airport. Tinsel covered trees were still everywhere, decked out in sparkling lights and red and gold ornaments. Weary Christmas carols wafted through the air like whiffs of stale leftovers. A young man took a selfie with a team of huge glittery penguins, hitched to a sleigh, with reindeer antlers strapped to their heads.

Sarah had been terrified the first time she passed through Schiphol Airport on her way off into the unknown. This time, the place was familiar. She didn't bother to wait in the long line at MacDonald's, opting for a sausage roll at the cafeteria behind the giant plastic cheese. When she tired of browsing through the duty-free shops, she made her way to the gate.

Pieter was there. His eyes lit up when he saw her, and he pulled his backpack off the seat next to him.

Sarah sat down. "Wow, I can't believe we're on the same flight."

"Not so unusual. Only one direct flight a day from Europe to Tanzania. And we're both returning from holidays."

"Oh . . . right."

"How was your Christmas? Was Santa Claus good to you?"

"I'm still my mother's little girl. She filled a stocking for me. What about you?"

"My mother also thinks I am still a child. I was not home on December 5th, when Sinter Klaas comes. When I did get home, there was a wooden shoe for me, filled with candy."

"Santa Claus doesn't come to Holland on Christmas Eve?"

"We have Christmas Man on Christmas Day. Two treat days. We are more spoiled that the children in your country. But do you think it's right to tell children these lies? Eventually they know the truth. Then how do they trust their parents?"

"I found out there was no Santa when I was four years old. I woke up when I heard a loud 'HO HO HO!' I peeked down the stairs and saw my dad putting presents under the tree. I never told my parents."

"You didn't want them to know you sneaked out of bed."

"I just wanted to keep believing. And actually, my dad saw me."

"So, your parents knew that you knew."

"Yes, and we all kept pretending."

"You are a hopeless romantic."

"Not hopeless. Hopeful."

They compared boarding passes—seats on opposite sides of the plane.

Pieter had a conversation in Dutch with the woman at the service desk. The woman frowned.

"She says the plane is very crowded. Maybe we should ask someone to switch once we are on board. We both have aisle seats, so it may not be difficult to find someone willing to trade."

David always claimed the aisle seat. Whenever Sarah needed to get up during the flight, he would act as though it were a huge imposition, harrumphing and making a big production of folding up his tray table and stowing his laptop, headphones. Maybe Pieter would be more gracious.

She provided an update on funding for the midwife project. "The Stanford Foundation will support Susie's focus groups. And your mother's foundation came through with stipends for the midwives."

"Things are really falling into place."

"Also . . . my department offered me a faculty position, after I finish my chief year."

"Awesome! Your future is all set."

The flight crew arrived, including the flight attendant who had been on Sarah's first flight to Africa—when the man had the fish allergy reaction.

Anika instantly recognized Sarah. "I hope we will not need your assistance on this flight."

"Let's hope not. But if we get into trouble, he's a doctor, too." She tilted her head toward Pieter.

Anika said that he looked familiar, and he said that of course she should remember him because he flew this route several times a year. They began chatting gaily in Dutch, Anika giggling and patting Pieter on the arm. She spoke to the woman at the service desk, then waved to Pieter and gave a "thumbs up."

Moments later, an announcement came over the PA system. "Passengers Pieter Meigher and Sarah Whitaker, please approach the service desk."

This time the woman was very friendly. She smiled

broadly and said something in Dutch as she gave them two new boarding passes.

"What did she say?"

"That we should have told her in the first place that we are on our honeymoon."

Sarah gasped. "Wha—"

Pieter put a finger on her lips. "Shhh. You'll like these seats. Trust me."

Business class. She could be completely horizontal—lie flat for a nice nap. And they had two center seats, each with aisle access. Champagne before take-off. As they clinked their glasses, Pieter glanced at her bare left hand. "What's up with the ring? You're not wearing it."

"Oh that? Umm . . . Well, you know, I was always uncomfortable wearing something so valuable in Africa. I left it back home."

It wasn't really a lie. She did feel uncomfortable wearing the ring. And she did leave it at home. Both statements were true—just unrelated.

SHE SHOULD HAVE said goodnight to Pieter after he carried her bag into the house. But they were both hungry. It was too late to go out for something to eat, but Sarah was certain she could come up with something in her kitchen.

He brought some beer and they wound up on the glider on Sarah's veranda, staring at the mountain in the moonlight.

Pieter waved a samosa. "You are a good cook."

"I didn't make these. I got them frozen at the market."

"Then you are a good procurer and preparer."

"Actually, I'm a pretty good cook."

"What kind of food?"

"Lots of things. And I'm branching out. Ameera's teaching me to cook Indian food."

"I am a very good cook as well." He took a long swig of beer. "I can boil an egg and make toast."

"Seriously? Is that all?"

He laughed. "Do I look like I am starving?"

"I bet you live on take-out pizza."

"I should hire you to cook for me."

Sarah began peeling off the label off her beer bottle, something that always drove David crazy.

Pieter was driving her crazy. So close, staring over her shoulder. He draped an arm across her back, and she could feel his breath on her ear. "What are you doing?"

"It's just a nervous habit." She succeeded in removing the label intact and leaned forward to spread it out on the coffee table.

"You did a great job." He reached out to smooth some wrinkles out of the label. Then he touched her empty ring finger. An electric current flowed up her arm. "Is the wedding on or off?"

"I'm not sure." She was going to say something else, but when she turned her head to speak, his mouth was right there.

CHAPTER THIRTY-SIX

THE MORNING AFTER

A re you awake?"

Pieter nibbled the back her neck as she stretched, yawned, and opened her eyes to the peach glow of dawn. "I am now."

"Sorry to wake you."

"Sorry?" She giggled and flexed into the curve of his body. "You feel pretty happy to me."

His hand drifted from her breast down into the valley of her waist and then up over her hip. "You are shaped rather like a cello."

"You've got this backwards." She flipped over to face him. "The cello is shaped like a woman. Ladies have been around much longer than any stringed instrument."

"Is that so?"

"Mmm-hmm."

"Come here. You on top for a change."

Sweet and languid at first, like a graceful pas des deux, as if they were the only people in the world and they had all the time in the universe. Then passion took the reins and they galloped across the plains until they tumbled over a cliff, and the world became a kaleidoscope.

She fell into that space between his arm and torso, watching his chest heave as he caught his breath.

He turned and touched her cheek. "Did you know that you are totally irresistible?"

She wondered if he said that to all the girls.

He rubbed her shoulder. "Making love to you is like playing a Stradivarius."

"Really? I didn't know you could play the violin."

"Saaraah," he whined. "Can't you ever take a compliment?"

"Sorry. You were sweet to say that."

"Say something nice to me."

"Well . . . you're not shaped like a cello."

"Is that the best you can do?"

"You're like a bass viol." She laid her face on his chest. "I can feel your voice. Like when we were dancing. Remember?"

"Mm-hmm." He stroked her hair. "David was crazy to let you come here alone."

Sarah sat bolt upright.

"Sorry. Come back."

She lay back down to face him in the morning light. She had always avoided staring at him. Now she felt entitled to gaze directly into his clear blue eyes.

She tapped him on the nose. "Tell me about this Eva person."

"Ahh, no." He flopped onto his back and folded his arms under his head. "You don't need to hear about her."

"Why not? I told you about David."

"This is different. She's a just a friend. But . . . " He tapped the empty ring finger on her left hand. "He gave you that ring." He laughed. "A chastity belt would have been more effective."

"Pieter!"

"Sorry, bad joke."

"What does Eva do? Is she a doctor? A lawyer?"

"She sits on the board of her father's company."

"So, she works for her father?"

He rolled his eyes. "Did I say she works? She does not."

"Oh."

He sat up. "I have to be at the hospital soon. Can you cook us some breakfast?"

"You said you could cook."

"Only my boiled eggs. You could make something much better."

She crawled out from under the mosquito net and pulled on a T-shirt. "Let's go see if there's anything worth eating in my kitchen."

"Mind if I take a shower while you cook?"

"The water heater's not on yet."

"No problem."

Cold shower. She shuddered at the thought.

The eggs and long-life milk in the fridge were still okay, and she had some frozen bread, so she made French toast, which Pieter proclaimed to be the best he ever tasted.

He barged into the bathroom while she was on the toilet and asked to borrow her toothbrush.

"It would be polite to knock. I prefer to pee in private."

He laughed, tried to cover his mouth, but white speckles spewed onto the mirror. His voice was muffled. "I wot witning."

"You're not listening, eh?" She feigned indignation, flushing the toilet with a flourish. "I've heard that before. You have totally blown your credibility."

He rinsed his mouth and tapped the toothbrush on the sink. "A little white lie is okay, isn't it? Once in a while?"

She bumped her hip against his. "Move over so I can wash my hands."

He reached around her to wipe the spots off the mirror, slipped his hands around her waist, and winked at her reflection. "You might like Holland. We keep our toilets in little closets."

The kitchen was spotless, pans and dishes drying on the counter. "Pieter, you cleaned up. How nice."

"I am compensating for my lack of credibility." He paused with his hand on the door knob. "Are you coming to the operating room today? Or do you need to recover from jet lag?"

"I'll be in midwife class this morning, and I have to go to market this afternoon. My cupboard is bare. Hopefully I'll have time for a nap some time."

"So." It was an awkward moment. He cleared his throat and shrugged his shoulders. "I guess I'll see you around. "

"RATS." SHE'D LEFT her phone on airplane mode. When she switched it back on, the messages appeared in reverse order of transmission. The last and most frantic message appeared first, in all caps: "*CALL ME NOW!*"

David was not happy when he answered the phone. "What the fuck?"

"Did I wake you up?"

"Of course not. How the hell am I supposed to sleep? Jesus, Sam."

"I forgot to take my phone off airplane mode Sorry. I—"

"The ring. You left it. Taped to the mirror."

"I wanted to be sure you saw it."

"You just left it! What's that supposed to mean?"

She switched from defense to offense. "I felt stupid wearing that ring. We'll never—"

"If you really want to get married, then just come back home right now. We'll fly to Vegas or something."

Her voice oozed with sarcasm. "Oooh, that's really romantic."

"So, is this it? Are we through?"

"No." That thought made her shiver. "Maybe I just need a little space."

"Space? As if the Atlantic isn't wide enough for you?"

"Technically, I'm still living with you. You have all my stuff."

"That's not funny."

"Sorry."

"I guess I'm not scoring many brownie points, ranting on like this."

"I can understand why you're upset."

"Do you still love me?" His voice had never sounded so weak.

The pause was only a couple of heartbeats. But it was there. "I still love you. You don't just stop loving someone."

"I don't want to lose you, Sam."

"I should go now. Got to get to class. "

"Call me when you can. Please."

"Okay."

"Don't give up on me. Promise?"

"Cross my heart."

IT WAS IMPOSSIBLE to pay attention to the lecture, even though it was important. Oral medications to control postpartum bleeding. Should TBAs be allowed to dispense it? It was controversial. Sarah was not just jet-lagged. They hadn't spent much time sleeping during the night. Her brain was in a fog as she struggled to wrap her head around her train wreck of a life. Whatever possessed her to leave the ring? It was a stupid snap decision. And she hadn't really intended to get tangled up with Pieter.

Okay, she had fantasized about it. Still, she couldn't believe it had actually happened. Was that really her last night? She didn't consider herself to be a cold fish, but she had never thought herself capable of such—it felt weird to even think the word—such passion.

She had to put it behind her. Pieter was a player. It was a one-night stand. She would be a big girl, wouldn't let it get weird. Not like it did after that night up in the mountains. Still, as she dozed off, her mind drifted off into the moonlight, the owl hooting, the creaking glider . . .

She nearly fell off her chair when her cellphone buzzed. A text from Margo: *"Need help in ER. STAT."*

THE YOUNG WOMAN lay prone on a stretcher with a deep gash in the back her neck. Her right arm was slashed, and the left hand was nearly severed from her wrist, hanging by a thin strip of flesh. Her husband had attacked her with a machete. Fortunately, the neighbors heard her screaming and chased him off. Margo wondered if they could save the dangling hand.

Sarah examined the wound. "It's reasonable to try. The hand should survive if at least some of the blood supply was spared. She might even regain some useful motion. Many of the muscles that move fingers are up in the forearm."

In the operating room, Ruben repaired the right arm while Margo and Sarah worked on the left wrist. They were ecstatic to discover an intact artery and vein. Sarah tugged on a tendon. "This one moves the index finger. I can't believe her husband did this. Have you ever seen an attack like this before?"

"Once in a while. It's a good thing they always chop from the back, so the spine can stop the blade. I've never seen a complete decapitation."

"Well, you wouldn't, would you? I mean, a person being headless and all—they wouldn't bother bringing her to the hospital."

"You got me there. But domestic violence is very common in your country, too, isn't it?"

"Sure, beatings, shootings . . . I've never seen anything like this."

"Aaahh, shootings. So, they wind up dead instead of just mutilated."

"I see your point."

Margo paused in sewing, as though she had a sudden inspiration. "We need to teach about domestic violence in our course."

"Talking to women." Sarah sighed. "That's the main strategy in the US. Educating women, providing shelters, public service announcements. Still, it never ends."

"Maybe Pieter should talk to the men in some of the villages. Give a class or something. What do you say, Pieter?"

He was hanging a unit of blood. "Sorry, I wasn't listening. Just back here keeping the patient alive."

After the long and tedious wrist repair, the women left Reuben to sew up the neck. Pieter joined them in the lounge.

Margo sat down with a cup of tea. "So, Pieter, what

about addressing domestic violence in our course? You know, what we asked you about during the case?"

"I didn't hear. Ask me again."

"Sarah and I can only do so much by talking to the women about domestic violence. We think you should have some sessions with the men."

"I can't see how me talking to a few men would change anything."

"It couldn't hurt to try," said Sarah. "Who knows—change one or two minds and it could snowball. Or maybe you save at least one life."

He shrugged. "Sure. Okay."

"I'll go check on Ruben." Margo downed the rest of her tea and headed out the door.

Pieter and Sarah sat in awkward silence, avoiding eye contact. After a few minutes he asked, "Did you get to the market?"

"No."

"Would you like to share a take-out pizza?"

CHAPTER THIRTY-SEVEN

BREAKFAST CLUB

It was a beautiful morning for a run—bright sunshine, clear, cool air. The path crossed a recently plowed field, punctuated at random intervals by towering termite mounds that were apparently too big to fall. The field had been full of tall corn and sunflowers when Sarah first arrived. Now the ground was prepared for the long rains that would transform the footpath into a long serpentine mud wrestling pit.

Beyond the field, the trail passed through a canyon of lantana and bougainvillea hedges filled with twittering weaver birds. Toucans wailed from the branches of the jacaranda and flame trees, and the ground was blanketed with lavender and scarlet blossoms. Sarah willed her mind to be an organic digital recorder, capturing everything for future reference.

From the main road, she could see the mountain. A long ridge, known as the saddle, gradually sloped upward from the jagged crown of Mawenzie to join the majestic Kibo peak. She had heard that the path across the saddle was deceptively gentle in appearance, that many failed attempts on Kibo ended on that ridge.

Kilimanjaro was the reason Sarah was here. It had been

David's dream to climb that mountain. She had been a just passenger in that vision. Now she was chasing something totally different. Funny how things turn out.

Pieter had breakfast waiting. They had settled into a very comfortable routine, taking turns cooking the morning meal. He always served soft boiled eggs in little porcelain cups. Sarah was more creative: omelets, bacon, fried eggs, pancakes, sausage.

Sarah gazed at the scorched piece of toast on her plate. "I think I'll buy a toaster."

"Don't like my cooking?"

"Your skillet toast skillet is simply marvelous. I'd just like to save you some time and effort."

"I have a toaster at my house. I'll bring it over." He snipped the tops off the eggs with a little gizmo. They used little cappuccino spoons to scoop and spread the innards onto the toast. Pieter cut and ate one bite at a time, knife in his right hand and fork in his left.

Sarah cut her toast into nine equal pieces, like a tic tac toe game.

"Why do you always cut your toast like that?"

"It's how my dad always did it. I liked the center piece best, with no crust."

"But you did eat the crust, didn't you?"

"Only after I became a big girl. When I was a little girl, I did this."

She picked up a corner piece and chomped into it, her teeth slicing off the bread just inside of the crust.

"Shocking. But you must have been a very cute little girl, so your father tolerated this waste of food."

"Yep. I'm such a big girl now." She popped the crust into her mouth.

They had not gone public with their arrangement. He kept his SUV parked at his own house, and they were careful not to come and go at the same time. They had even kept things secret from Margo. Only Rosie the housekeeper knew—not because anything had been confided to her. She just returned his freshly ironed and folded clothes to the same house where she found them on the floor.

Pieter reached for her hand. "Can I take you somewhere for the weekend?"

"What do you have in mind?"

"Let me surprise you." He started to take his plate into the kitchen.

"Leave it there. I'll clean up."

He gave her a goodbye hug "I'll bring the toaster this afternoon."

"Have a great day!"

And I love you.

That's what she thought as she watched him walk down the path. She wanted to scream it. She wanted to run after him, tackle him, and beg him to never leave her.

But she couldn't.

Because she shouldn't.

And so, she wouldn't.

THEY FLEW TO Dar es Salaam, took a hydrofoil across sparkling turquoise water to Zanzibar, then rode in a smaller boat to a tiny coral island, an eco-resort with solar power and water supplied by rain. The manager, an old school chum of Pieter's, showed them to a small A-frame hut right on the beach. The sleeping loft had a stunning view of the sea and wonderful cross breezes.

Sarah and Pieter hiked around the island, searching unsuccessfully for elusive miniature antelope, then snorkeled among beautiful coral, fish, octopi, and huge sea turtles.

They ordered mojitos on the terrace before dinner. The waitress set their drinks on the table and whispered to Pieter, "I like this one."

The sun was sinking, and shadows were getting longer. Pieter downed the last of his mojito and took Sarah's hand. "There's a much better place to watch the sunset."

The path headed north along the beach and curved around a huge rock where the strip of sand became quite narrow. A concave coral cliff curved above their heads, like a sandy wave, creating an alcove. The face of the cliff was alive, teeming with hundreds of tiny crabs.

"Is this where you take all your lady friends?"

Pieter stopped in his tracks, a pained look on his face. "Where is this coming from?"

"I heard the waitress whisper to you. She said, 'I like this one.'"

"I did bring my friend Eva here, once."

Sarah blushed and stammered, "I . . . I'm sorry. I shouldn't . . ."

"I like it that you are a little bit jealous." He brushed some hair from her face. "It's just the two of us, right now."

She leaned back against his chest, enfolded in his arms as they watched the sky and the sea turn gold and orange and pink and red and purple.

CHAPTER THIRTY-EIGHT

SCHEDULE CHANGE

The first patient of the day waddled in, six months pregnant, and only just now presenting for her first prenatal visit. It was another sad case of severe scarring from genital mutilation.

"Okay, Teddy, give her the speech." Sarah's Swahili was getting better, but Teddy was so good at imparting difficult news and critical instructions. The Swahili vocabulary is inadequate for this topic. For example, there is no Swahili word for uterus. It is "that place in the body where the baby stays."

The eyes of this barely-a-woman-until-very-recently-a-child-herself filled with tears as Teddy imparted the sober news.

"Tell her that we will take good care of her. That we care about her and her baby very much."

"Daktari, she knows this. But you should tell her."

Sarah somehow found the right words. The young woman smiled sadly, and said, without looking up, "*Asante. Asante sana.*"

✕

"DOCTOR SARAH, YOUR Swahili is getting very good." Teddy said this as she was organizing charts at the end of clinic "Thanks. You're a very good teacher." Then Sarah blurted out a question. "Have you been cut?"

Teddy laid down the papers and leaned forward, hands spread out on the desk. "Yes."

"Why . . . why did they . . . why do they . . ."

Teddy's eyes focused somewhere in her memory. "To be a good mother. To be a faithful wife. To be pure." She turned to Sarah and lifted her chin proudly. "I did not cry out." Then she went back to unscrambling and sorting the multiple pieces of colored paper, with so many lives scrawled upon them in black and blue ink.

DINNER WAS WAITING. Sarah had soaked some tilapia and green bananas in coconut milk overnight. Pieter wrapped it all in foil and cooked it over charcoal. The aroma was scrumptious as she opened the packet on the kitchen counter. He slipped his arms around her waist and looked over her shoulder. "Is Margo joining us?"

"No, she has a date."

"With who?"

"You mean, 'with whom.' I don't know. She was vague. Kind of mysterious. Like she has some secret boyfriend."

"Then it's just us." He nibbled her neck. "You know, we've never done it in the kitchen."

"There's a reason for that. It's icky in here—the floor is decomposing and there are ants and—"

"No need to get on the floor. Just lean over the counter and—"

"Our dinner will get cold."

"Can I have a check for the rain?"

"You mean, can you have a rain check." She turned around and kissed him. "You said that wrong on purpose. You just think you're so charming."

After they finished eating, Sarah set her laptop on the table—facing sideways, so that they could both view the screen and review the teaching schedule for the midwife course.

"There's one thing that bothers me." Sarah pointed the list. "Jean is scheduled to teach the fistulae and FGM classes. The women will not be happy with a man giving that lecture."

Sarah's cell phone rang. David. He said, "Incoming Skype!" and then hung up.

She pushed her plate to one side and rotated the computer to face her. Pieter motioned to indicate that he would clear the table and start cleaning up. Very mature and thoughtful. Much better than his usual schtick: making faces behind her computer.

David's face appeared on the screen. "Hey, Sam! How are you?"

"Fine. Just finished dinner with a friend. Are you in the lab?"

"Yeah, and I have great news." His face beamed. "I'm coming to see you."

It took a moment to process this news. "Sooo, you're coming here?"

"Yeah, here's the deal. Dr. Cooke had a death in his family. He can't go to Berlin to present the paper next week. So he's sending me. Isn't that great?"

"Great that you get to present the paper. Too bad about his loss, though."

"Oh, it was an aunt with Alzheimer's. He's not broken up about it. Just needs to be there."

"I see."

"So, I'll already be on that side of the Atlantic, right? I just need to head south after I present the paper. A ticket from Germany to Africa is cheaper than a ticket from the States. We can finally do the Kili climb."

"That makes sense." She did her best to sound enthusiastic. "It will be great to see you. But the timing's pretty bad."

Pieter was washing dishes and placing them in the drainer.

She picked up a towel, started drying dishes. "David's coming."

"I heard."

"I guess I can't go with you guys to set up the program."

"We won't start without you. We'll just postpone it."

The suds sloshed in the dishpan and forks clinked against drinking glasses. The next-door neighbors were talking loudly—some kind of argument. A dog howled somewhere in the distance.

Pieter turned from the sink. "Are you okay?"

"I guess so."

He took the wet plate from her hand, put it back into the drainer. "You don't need to wipe that. It will dry overnight."

He tried to put his arms around her, but she pulled away, clutching the damp dishcloth to her face. "I can't."

"Can't what? Can't let me touch you?" His mouth was slightly agape, lower lip not quite trembling. "He just decides to show up and suddenly I-I'm—"

"I'm sorry." She twisted the dishrag into knots. "I just . . . I can't help how I feel."

"You can't, can you." He shrugged. "None of us can." He strode out of the kitchen and down the hall. Sarah heard the noise of slamming cabinet doors and bureau drawers. Spike wandered in and rubbed against her legs. She was powerless to move, as though her feet were glued to the disintegrating linoleum.

He reappeared with his backpack. "Where's my blue shirt?"

"I put it in the hamper. When Rosie washes it, I can—"

"She can bring it to my house. Now if you will excuse me . . ."

He paused to pick up the toaster before heading out the door.

IT'S FUNNY HOW quickly you can get used to having someone around. It hadn't been that long, so it shouldn't have been so disorienting to wake up without him in the morning. She longed to drape her arm across his body and feel his soothing voice resonating through his chest as he droned on about the surgery schedule for the day, or some patient in the ICU, or anything else that was on his mind. Anything.

She closed her eyes and tried to pretend that he was there—like when she was a little girl and her mother woke her up in the middle of a nice dream. "Time to get ready for school." Maybe she had been a Viking princess, maybe she had been flying in the clouds. She would close her eyes and her mind would grasp at the wisps of the dream as they dissipated and floated away. But even when she succeeded in dozing off again, the dream was gone. Later in the day, she would not remember one single detail—only that it had been a lovely dream.

The blue shirt lay on the pillow beside her. A bad dream, sometime during the night, had driven her from bed. She could not recall exactly had terrified her, compelled her to dig through the laundry hamper. The shirt smelled like Pieter. She was not ready for Rosie to wash it.

It was another beautiful morning for a run—cloudy, but not muggy. She heard a familiar loud squawk and there was her ibis, up in a tree. Backlit by the overcast sky, he seemed black as a raven. Sarah wished for a ray of sunshine to reveal his true colors.

She paused at the main road and looked back toward the mountain. The top was shrouded in clouds, but she could make out the long sloping shoulders. It would be an arduous climb. Two weeks was not a very long time to get in shape.

She should do two laps this morning. Maybe three. There was plenty of time.

No one had breakfast waiting for her.

CHAPTER THIRTY-NINE

DAVID'S ARRIVAL

"May I join you, or this table for ladies only?"

Margo ordered Pieter to "Sit down. Don't be silly!"

Ameera said, "It's really too bad that you can't come with us to start the course."

"I'm sorry too. Just couldn't accommodate the schedule change."

Sarah did not look up from her plate. "David gets in tonight. Sunday morning we're off to climb the mountain."

"You're joking!" Pieter laughed. "If I had not seen my woman for such a long time, I would not drag her off to a climb. I'd take her to a nice hotel and fuck her brains out."

Ameera gasped, "I can't believe you said that!"

Margo rolled her eyes. "You're a married woman now. Don't be so sensitive. Besides, he makes a good point." She waved a fork at Sarah. "She promised to pick him up at the airport. But she shouldn't drive there alone at night. He should be a big boy and take a taxi."

"I told him I'd be there. Can't change that now. His plane is already in the air."

Pieter stirred his coffee. "I can take you."

"You don't need to. But thanks so much for offering."

"It's no trouble at all."

✕

THE DRIVE TO the airport was silent until they came to a bend in the road, curving north, straight toward Kilimanjaro.

Sarah gazed in awe. "No clouds. We can see the whole mountain: Kibo, Mawenzie, and everything in between."

"Let's hope it's nice and clear like that when you get to the top. The view can be spectacular. But it will be *really* cold."

"I know. I have all the stuff on the checklist: long underwear, down jacket, knit cap."

"You need very good gloves. And hand warmer packets?"

"Yep, and some warmers for my boots, too."

"What about your sleeping bag?"

"I rented one from the outfitter. It's supposedly rated to 20 below."

Pieter shook his head. "Not warm enough. And you don't want to sleep in just anyone's bag. You could get . . . " he paused to think.

"Cooties?"

"Whatever. You have to borrow mine."

"So, this is a command and not an offer?"

"Really. If you're are not warm enough, you'll be more susceptible to mountain sickness. By the way, will you take Diamox?"

"Yes, David's bringing all kinds of drugs. Apparently, Cialis is a good drug for fending off mountain sickness."

Pieter snorted. "Well, he'd better take good care of you."

When they reached the airport, he paused after switching off the engine. "Does David know I am driving you?"

"No. Remember, he was already in flight when we talked."

"Oh, right. Have you told him anything about me at all?"

"No. You should know this. You have listened to enough of our Skype calls."

"I'm hurt that I didn't rate some mention. On the other hand, if he knows nothing about me then it should not be awkward for him to meet me."

"Not for him. But what about me?"

"You've never introduced him to an old boyfriend?"

"I told you. I never had another boyfriend."

"*Pole*. Sorry. I think you should have shopped around."

DAVID EMERGED WITH the waves of people flowing from the arrivals hall. When he spotted Sarah, he dropped his bags, lifted her off the ground, and spun around. She introduced him to Pieter. "He's an anesthesiologist at the hospital."

David shook Pieter's hand. "Thanks so much for coming with her. I was kind of worried about her driving alone at night."

"So was I." Pieter declared this perhaps too emphatically. Then, to account for his level of concern, he added, "She's a good surgeon—wouldn't want to lose her."

David clutched Sarah tightly as they walked to the parking lot, as if she might fly away.

Pieter loaded the bags. "Do you two want to sit in the back?"

Sarah shook her head. "David will be more comfortable in the front seat. More leg space."

David chatted as they rolled along, said his paper had been favorably received in Berlin. "I was worried that we wouldn't finish analyzing the data in time. Carla and I were up to all hours the last couple of nights."

"Carla." Sarah leaned forward. "Isn't she the one who forgot to order the gels?"

"Yeah, she's a technician in our lab. You met her at the Christmas party, remember?" He switched the subject to their upcoming climb. "I heard that we should use walking sticks. We can rent them at the park entrance."

Pieter said that he had some sticks they could borrow.

"Thanks," said David. "Have you climbed the mountain before?"

"Only eight times." He stated this matter-of-factly, didn't emphasize the word "only." He launched into a lecture on altitude physiology: milliequivalents, partial pressures, cerebrospinal fluid pressure . . . Sarah's mind wandered until David said, "No kidding? He climbed the mountain with a bolt in his head?"

"It was a rather remarkable study," said Pieter. "It shows that older people are less susceptible to altitude, because the brain shrinks with age. What is also interesting is that he died before the study was published. At first, it was feared that the data was lost in a fire. But then his wife found the notes in the trunk of a car. The study was published posthumously."

"Sam, I guess you need to know where to find my notes, in case I have an untimely death."

Pieter mused, "Perhaps your assistant would be more helpful in that regard."

"My assistant?"

"Yes, this Miss Carla."

Sarah kicked the back of Pieter's seat and caught his eye in the rearview mirror. She drew a finger across her throat. *Shut up.*

"Oh, she's not *my* assistant," said David. "She works for

Dr. Cook, like me. I'm not an independent researcher. Yet."

They stopped by Pieter's house to pick up walking sticks, water bottles, and neck warmers—and the sleeping bag, which he rolled out for inspection on Sarah's living room floor.

David laughed, "I'm really jealous! She'll be a lot warmer than me!" Then he whispered to Sarah, "I'll bet we can both fit in there."

Sarah saw Pieter frown. He couldn't have heard David's comment, but maybe the same thought had occurred to him.

David excused himself to the bathroom.

Pieter grinned at Sarah. "So how am I doing?"

"Great. Maybe too good. David seems to think you're a great guy."

"Well I am a great guy, am I not?"

"You are not a nice guy. You've been sleeping with his girlfriend."

"Why does he call you Sam?"

"It's a family nickname. Ostensibly my little sister couldn't pronounce Sarah, which I find hard to believe. I think it's just something my father came up with."

"But your father called you princess."

"Sometimes, yes. But it's not always a good nickname. Like, during a volleyball game. You'd never yell, 'Spike the ball, Princess.'"

"I see the logic in this nickname, Sam. Perhaps your father called you this when he wanted you to be strong."

The sound of the toilet flushing announced David's imminent return.

Pieter knelt down and started rolling up the sleeping bag. "Let me show you how to stow this."

As Pieter went out the door, David thanked him profusely for his help. Pieter repeated that it was no trouble at all.

"*Hakuna matata.* No worries." David recited. "That's the only Swahili I know."

"Let me guess," said Pieter. "*Lion King.*"

Pieter's car pulled away, and David turned to Sarah. "Too bad you didn't get to know him sooner. He could've been a big help planning our trip."

CHAPTER FORTY

THE CLIMB

The climb began gently, up a winding path through shady jungle. There were two other climbers in the party, Kurt and Oswald, twenty-something brothers from Germany who had successfully ascended the Matterhorn a few months earlier. The guides were a father and son team. Micah had a grey beard and a red knit cap, and Richard wore a Philadelphia Eagles T-shirt. Eight porters scampered ahead in their flip flops, bearing heavy packs on their heads, making the tourists look like sissies.

Scores of descending trekkers shouted encouragement to uphill climbers. Some offered specific advice, such as "Don't take off your gloves at the top." Thirty young women in matching shirts and caps, waved Korean flags, and shouted "Good luck!" (Only four of them had actually made it to the top.) And of course, there was the continual refrain of, "*Pole, pole.*"

David frequently became lost in conversation with the energetic German brothers. They tended to surge ahead, while Sarah remained committed to that slow and steady, *pole, pole* pace. She didn't mind bringing up the rear. Richard was always nearby, providing a running commentary on the flora and fauna. It was a well-worn path, but some segments crossed tangles of large tree roots. Sarah was engrossed in watching a couple of playful baby monkeys when she tripped. It wasn't a stumble—just one step forward without realizing that the back foot was not going to follow. Richard caught her before she was fully aware that she was falling. Her boot was firmly wedged under a tree root, and her foot would not come out of the boot until Richard unlaced it. By the time David and the guys doubled back, Sarah was sitting on the ground, pulling her boot back on.

"What's up, Sam? Got a rock in your shoe?" David sat down beside her.

"I tripped. Got my boot caught under a root."

Kurt clucked his tongue, hands on his hips. "You have to watch where you're going. Sprain your ankle, and someone will have to carry you down the mountain."

Richard glared at David. "She would have snapped her leg if I had not caught her."

The color drained from David's face. "Thanks. I'm glad you were there."

Richard lifted his chin. "This is what a man does."

THE LANDSCAPE ON day two was a moorland with weird looking vegetation, like the set of some sci-fi adventure on a faraway planet. And the temperature dropped. Shorts and T-shirts had been de rigueur on the first day, but now long pants and jackets were necessary. They stopped for the night at the Horumbo Huts, more than 12,000 feet above sea level.

At breakfast, Micah presented the plan for the third day, structured for adaptation to altitude. They would climb

500 meters up to Zebra Rock and then come right back down to Horumbo.

Kurt and Oswald were gung-ho to skip acclimatization, and David thought it was a good idea. "What do you think, Sam? We could finish the climb in five days instead of six."

Sarah shook her head.

David cocked his head. "You're not feeling sick or anything are you?"

"No. But we aren't that high yet. I hear it can creep up on you."

"Come on. If we feel bad, we can always turn back."

She waved a hand. "Go on, if you want to. One of the guides can take me back."

Kurt and Oswald gazed at David expectantly.

David squeezed Sarah's hand. "Don't be silly. I'd never go on without you."

KURT AND OSWALD set off with Micah. As they disappeared over the rise, Sarah and David heard a strange wailing sound, off in the distance. As it grew louder, they saw the source: a porter imitating an ambulance siren. He rushed past, pushing a strange conveyance: a platform, atop a single mountain bike tire, carrying a passenger who was completely encased in a sleeping bag.

Richard wagged a finger as they passed. "Mountain sickness. Always remember, *pole, pole.*"

They stopped for lunch break at Zebra Rock, a large slab of black lava on the side of a cliff. Through millennia, dripping minerals had painted irregular white vertical stripes. A nearby overlook provided a sweeping vista of the saddle, the broad ridge sloping up to Kibo. David thought it looked like West Texas. "You know, your family's ranch."

The day after her grandfather's funeral, they had hiked up to a hilltop and fantasized about coming back to live on the ranch someday with five or six children. The sky was brilliantly blue that day, and their future spread out before them across the plains, like a glittering silvery highway.

"What happened to us, Sam?"

It was not a question. It was a refrain. They had both lived through the long work hours, the solitary nights, the angry words, the slamming doors . . .

The acclimatization hike had been exhilarating rather than exhausting. Instead of collapsing into sleeping bags right after dinner, they sat out under an incredibly starry sky. The Milky Way arched above like a band of fluffy clouds.

He put his arm around her. "It'll be better next year. I promise."

She nodded. "Slower pace. I'll be a chief, and you'll be a fellow."

"The lease on our apartment is up in July, so I've been looking around. I found a nice two-bedroom townhouse." He reached into his pocket. "I was gonna do this at the top. But I heard we should keep our gloves on up there." He opened the box. The ring was nestled inside. "Will you take this back?" He knelt down beside her. "Please?"

RICHARD RAPPED ON the breakfast table. "This is the big day. Are you ready?"

"Uh, sure. Right Sam?

She shrugged. "Yeah. Piece of cake. We cross the saddle, rest for a few hours at base camp, and then climb all night. And it's only thirty or forty below at the top."

After breakfast, Sarah and David sat on the steps of the dining hall, staring down at the clouds and up at the brilliant blue sky. Climbers bustled about, in various stages of preparation. Everyone paused and looked up the trail when another human vocal "siren" pierced the air. The crowd parted to allow the ambulance stretcher to pass through.

Sarah couldn't believe her eyes. "That looks like Kurt's sleeping bag."

The stretcher rumbled on down the mountain. David touched Sarah's shoulder. "You okay? Want to back out?"

"Nope. Let's go. But . . . *pole, pole.*"

The trail across the Saddle looks like a leisurely stroll. This is an optical illusion. The path ascends 1,000 meters over 6 miles to reach Kibo base camp.

They paused for lunch near the last water source. Richard instructed them to stand on one leg and spread out their arms. "This is good test for mountain sickness."

David asked, "Are you measuring cerebellar function or spinocerebellar reflexes?"

Richard didn't answer. His eyes were focused two descending climbers coming down the path. Sarah recognized Oswald's green parka and Micah's red cap.

Oswald sat down heavily on a rock and spoke between gasps. "Last climb . . . so hard . . . so cold. Kurt coughed . . . bubbles."

"We saw him passing Horumbo on a stretcher," said David. "He's probably all the way down by now."

Micah helped Oswald to his feet, and they started back down the mountain.

Sarah, David, and Richard resumed their climb. *Pole, pole.*

Kibo base camp was awash in colorful domed tents.

Richard served an afternoon snack of popcorn. The tea was lukewarm and tasted funny, because the water had to be treated with iodine. At such a high altitude, water boiled at too a low temperature to kill germs. Then it was time to rest before the final assault on Kibo, in a brick bunkhouse, along with fourteen other climbers. Sleep seemed impossible in the noisy, bustling room, with the specter of the strenuous climb looming. But fatigue and hypoxia are powerful forces. Sarah drifted into the oblivion of dreamless sleep.

Richard tapped her shoulder. The time had come! Her heart pounded as she climbed out of her cozy sleeping bag, eyes barely open, like a sleep walker. One last meal of soup and tea, and then the climb began, in the pitch-dark night, their faces completely covered by neck warmers, knit caps, and goggles.

The air was thin, and it was bitterly cold. Ahead, headlights of climbers glimmered like a string of Christmas tree lights, zig-zagging its way up a precipitous slope of unstable volcanic ash, where their boots had little traction. Then they clambered over huge boulders. Richard knew every stone by heart. They walked over frozen vomit, courtesy of a German group who were using oxygen (carried by their porters). Oxygen clearly did not prevent mountain sickness.

Sarah occasionally lapsed into microsleeps, with brief flashes of dreams of tiny animals scurrying past her feet. Hallucinations. No such animals at this altitude.

Three steps and breathe. Three steps and breathe.

"*Pole, pole. Pole, pole.*" Sarah mentally repeated the mantra.

Two steps and breathe. Two steps and breathe.

Pole, pole.

Then it was just one breath for each step.

After six hours that felt like six endless nights, they could hear jubilant voices at the summit. The sound provided a surge of energy for the final push. A few more boulders, and Richard pulled Sarah up onto the edge of the crater, where a large sign welcomed them to Gillman's point, 5685 meters above sea level. The sun emerged over the jagged summit of Mawenzie, and a pointy shadow fell onto the steep slope below, like a mammoth sundial.

David whistled. "Can you believe we climbed up that?"

Richard snapped a few shots of them in front of the sign and next to the crater. "Do you want to go on? Uhuru peak, the real summit, is 210 meters higher."

David and Sarah stared at one another.

"Even if you don't go to Uhuru, you still get a certificate for coming this far."

Sarah picked up her backpack. "Let's go!"

They plodded ahead, only aware of the earth immediately in front of each foot until they reached the summit. Adrenalin and endorphins surged, and they joined all the other pumped up hikers, whooping and raising their fists. David danced a little jig. "We're on top of the world, Sam!"

The summit was clear, but only isolated patches of land were visible through breaks in the low cloud cover. Sarah scanned the horizon. "Which way are the Usambara mountains?"

Richard pointed to a tiny ridge of earth peeking through the clouds, far, far away.

Sarah patted David's heavily padded arm. "That's where I'm going. My little village is on that mountain. The clouds are so thick. It looks like I could just jog right over there."

"*Hapana. Kamwe*," said Richard. "Only angels can walk on clouds."

CHAPTER FORTY-ONE

TOES AND TOAST

Sarah called out from the kitchen, "What shape do you want for your pancake?"

"A kitty, in honor of Spike." The African cat purred contentedly on David's lap.

Sarah poured just the head of a cat—a round face with pointy ears—and watched as bubbles formed in the batter and the edges firmed up. "What would you like to do on your last day?"

"Let's go into town—shop for souvenirs."

She stepped gingerly into the dining room—her big toes had been aching since Kilimanjaro—and placed the cat face pancake on the table. David scratched Spike under the chin. "He's not as soft as our cat."

Back in the kitchen, she poured a simple disc for herself. "I hope Whiskers hasn't been too lonely without you."

"He's fine. Carla's taking good care of him."

"Well, that should be convenient. Sounds like she's essentially moved in already." She chuckled at her little joke.

David did not answer. Sarah glanced out at the dining table. He sat there, expressionless, staring at his pancake. He had painted a face with syrup: two eyes, a nose, a "w" mouth, and a few whiskers. His fork was poised in midair.

"I'm sorry, Sam. I mean . . . I'm just . . ." He sighed and looked up looked up at Sarah, briefly, sadly. "I'm so sorry."

LATE SUNDAY NIGHT, there was a knock at the door. Sarah groaned as she limped to the door. The ache in her toes had gotten steadily worse.

It was Pieter. "I thought of a few more things that you might need." A duffel bag plopped on the kitchen counter with a loud clank.

Sarah peered inside. "I hope I never need this stuff."

"Oxygen always comes in handy. And if someone has a cardiac arrest, you would want to have a decent laryngoscope. Not that plastic abomination."

"But chest tubes?"

"You just never know."

"How were things in the village this weekend?"

"Everything is ready. The whole village is excited." He glanced around the room. "David's gone?"

"Yeah, he left last night."

"How was the climb?"

"Overall, great, but with some tough moments."

"Then it was a usual climb."

"Would you like a beer?"

"Sure."

Sarah hobbled to the fridge.

Pieter rummaged in the cabinet. "I thought we had some peanuts."

"David ate those."

He smirked. "How dare he eat my food!"

"There are some taro chips up on the top shelf."

"You're walking funny. Did you sprain something?"

"No, it's just my big toes. They really hurt!"

"Let me see."

She balanced on one foot, like a flamingo, still clutching the two beer bottles and raising the other foot for him to see. Her big toes were swollen like ripe plums.

"You're going to lose these."

"What? My toes?"

"Just the toenails. Don't worry. They grow back in about six months."

"Sounds like you're talking from experience."

"Go sit. I'll bring some hot water to soak your feet."

She juggled the beer and the bowl of chips to the coffee table and was still struggling to take the top off a bottle when he placed the steaming pan of water on the floor. She soaked her feet as he deftly uncapped both bottles.

"So," he took a swig. "Tell me about this climb."

His expression was grave when she spoke of the German brothers and how David had wanted to skip the acclimatization.

"I'm glad you didn't let him talk you into that. We have Kurt in the ICU, in pretty bad shape, right now. But he has a good chance to recover. How about you? How are you feeling?"

"Not too bad, except for the toes."

"Do you have a paper clip?"

He sat on the floor and pulled one of her feet into his lap. He straightened one end of the paper clip and heated it over a match. "Don't worry. This won't hurt."

She had used this technique a few times to treat painful blood clots under fingernails. A heated paper clip pops through a nail like a hot knife through butter. It doesn't hurt. In fact, the pain is relieved instantaneously. But patients can be shocked when they see the eruption of black blood, despite efforts to prepare them for the sight.

"So how did you make out with David?" He cleared his throat. "I don't think that came out right. I meant to ask, did you enjoy his visit?"

"It was fine."

"Not a very enthusiastic answer." He touched the red-hot paper clip to her toenail and a small dark geyser spurted out. "Okay. I won't interrogate you." He turned his attention to the other toe. "You're wearing the ring again."

Sarah sighed. "He has a girlfriend."

"Is he banging the lab lady?"

Sarah gasped as he popped a glowing paper clip into the other toenail.

"Did that hurt?"

"No."

"Oh, I guess my question was a bit blunt. Sorry."

She explained about Spike and Whiskers and how she meant to make a joke. And that David had begged forgiveness.

"What did you say to him?"

"I don't quite remember."

Pieter frowned. "You don't remember?"

"He was talking so fast and I couldn't get a word in. Or maybe . . . I was too surprised to say anything. I think I essentially said okay."

"Okay?"

"He expected me to be angry—I think he actually wanted me to be angry, but how could I? How could I blame him?"

"Did you tell him about us?"

"No," she whispered.

They had always been them. David and Sarah. The permanent couple. Others had spats and quarrels and sometimes split up. Her friends cried on her shoulder, and he took guys out for beer, but Sarah and David were always rock solid. David and Sarah forever. Well, maybe not forever, but a long time. The pre-David years were mostly in the misty realm of fuzzy childhood memories.

A Venn diagram of their lives would almost be a single circle. David was the one she called when she lost her keys, or when she needed him to pick up some orange juice. He changed the oil in the car and took out the trash. And if he hurt her feelings or she exasperated him, it didn't matter. They were still them.

Now they seemed to have wandered onto the edge of some crumbling precipice, dangling over yawning nothingness, desperately clinging to each other.

"I was afraid that if I told him, everything would fall apart."

Pieter's eyes softened, and he sat down beside her on the couch. "What happens now? "

The issue had been compartmentalized. But it was not as simple as stuffing the clown back into the Jack in the Box. It was more like trying to round up Pandora's woes.

"We'll deal with it when I get home, I guess."

"You're wearing the ring."

"He left it—taped to the bathroom mirror. I'm afraid to leave it lying around. Safest place is my finger. He said he was really sorry. He was just lonely, and he'll break it off with her."

"Well, she'll be pissed off. I can just hear her now." He whimpered, in a high-pitched whine, "You were just using me!"

Sarah chuckled, but then a horrible thought crossed her mind. "Do you think I was using you?"

He raised his bottle as if making a toast. "Frankly, my dear, I don't give a damn." He slugged down the rest of the beer and plunked the empty bottle onto the coffee table.

Sarah sniffed and curled up into a ball, clasping her knees under her chin.

Pieter frowned. "Did I say something wrong.?"

"That's what Rhett says to Scarlett when he dumps her."

"Who?"

"Did you ever see *Gone with the Wind*? Or read the book?"

He shook his head.

She sat upright, legs in semi-lotus position. "Okay, it's like, Rhett's leaving Scarlet because he's so fed up with her bullshit, and she's like, 'Oh no, what'll I do?', and he's like . . . " She paused to take a breath and threw up her hands. "That's when he says the 'frankly, my dear' thing."

"Oh." Pieter scratched his head. "It was just something my father used to say. My mother would always laugh."

She started to pick up the pan of water, but Pieter grabbed it. "I'll get that. You're crippled."

She followed him into the kitchen and watched the water swirling down the drain. "It's going clockwise. I thought, this close to the equator, it should just go straight down."

"The Coriolis effect has no influence on such a small volume of water." He turned the basin upside down on the drain board. "Trust me. I've been traveling back and forth across the equator all my life."

Her eyes burned. In the morning, she would be off for her adventure in the mountains. And then she would be gone. Back to her regularly scheduled life in the United States. "I guess I won't see you for a while."

He grabbed a cloth, mopped up some water that had splashed onto the counter. "Aren't you planning to be here when that American surgeon comes for a visit? Dr. Marshall?"

"That's two whole weeks from now."

He wrung out the dish cloth and draped it on the faucet. "Do you think . . . maybe . . . can I stay tonight?"

"Hmmm, did you bring back the toaster?"

"I thought that would be presumptuous."

"Guess I'll have to make French toast."

CHAPTER FORTY-TWO

MOVING TO KANDU

The sky was nearly cloudless. A tiny wisp of angel hair clung to Kibo, and Mawenzie sported a puffy toupee at a rakish angle.

"You should look at the mountain. It's so beautiful this morning."

"Kibo will be here tomorrow. You won't."

She got back into bed and snuggled next to Pieter. "I'm nervous. I keep thinking I must have forgotten something."

"I doubt it. And any time you need something, we can get it to you. It's not like you're stuck on some desert island." He sat up abruptly. "I almost forgot your toes."

As he examined her nasty feet, she studied the scars on his shoulder. If you had to be clawed by a leopard, this was an optimal site. The back was the first lesson in anatomy lab, presumably to avoid face to face encounters with dead bodies on day one. She recalled that slicing through that skin had been startling. Who knew it was so thick? Lying there in the morning light, she tried to imagine Pieter's wounds when they were fresh, with blood flowing from deep gouges.

"Sit up and I'll show you how to take care of this." He tapped the base of one toenail. "This is where the new nail will grow in. You'll need to trim the old one off as it gets pushed out and pops up. Otherwise it may get caught on something and be ripped off."

"That sounds painful."

"For the next week or so, you should wear socks to keep the dirt out. And don't wear shoes that put pressure on your toes."

"But I can't wear socks with my sandals. They have toe thingies."

"Thingies?"

She held up her flipflop-style sandal. "The thingy goes between the toes."

He picked his pants up off the floor, pulled a knife out of his pocket, and made a strategic slash in her sandal. "No more thingy, see?"

He knelt to slip the altered sandal onto her foot.

"There, Princess Cinderella, a perfect fit!"

"Cinderella was not a princess."

"She married a prince, did she not?"

"But when she became a princess, they didn't call her Cinderella anymore."

"You have split that hair."

"You mean, I'm splitting hairs."

He winked. "Whatever."

TUMAINI PULLED UP in the hospital van and Margo hopped out. Her jaw dropped momentarily when she saw Pieter following Sarah out of the house. He loaded the duffel bag into the back of the Rav4. "Good morning, Margo. I just dropped by to see you all off. Brought some last-minute items you might find useful."

Margo's head gave a microshake and her eyes darted skyward. "Whatever."

Tumaini took the lead, with Ameera and Rasheed on board. Sarah followed with Margo in the shotgun seat and Pieter in the rearview mirror.

Every inhabitant of the village came out to meet the team. The welcome ceremony included singing and dancing, masala tea and cassava, and of course, roasted goat. It was late in the day before Sarah moved into her house. Like all the other dwellings in the village, it had mud brick walls and a corrugated metal roof. But Rasheed pointed out his significant upgrades in design. The floor was concrete, not dirt, and had a large screened window. He was most proud of the transoms under the eaves. "You will be very happy for this ventilation."

Sarah gazed up. "Nice. But no screens up there?"

"Hmm. They forgot that. Well, malaria risk is pretty low at this altitude." He had also installed a wood burning stove, and an outside shower with solar heated water. Of course, she would have to fill the heating tank with water fetched from the faucet in the dispensary. All other water was toted up the mountain from a stream, one large plastic bucket at a time, on the heads of women and children.

Ameera and Rasheed spent the night in Betje's lodge, while Margo and Sarah settled down in the new house, sleeping on folding cots. Sarah switched off the lantern, and they wished each other good night. But both were too wound up to fall asleep.

"Sarah, you awake?"

"Yep."

"Remember the safari? The night at Ngorongoro?"

"Your wild night with the Italian boys."

"I didn't stay with them. They weren't so nice—got drunk—wanted me to come to their room. They literally started to drag me. Israel was at the front desk, ordering our lunches, and saw what was going on. He told them to bugger off."

"Sir Galahad! Lucky he was there."

"For sure. We sat on the terrace. Talked all night, watched the moon come up."

"Why didn't you tell me?"

"He told me not to. He's not supposed to get involved with clients. I guess I could have told you. But . . . you haven't been straight with me, either . . . about Pieter."

"No," she murmured.

"You're wearing the ring again."

Sarah twisted the ring around her finger. "It's complicated."

"You love Pieter, don't you?"

"I'm afraid so."

"Why are you afraid?"

"I don't think it's serious for him."

"Did he ever say that?"

"No."

"Then you don't know. You have to ask him."

Sarah changed the subject. "Tell me more about Israel."

Sarah could hear the smile in her friend's voice. "He is so great. He wants to get married. But I don't know. I'm supposed to go to Nairobi next year for a trauma fellowship. I don't think I should go if I get married. What do you think?"

"Don't ask me for advice. My track record in such matters is not good."

✗

THE WEEK WENT by quickly as they unloaded and organized equipment and supplies for the new delivery room and stuffed "goodie bags" for all the TBA students: band aids, antibiotic ointment, scissors, and sterile string for tying off umbilical cords. They hung educational posters in Sarah's house, which would double as the classroom. By Saturday morning, everything was ready for the first class.

Ten birth attendants clad in their best colorful kitatngas and head wraps filed silently into the room. The cots were folded against the walls and the floor was covered in straw mats. Sarah expected them to sit in rows, classroom style, but they arranged themselves into a circle, some peeking under the edge of the straw mat to marvel at the smooth concrete surface beneath. One woman had a baby slung on her back, but the rest were well past child-bearing age. All had learned about childbirth from their mothers who had learned from their mothers, and so on for countless generations.

Sarah's Swahili had become passable, and she had practiced her remarks over and over. But the collective knowledge in the room, passed down through generations made her feel inadequate to teach them anything. After a deep breath, she began the first lesson: infection control. Susie had given her good advice, "Don't give lectures. Speak to them in stories." Sarah asked if everyone in the room had seen a mother with childbed fever. They all nodded their heads and murmured to each other. One woman, Dura, said that such fever happened when there was not enough prayer. Another woman, Nasila, said that it was witchcraft. Sarah said that infections were caused by something called germs. Many years ago, in a country far away, a doctor was very sad because so many mothers died from fever. He noticed that most of the mothers who got fever had been attended by doctors, rather than midwives.

Dura said that the midwives prayed, but the doctors did not.

Sarah did not dismiss the power of prayer but stated an important fact. Doctors examined the bodies of women after death. Midwives did not. Maybe the doctors got something from the dead women on their hands, something that made some other mothers sick. Then something very sad happened. Another doctor, accidentally cut his finger while examining a body. That doctor died from the same fever that killed the woman.

There was a collective gasp from the group. Nasila declared that the dead woman's spirit had put a spell on the doctor.

Sarah ignored that comment. She told them that after that doctor died, there was a new rule. Everyone should wash their hands. Suddenly, childbed fever became very rare. Hand washing works is because it kills the germs. She pointed to a colorful poster on the wall with cartoon images of microbes.

The woman with an infant on her back stood up and pointed to a lumpy pink creature in the poster and said that she had never seen such an animal.

Sarah explained that it was just a drawing, a cartoon. Germs were too tiny to see. Unless you looked through a special device. She pointed to a microscope on a small table.

Margo held up a glass slide with a purple dot in the center, a stained clump of bacteria. The women clustered around and one by one, they marveled at the purple-blue clumps of staph germs. Everyone except for Nasila. She was afraid that looking at the germs would make her sick.

Ameera conducted a hand-washing exercise, to show how thoroughly they needed to wash. The women dipped their hands into a purple solution and then scrubbed with soapy water until all the purple was gone.

The class toured the new delivery room, with its spick and span floor and shiny cabinets. The pièce de résistance was the autoclave. Steam poured out when the door was open, and the women oohed and ahed. Ameera pulled out hot packages of sparkling scissors and clamps, packaged in clear plastic and declared that all the germs were dead.

Nasila gazed into the steaming autoclave and declared that it was very good magic.

CHAPTER FORTY-THREE

LIFE IN THE MOUNTAINS

L ife in the village of Kandu was unplugged. No internet. No cellphone service, unless you hiked uphill for twenty minutes to a cellphone hotspot on the edge of the escarpment. Or you could pay Jabari fifty shillings to give you a ride up there on his motorcycle. He was the unofficial chauffeur of the village, hitching up his white caftan to straddle the bike, ferrying passengers to and from Lushoto, for shopping, and visits to the hospital. According to Balinda, Jabari was annoyed by Sarah's presence in the village. Her clinics were cutting into his business.

The only electricity in the village was the generator that powered the dispensary and delivery room. Daily routine was dictated by rising and setting of the sun. She helped Keisha prepare the evening meal and learned the secrets of making excellent chapatis. The people of the village were quite curious about her; someone was always dropping by to chat, so she was rarely alone during waking hours. One woman offered to teach her how to weave baskets. The children loved to hear her fairy tales, and she became quite attached to Hamid and Jamal's pet goat, who loved to be scratched behind her ears. Pieter had built a cart for the goat to pull the children around the village. After dinner each night, everyone sat out under the stars for an hour or two, sharing legends, funny stories, plans for the next day, and, of course, gossip.

She had never felt more alive.

Clinics were busy, but most patients had routine problems—colds, ear infections, diarrhea. Women complained of pain in their shoulders, backs, legs, and arms, pain, aches that were the wages of hard work in a cold climate, trudging up and down the mountainside to tend crops in the terraced fields, carrying babies strapped to their backs.

THERE WAS ONLY one interesting patient during that first week. Balinda announced that the town chauffer had a problem. "Daktari Sarah, you need to see Jabari. I think so maybe he has a rupture. He has pain." She pointed to her own groin. "Here."

"You mean a hernia? I'm happy to see him. But if he needs surgery, he'll have to go to the hospital anyway. He should just hop on his motorcycle and go straight there."

"He cannot drive now. Too much pain."

"Then tell him to come see me."

"He does not want you to look at him down there. You are a woman."

Eventually Balinda convinced Jabari to come to the clinic. His wife covered him with sheets so that only the swollen area was visible. He winced when Sarah gently prodded the mass. "It's not a hernia. It's an abscess. I need to cut it open."

Jabari nearly jumped off the table, but his wife managed to calm him. He bit on a stick as a pointed scalpel released a torrent of foul-smelling pus. Sarah removed a large ingrown hair, rinsed out the cavity, and then packed it with gauze. "I want you to come back every day for the next week so that I can replace the packing."

He was out the door before she finished the sentence and never came back to the dispensary. The very next day, he was back in business on his motorcycle.

THE TBA STUDENTS were expected to bring laboring women to the new facility, where Sarah would supervise. The first few births conveniently occurred during daylight hours. But one night, Sarah awoke to see Balinda hovering over her like a ghost in the eerie light of a kerosene lamp.

"Daktari, Dura is with a mama now. The baby is not coming."

Sarah sat up and rubbed her eyes. "Are they in the delivery room?"

Balinda shook her head. "The mama will not come here. We must go to her house."

She paused a moment to process this. She was supposed to work in a new delivery room with electric lights, running water, and lots of other things that would be helpful if there were a complication. She had not signed on for "house calls," especially in the middle of the night.

On the other hand, half of rural births occurred in homes. This was an opportunity to see what it was like "in the trenches."

Sarah pointed at the kerosene lantern. "Is that the only light we will have?"

"No, Dura has one. Maybe two."

"I'll bring a headlight." Sarah pulled on jeans and her down jacket. "How far away?"

"About one hour to walk."

"Then we'll take my car."

The mountain roads were treacherous enough in daylight. In the dark, it was downright terrifying: one lane dirt roads, hairpin turns, goats in the road. There were huge potholes, and sometimes part of the road was just gone.

The laboring woman reclined on a blood-soaked straw mat over a dirt floor. She was bathed in sweat, despite the chilly night air. The dim greenish light from the lanterns cast spooky shadows on the walls.

Dura announced that the mother was fully dilated and had been pushing but the baby was not coming.

Balinda examined the woman. "I think so maybe the bottom is first."

In medical school, Sarah learned that breech babies were always delivered by C-section. Always. She had never even seen a vaginal breech delivery—only read about it. She seemed to remember that you usually had to pull upward on the feet to get the head out. "We should take her to the hospital."

Balinda shook her head. "This mama won't go. The baby will be born here."

"Do you understand how serious this is?"

"Yes."

"If the cord gets pinched, the baby could die or have brain damage. If the head gets stuck, the only option is to cut the bones apart. We don't have instruments for that." The thought of driving down to Lushoto in the dark was daunting. "If there's no progress by sunrise, I will insist on taking her to the hospital."

Balinda told the woman to turn over and to get up on her hands and knees. "Baby should fall out—no pull." She spoke softly to the woman, encouraging her to push with each contraction. The baby's bottom appeared slowly. But there was no further progress. The contractions became stronger and more frequent, but the baby did not budge.

Balinda tried to dilate the opening with her finger.

Sarah handed Balinda a pair of scissors. "Do an episiotomy."

Balinda stared at the scissors. Sarah realized that they hadn't covered that in class yet.

"You cut the skin in a good place, like here." Sarah pointed. "So it doesn't rip in a bad place."

Balinda hesitated for a second or two before snipping. The baby slipped out, covered with a thick coat of waxy vernix. Dura cleaned out his mouth. Then he cried, and the mother finally made a sound. She shouted for joy.

The sky was brightening with pink and gold clouds as Sarah and Balinda headed back to their village.

"Daktari, you are a good teacher."

"I only showed you where to make the cut. You were the teacher tonight."

CHAPTER FORTY-FOUR

SOLO ROAD TRIP

Amaya was waiting at the door of the Elephant Hotel, cell phone in hand. "Doctor Pieter say me call when you get here."

"He's on the phone now?"

Amaya handed her the phone. "Pieter?"

There was a brief silence before he launched into a tirade, frequently into lapsing Dutch or Swahili, the central theme being Sarah's idiocy/insanity for driving back from the mountains alone. The surgeons from America had arrived for a visit. Pieter had asked Tumaini to fetch Sarah, but she told the driver not to come.

She wanted to explain that it would have been a waste of time and gasoline, but she could not get a word in edgewise until he paused after a question, "Why are you so late?"

"Sick baby. I had to start an IV."

"Then you should have waited until tomorrow. You should not be on that desolate road after dark."

"I'll be there by six."

"Last year, a woman was driving down from Machame at night. They found her body, but not her head."

It sounded like a ghost story. Too weird and scary to be true. Sarah said, "If I want to get there before dark, I'd better leave now."

Amaya gave her a Coke Zero and a basket of chips to take along. Sarah made good time until she came upon an overturned truck that blocked both lanes of traffic. It was just before a narrow bridge across a deep gorge, so she couldn't pass by on the shoulder. No injuries, but potatoes were strewn all over the road. Men from a nearby village struggled to help helped the driver get his truck upright, while women gathered up the spilled spuds.

No cell service. She couldn't send Pieter a text to let him know about the delay (she did not really want to talk to him again), so she got out of her car and helped retrieve potatoes.

When the road was finally clear, she tore off down the road to make up for lost time. But thirty minutes later, there was a loud bang. The car shuddered and swerved, but she managed to stop safely on the shoulder.

The left front tire was flat. She had changed a tire once before. In her driveway at home. It was an exercise. Her father wanted to be sure that she knew how to deal with such a problem. Grateful for that lesson, she placed her orange hazard triangle on the road and wedged a large rock against the back tire to stabilize the car. The lugs on the wheel were very tight, but she was eventually able to loosen them.

But the jack was useless—not like anything she had ever seen before—and she could not figure out how to get the spare tire off the back of the truck. Defeated, but determined not to cry, she sat down on the gravel. The sun blazed orange on the horizon. Setting off on foot would be stupid. She had to stay with the car. Someone would come looking for her, eventually. At least it wasn't raining.

It was dark by the time a vehicle slowed down and pulled off the road behind her. Doors slammed, and several male voices chattered in Swahili. Her heart pounded, and a sour taste rose into her mouth. Four men approached her, silhouetted in the headlights. One of them spoke. "Daktari?" He tapped the doctor sticker on the back window.

They didn't need the jack—just lifted the car and stacked some rocks under the bumper. Sarah tried to tell them to put the damaged tire in the back of her car, but they insisted on loading it into their truck.

The lights of an oncoming vehicle washed over them as a van pulled off on the opposite shoulder. Tumaini leapt out. "Daktari Sarah. You okay?"

The men refused any payment. They told Tumaini that they were planning to repair the tire and would bring it to the hospital in the morning.

"And now, Daktari Sarah, I follow you. Daktari Pieter *very* worried."

It was nearly nine by the time she reached the Indian restaurant. Dr. Marshall, Jeff, Margo, and Pieter sat around a table out on the lawn, under a large tree that was lit by a string of Christmas lights.

Dr. Marshall popped out of his chair to give her a hug. "Sarah! We were really worried."

Jeff hugged her too. "Hey, Sam! We didn't wait for you. We went ahead and ordered—hope you like tandoori chicken."

"My favorite."

Pieter would not look at her.

Jeff and Dr. Marshall had spent a very good day in clinic with Margo, seeing all the patients that were scheduled for surgery in the next few days.

"This will be like old times," said Jeff. "Just like when we were in Honduras."

Margo asked, "Honduras? When were you guys there?"

"Dr. Marshall goes there every year to fix cleft lips and palates. Jeff and I went with him a few years ago."

Jeff laughed. "Remember when you threw that paper wad at the guard?"

"I didn't throw it at the guard. I threw it at you, but you jumped out of the way."

Jeff put his hand on Margo's shoulder. "Here's a safety tip. Don't ever throw something at a guy with an Uzi, especially if he's asleep."

"Oh my God! What happened?"

Sarah rolled her eyes. "Nothing. He woke up and saw the paper wad on the floor. He just laughed."

Jeff rubbed his chin. "What did I say that made you so mad?"

"I think you remember exactly what you said. I won't repeat it. And I don't think it was an Uzi."

"Well, it was a big gun anyway."

Dr. Marshall wondered why he had never heard this story before.

Jeff looked sheepish. "The same reason I shouldn't have brought it up in front of you now."

Sarah added, "We didn't want you to think we were immature."

Pieter sat silent and sullen, arms folded. Until a large insect fell from the tree, landed back of his neck, and disappeared under his collar. He leapt from his chair and danced around, clutching at the back of his neck. Sarah bounded out of her chair and reached under his shirttail to liberate a bright Kelly-green grasshopper. They almost knocked over a waitress carrying a large tray with another round of drinks.

Jeff laughed. "Oooh, Sam, come help me. I have a bug in my shirt too."

The group planned to head to a bar with live music, but Sarah begged off, citing exhaustion. Pieter stated that they would follow her car to see her safely home. While everyone else piled into Pieter's SUV, Jeff rode with Sarah.

"Dave told me Pieter was a nice guy," said Jeff. "But he seems kind of cold to me."

"He's got a lot on his mind. We have some challenging cases on the schedule."

"Such great pathology here."

"You mean, great opportunities to help patients."

"Yeah, that's what I meant."

No lights on at the house. No surprise. She hadn't left anything on when she left. Jeff shone his cell phone, so she could see to unlock the door. "Are you sure you won't come with us?"

"I'm really tired."

"Did you and Dave break up? I heard . . . but I see you're still wearing the ring."

"It's complicated."

Sarah watched them drive away before closing the door. When she flipped on the light switch, nothing happened. In fact, none of the lights worked. Another power outage. The house was pitch black and quiet, with a musty smell. She opened the windows, brushed her teeth by candlelight and fell asleep as soon as her head hit the pillow.

A noise startled her, and she rose to look out the window. Suddenly a horde of flying huge green grasshoppers burst through, with fangs and sharp claws. A man with an evil grin on his face crawled through the window, brandishing a machete. She tried desperately to scream for help. But she had no voice.

"Wake up." Pieter rubbed her shoulder. "It's okay. Just a bad dream."

"You're here. I didn't think you'd turn up. You were so angry."

"I wasn't angry. I was afraid."

"I sleep better when you're around."

He kissed her forehead. "No more bad dreams. Only sweet dreams."

CHAPTER FORTY-FIVE

VISITING SURGEONS

Her face was a Picasso portrait—as if some tectonic rift had shifted the halves of her face. A giant shard of windshield had inflicted the wound in an instant. The well-intended but misguided repair probably took a couple of hours. Three years later, the hideous deformity persisted: eyeball exposed, half a nose splayed out, the corner of a mouth partially hidden by a fold of flesh. Anxious, but hopeful, she lay on the operating table. Margo held the patient's hand and murmured soothingly as the young woman slipped into the oblivion of anesthesia.

Dr. Marshall handed the scalpel to Margo. "You're the surgeon today. I'm just the coach." A crowd of observers huddled around the table, and Dr. Marshall provided a running commentary during the three-hour procedure. "The basic principles of wound closure are simple. The skin edges should be on the same level. You want the scar to heal flat, so it won't cast a shadow. And it's critical to match up landmarks, like the eyelid, the edge of the lip. This woman has lived for three years as a social outcast, because her injury was not repaired correctly in the first place."

Margo paused to admire her work. "She's going to be beautiful again."

Dr. Marshall pulled off his gown and gloves. "You did a great job. You're a talented surgeon."

"I'm going to Nairobi next year to do a fellowship in trauma surgery. But I don't think they can teach me things like this."

"You should come over to Philadelphia for a while. You wouldn't be able to do any operations. But you could observe us."

"Why couldn't I operate in Philadelphia?"

"You'd have to get a training license, and that would require passing some US exams. A full license would require at least two years of training in the US."

"Because I'm from Africa?"

"It's the same for all overseas doctors. There are some exceptions. For example, an expert can get licensed as a visiting professor." He nodded at Pieter. "Someone like him. His altitude research is fascinating."

Margo looked at Sarah and wiggled her eyebrows.

When she awoke, the woman stared at her face in a mirror. Her features were swollen and dotted with tiny sutures that looked like gnats. But everything was back in the right place. "*Asante*," she whispered, as tears trickled down her face. "*Asante sana*."

CHAPTER FORTY-SIX

PEDICURES AND CPR

Balinda barked commands like a drill sargent, establishing order in the unruly crowd outside the clinic. She had a natural aptitude for triage, separating the truly sick from the ones with frivolous complaints.

A woman shuffled in, herding six children with runny noses and/or skin rashes. Sarah peered into throats and ears, and dispensed vitamins and skin creams. The mother complained of aches and pains. Nothing to be done about that, aside from offer sympathy and naproxen. As the family headed for the door, Sarah noticed that the mother was limping. She knelt down and removed the woman's blood-stained sandal. Dry and cracked heels were ubiquitous among the village women. But these feet were the worst she had seen. "Balinda, bring me a pan of warm water."

It was a moment of Zen for the hard-working mother. Her pained and stressed face gradually relaxed as her feet soaked. After twenty minutes, Sarah dried the feet, slathered them in Vaseline, and applied a pair of her own socks. She instructed the woman to keep her feet covered so the skin would not get so dry.

The mother beamed as she walked out to gather her

children, carrying the jar of Vaseline. Sarah remembered what Hippocrates said, "Cure sometimes, treat often, comfort always." She turned to Balinda and joked, "Maybe we should do this foot treatment for all the women."

Balinda grinned. "Me first."

SARAH'S HEART FLUTTERED at the sound of Pieter's car. She hadn't seen him for three long weeks. Jean had been the first of the voluntary dispensary doctors to teach the Saturday class. Then it was the obstetrician from Dar, followed by the pediatrician from Tanga. It was finally Pieter's turn.

A stampede of children mobbed him as he popped out of his SUV. He grinned at Sarah and waved, before indulging the children in a few rounds of "monster." He loaded Hamid on his shoulders and strode up the path, with other children clinging to his arms and legs. He kissed Sarah on the cheek. "Hi, Princess. Good to see you."

Aneisha had prepared a special dinner with Pieter's favorite foods. Balinda and her husband, Ghalib, joined them in the meal. Ghalib, as the ranking elder of the village, gave a brief speech. Sarah was beginning to despair of ever having a moment alone with Pieter. But as the dinner group dispersed, he asked to see her new home.

Pieter glanced around her one room house. "Very cozy. *Zoals het klokje thuis tikt, tikt het nergens.*"

"What does that mean?"

"It's a Dutch saying—I mean, obviously, it's Dutch. It means, 'The clock ticks here and nowhere else.' Kind of like your saying: 'There's no place like home.'"

"We also say 'Home is where the heart is.'"

The narrow cot creaked and wobbled as he sat down.

Sarah apologized. "The cots fold up when we have the class in here. It's not really configured for conjugal visits."

"I should sleep in my tent anyway. This is a devout Muslim community. Don't want to offend local sensibilities."

"You don't have to leave right away, do you?"

He leaned in for a kiss. But Jamal and Hamid and their little sister, Karima, peered through the doorway, giggling. Hamid begged, "Daktari Sarah, tell us your goat story again."

The boys sat on either side of her, and Karima climbed into Pieter's lap. The American tale of the "Three Billy Goats Gruff" had a happier ending than the African goat story. The children had related that fable, which seemed to confabulate the "Three Little Pigs" and "Little Red Riding Hood". Three little goats were home alone while their mother went out to get them some food. A jackal, covered in a goat skin, came to the door, claiming to be their grandmother. The little goats exclaimed about the big eyes, the paws instead of hooves, and the big teeth. Predictably, the jackal ate them all up.

Sarah provided a dramatic rendition of three clever goats who fooled a troll into letting them trip-trap across his bridge to reach the sweet green grass. "The little goat said, 'Don't eat me. You should wait for my brother, who is much bigger and tastier.' The troll let him pass by." Sarah was glad that none of the children asked her what a troll was. Come to think of it, she had never asked that question when she was a little girl. Obviously, the troll was a bad guy who could eat goats. No other explanation needed.

By the time the medium billy goat Gruff had also trip-trapped over the bridge and the big goat had butted the troll into the river, Karina was fast asleep, and Pieter carried the little girl out the door.

✕

AT NOON, SARAH took a break from clinic to check on Pieter's CPR class. The women were initially afraid to touch "Resusci-Annie." But eventually, they were all able to push rhythmically on the mannequin's chest, firmly enough to make the light flash. Sarah was not certain that any of them fully comprehended the physiological significance of the process, but Pieter was unfazed. "As long as they know when they should thump on the chest, I'm happy."

The class ended with the Heimlich maneuver. Pieter demonstrated the technique on Sarah, rather than presuming to embrace any of the women. "You stand behind the person and wrap your arms around the waist like this, and then . . ." He pulled up sharply on Sarah's mid-section.

Sarah muttered, "This is what I had to go through to get a hug?"

DURING THE EVENING meal, Aneisha asked an interesting question. "Pieter, when will your wife come to visit again?"

Pieter shrugged. "No plans for that."

Sarah got up without finishing her meal, murmured "*Asante*" to Aneisha, and retreated to her house. She was stoking her wood stove when Pieter arrived at her door.

"You aren't stacking it properly. Still not very good with fires, eh?" He rearranged the wood and lit the kindling.

"You shouldn't really be here, should you? I mean, you being a married man and all that."

"Aneisha assumed we were married. Eva did not correct her."

"And you didn't correct Eva?"

Pieter laughed. "You mean, call my wife a liar?" He turned from the fire, dusting his hands and grinning. But Sarah was not smiling.

"I need to tell you something. I'll miss my next visit here. I'm attending a conference in America."

"That's nice."

"It's in a town called Bethesda. Is that close to Philadelphia?"

"It's on the same continent."

"Come on, Sarah. What's wrong?"

She forced a smile. "I'm okay. Just a little grumpy. I'm tired. So, the meeting's in Bethesda. I guess the conference is at NIH?"

"Exactly."

"That's really cool. I hope you enjoy it. It's a couple of hours from Philly by car."

"I'm sorry to leave you hanging, but I've arranged for back up. One of the medical officers from Lushoto agreed to run the clinic while you teach."

"Thanks."

He stood up. "Looks like you need some sleep, so I'll say good night." He looked back from the doorway. "I don't have to leave until noon tomorrow. Will you go on a hike with me in the morning? There are some interesting caves." He tilted his head. "Please?"

THEY SET OFF right after breakfast. Pieter said that they had to take a shortcut if they wanted to be back in the village before lunch, so he chopped a trail through the forest, hacking down shrubs and vines. At the edge of a cliff, he shoved his machete back into its sheath and pointed over the edge. "It's just down there."

Sarah frowned at the steep rocky trail. "Are you sure it's worth it?"

"Oh, yes. Archeologists found evidence of hominid occupation more than a million years ago."

A large rock outcropping overhung the entrance, so the cave wasn't visible until they stood right in front of it. Sarah stepped into a narrow twisting tunnel, with jagged walls formed by huge slanting slabs of rocks. "It doesn't look like any cave I've ever been in. No stalactites, no stalagmites . . ."

"The caves were formed by earthquakes, not erosion."

"Doesn't look too comfy." She sat down on a boulder. "Hard to believe anyone could live here."

"It was more of a hiding place—a place to retreat from warring tribes."

"I heard there are some fossilized footprints around here. Left by pre-humans."

He shook his head. "That's what they used to think. But it turns out they're just depressions caused by erosion. Not real footprints like the ones that Lucy left in Olduvi Gorge."

The cave overlooked the cradle of humanity, untouched by the last ice age. Kilimanjaro was a tiny pimple on the horizon, as it had been for millions of years.

Pieter agreed to take the footpath back, with no more shortcuts, but it meant they wouldn't have time to visit any more caves. Sarah had to keep her eyes on her feet with every step as they climbed the treacherous trail. Until she ran smack into Pieter's outstretched arm.

The bushes rustled, ahead, on the left. "What—" she began.

"Shh."

A creature oozed onto the trail, tawny fur with irregularly circular black blotches. The huge cat paused and turned to face them. No cheek bars, so it wasn't a cheetah.

It was a leopard.

Amber eyes burned into Sarah's, and her heart pummeled against her ribcage. There was no room in her chest for air. She squeezed her eyes shut, waiting for the pounce that would end her life.

But nothing happened. When she opened her eyes, the leopard was still gazing at her, eyelids at half-mast. With a deep sigh, the huge cat slunk into the undergrowth across the path, his tail twitching in a final flourish before it disappeared.

They stood stock still until the shuddering sounds from the bushes slowly faded away.

When Sarah could breathe normally, she said, "I heard that you have to be very lucky to see a leopard."

"I've never heard of anyone spotting a leopard around here."

"You were so calm. I was scared shitless."

"He had no reason to attack us. They don't kill for sport, like men do." But he had drawn his machete, clutched firmly in his right hand. He stuffed it back in its sheath and climbed up onto a large boulder. Sarah clambered up beside him and spied the leopard descending in a smooth zigzag, slithering from rock to rock.

"Do you ever regret killing that leopard?"

"Never. I would kill ten leopards, right now, if it would bring Robert back."

Sarah hopped back down onto the path and noted a shoelace undone. She giggled as she stooped to tie it.

"What's so funny?"

"I just remembered a stupid joke. Two guys see a bear. One stops to tighten his shoelaces. The other guy says, 'You can't outrun a bear and—'"

"I've heard this one. The first guy says, 'I just have to outrun you.'"

With that, he bolted away. Sarah ran after him, but when she crested a rise, he was nowhere to be seen. No footprints on the stony trail—no clue as to where he had gone. She shrieked at the sound of something coming through the brush. Pieter crashed out, growling, and swallowed her in a bear hug.

A FLOCK OF children surrounded Pieter as he loaded up his SUV. Sarah called out from the edge of the herd. "Safe travels to America. Guess I'll see you in a couple of months."

He paused before closing his door. "Maybe we can get together sooner . . . some place. I have an idea. I'll be in touch."

Her heart was tied to his bumper, ripped from his chest, as he drove away. She could almost see it bouncing along the road behind him.

CHAPTER FORTY-SEVEN

SOLIDARITY

Ghalib's little store was a short walk from the clinic. It was a nice place for a tea break and some fresh roasted peanuts. Normally, three or four elders would be lounging on the bench in front of the shop, drinking tea and discussing the problems of the world. But today, the bench was occupied by three ladies, their feet soaking in tubs of water.

Ghalib greeted Sarah warmly, "Daktari, karibu."

Sarah jerked a thumb over her shoulder. "Looks like you're running a spa here."

Ghalib grinned. "These mamas like to have nice feet."

A shelf behind the counter had recently been stocked with jars of Vaseline. Ghalib had recognized the market for foot care. "Are you selling socks, too?"

He pulled a basket full of socks in varied colors and patterns, some with lace around the cuff. "Jabari brought these from market in Lushoto." The Wonder Woman socks caught Sarah's eye.

She pulled out 500 schillings for the peanuts, but Ghalib refused payment. In fact, he gave her a second bag, and a cup of tea.

Back at the clinic, Balinda had just dismissed the last patient. She stared out the window at a red sports car coming up the road. "Daktari Jean. He is good teacher."

Sarah frowned. Jean had done an excellent job with his first class, teaching wound management. The ladies, already excellent seamstresses, quickly became skilled at suturing lacerations. And he convinced them to stop slathering mud on skin burns. But tomorrow's class would deal with FGM. "He's a good teacher. But the women may not like hearing this lesson from a man."

Balinda nodded, "Private parts. You should teach them."

"My Swahili's not that good. And I don't have his experience."

The red car stopped at the end of the road and a woman emerged from the passenger side. Jean waved. "I brought you a houseguest."

The attractive woman was tall and proud, her hair done up in elaborate braids and beading. She ran to embrace Sarah. "I am so happy to see you."

It was Charmaine, fully recovered from her surgery, freed from shame and stench, essentially reborn.

IN THE MORNING, Charmaine taught the class, using Jean's lesson plan and posters. Sarah and Jean "double-teamed" the clinic, seeing all the patients by early afternoon, so that Jean could join the class to answer questions.

It didn't sound like a class was going on. Loud voices rang out through the windows as the women joined in a traditional African call and response. Charmaine would sing a line, and the women would repeat the phrase, clapping their hands in rhythm.

The singing stopped as soon as Jean and Sarah opened the door. The women stood in a circle, heads held high as Charmaine presented Jean with a sheaf of papers. Jean leafed through the pages, shaking his head slowly. "I can't believe it."

Each paper had a statement, printed in Swahili, and below it was the name of a TBA student. Some had marked it with and "X," some with a thumbprint, and three had actually printed their names.

Charmaine explained "They have all sworn. They will never again perform FGM. And they will tell everyone else: FGM is bad."

The students, with solemn faces, lifted their clenched fists high in the air.

Sarah whispered, "Charmaine is raising an army."

Jean nodded. "An army of angels."

CHAPTER FORTY-EIGHT

BACK TO DAR

Sunday, the day of rest. Sarah headed to the lodge for cell phone service, internet, brunch, and a hot shower.

Betje met her at the door with a broad smile. "Pieter says to call him as soon as you get here."

He answered the first ring. "How would you like to speak at a fund-raiser in Dar next Saturday? Black-tie gala for high-end donors: local businessmen, ex-pats . . . It's short notice, I know."

"Who gets the money?"

"Women's Health in Tanzania, my mother's foundation."

"I'd be happy to support that, but why me?"

"Some celebrity was scheduled, but she had to cancel. They were looking for a woman involved in health care to fill in. I told my mother you were a great speaker."

"What makes you think so?"

"I saw a YouTube video of you speaking at some surgical conference."

David had posted that video. She had won first place in the resident speaking competition at a national conference. So Pieter had been stalking her online. She had checked him out, too. That conference at NIH—he wasn't just attending. He was one of the keynote speakers.

She told Pieter that she didn't feel good about driving all the way to Dar by herself.

He reassured her. "They'll book an air taxi from Mambo. Betje says she'll drive you down."

"Black tie," she mused. "I don't have a formal dress."

"A duffel bag full of T-shirts and trekking pants, and not a thing to wear. You women always have the same complaint. But don't worry. My mum says she'll bring something for you to wear."

"Your mother will be there? And she won't mind bringing a dress for me?"

"She won't mind at all. She's bringing my formal suit anyway."

"You'll be there, too? In a tuxedo? Now that's exciting."

"Exciting? Me in a silly suit?"

"Every man looks sexy in a tux."

"Really?"

"Really."

"Hmm. From now on, I shall look forward to getting dressed up."

AS THE TINY aircraft approached the dirt landing strip, Sarah had second thoughts about the wisdom of traveling this way. But after takeoff, the exhilaration of flying took over. She looked down at the acres of sisal plants and watched the shadow of her airplane as it zoomed across the vast savanna. The plane circled far out over the Indian Ocean before landing.

Dar was steamy and smelled of the sea. A black Lexus SUV was waiting, thankfully air-conditioned, with a bottle of chilled water and a cold, wet, basil-scented face towel.

The hotel lobby was vast and beautiful, with glass walls rising up to the three-story ceiling. Sarah felt shabby in her jeans and T-shirt, hair pulled into a messy bun. The check-in clerk greeted her with respect. "Welcome to our hotel, Dr. Whitaker. All your expenses are covered. I have a nice room for you on a concierge floor. Do you need one room key or two?"

"Two please."

"Will you be needing any help with your luggage?" The clerk looked around her, as if expecting a pile of suitcases.

"No thank you." She felt self-conscious with only a small backpack.

"Here are your key cards. Your room number is printed on the jacket. Should I have a bellman escort you to your room?"

"No, thanks, I can find it." She turned and bumped into Pieter.

"Welcome, Dr. Whitaker." He shook her hand formally and gestured across the lobby toward two attractive women, tall, with ash blonde hair. They waved and smiled. "My mother and sister." He took Sarah's backpack. "Let me see you to your room."

He pressed Sarah's key card into a slot inside the elevator. "It's required to access your floor." Nothing happened when he pressed the button for her floor.

Sarah pointed to a sign. "It says to remove the card, and then push the button."

The elevator began to climb, and she murmured, "I know you like to leave it in."

Pieter exploded in a muffled guffaw. "Did you really say that!"

"I must be hanging around you too much."

"On the contrary, I believe you're having withdrawal symptoms."

The elevator door opened, and he placed his hand on her back to guide her to the room, where he opened the door with a flourish.

The spacious room had a sitting area and floor to ceiling windows overlooking the sea.

For a moment they just smiled at each other. Then he tackled her. They tumbled onto the bed, Sarah cackling like a giddy four-year old until he smothered her giggles with a kiss. And what a kiss! She got all fuzzy-brained and raked her fingers through his hair. "It's getting long. Soon we won't be able to see your ears."

"You sound like my mother."

"But I think it's cute. Makes you look like my wild man."

He growled and blew a raspberry on her belly and then pinned her arms above her head and kissed her again. "Mmm. Sarah, Sarah, Sarah, it's been way too long. Too bad we have to go to lunch now."

"What?"

"They're waiting in the café." He stood up and tucked in his shirt. "I can order for you while you freshen up. How about a cheeseburger?"

Sarah thought about their two-fist versus knife and fork debate and wondered where his mother stood on the issue of how to eat a hamburger. To avoid controversy, she asked for soup and a couple of samosas. She gazed into the mirror and sighed.

Pieter paused at the door. "Don't worry. You look beautiful." He pocketed the extra key card.

The whirlpool bathtub was inviting, but in the interest

of time, she took a quick shower and pulled her hair back into a high ponytail. A little mascara and lip gloss and she was ready.

Soup and samosas were waiting for her. Pieter was doing the knife and fork thing with his cheeseburger, while his little sister Mila took the two-handed approach. He waved his fork, "Sarah does not think that I eat my hamburger correctly."

Mila agreed. "She's right."

"My sister has been corrupted by time in the USA. She was an exchange student in Michigan."

"So, you've been exposed to the American Midwest. Did you ever go to a Packer's game?"

Mila nodded enthusiastically. "It was so much fun. I wore the cheese hat. And I am so excited to go to America with Pieter next week. He's speaking at a conference."

Sarah nodded. "Yes, that symposium at NIH." She stirred a little honey and lemon into her tea and placed her teabag on the edge of the saucer.

Pieter glanced into the cup. "Your tea looks weak."

As she took a sip, he picked up the limp teabag and winked. "I would have left this in a little longer."

Sarah coughed and choked, tea spurting out of her nose. Mila touched her shoulder, "Are you okay?"

"Fine," Sarah said between gasps. "Just went down the wrong way." The choking spell provided cover for the blush spreading across her neck and face.

"Your ring." Mila reached over to touch the diamond. "It's so beautiful."

Pieter said, "It belonged to her fiancée's grandmother."

"Fiancée?" Mila knitted her eyebrows. "Why isn't he here for your speech?"

"He's back home in Philadelphia."

"Pity," said Ana. She smiled, but it was a tight, thin-lipped smile. "The separation must be difficult." She glanced at Pieter, pursed her lips, and looked back at Sarah. "So, the schedule for the afternoon, you'll come to my suite for a fitting, to select your gown. After that, we'll go to the spa—us ladies, that is. We'll have a nice massage, pedicure, they'll do your hair and makeup, too." Her smile became warm. "We'll be so gorgeous."

SARAH TRIED ON all six of the dresses on approval from a boutique in Amsterdam. The unanimous favorite was sky blue satin gown, off the shoulders, form fitting down to mid-thigh, where it flared out to a flouncy skirt. Mila said that the dress would be perfect with the Tanzanite necklace.

"The what?"

Ana explained. "A copy of a necklace worn by the Dutch Queen at the coronation. It's been donated for the auction. We hope you'll be willing to model it."

Mila answered a knock at the door and Pieter poked his head in. "Is it safe to come in?" He sank into the sofa and approved of the dress. "You look like Cinderella."

Ana rolled her eyes. "We were just about to select shoes, but unfortunately we have no glass slippers."

Mila picked out some strappy silver sandals.

Pieter shook his head. "Oh, you can't wear sandals. Your toes!"

Ana looked perplexed.

Pieter and Sarah both babbled at once, explaining not only what was wrong with her toes, but why Pieter would be so cognizant of her feet. He said that she had lost her toenails during a Kilimanjaro climb *with her fiancée*, while Sarah pointed out that Pieter had to examine her toes because he was responsible for infection control in the operating room.

Ana shook her head and sighed, stooped to peer at Sarah's feet. "Not a problem. The spa can fit you with gels."

Pieter smirked. "You mean fake toenails?"

Ana thought that the gown was a tad too long and that the waist needed to be "nipped in." A dressmaker with a pincushion on her wrist marked the adjustments.

Ana nodded at Sarah. "You can take the dress off now."

Sarah froze, arms across her chest and glanced at Pieter.

He uncrossed his legs and stood up. "Sorry, I will excuse myself." He kissed his mother on the cheek. As he went through the door, Ana called out, "Get your hair cut."

CHAPTER FORTY-NINE

THE GALA

Sarah caught her reflection in the wall of mirrors as she stepped from the elevator into the lobby. The dress was perfect. Her dramatic up do was topped by a tiara and pale pink toenails peeked out beneath the hem of her skirt. She had never felt so elegant.

Ana was in regal purple, and Mila sparkled in a glittery emerald green gown. The dignified gentleman was obviously Pieter's father—the resemblance was unmistakable. He gallantly kissed her hand when they were introduced.

Behind him, Pieter looked absolutely scrumptious in his tux and neatly groomed hair. But his smile seemed forced, almost plastic.

"Sarah, here is someone I want you to meet." He stepped aside, and there she was: a beautiful slender woman in a sleek strapless column gown that matched her bright red lipstick. Her platinum hair was cropped short, her eyes were sapphires, and she wore insanely large diamond earrings. With her killer spike heels, she was nearly as tall as Pieter. The stunning woman extended her hand. "I am Eva. I have heard so much about you."

Sarah took Eva's hand and tried her best to smile as they touched cheeks with air kisses.

Pieter mumbled something about going to check on the car.

A chorus of children flanked the red carpet, singing, clapping and dancing. Inside the soaring ballroom, festive chatter nearly drowned out the soft strains of a string quartet. Tables, covered in bold African print cloth, were topped with towers of tropical flowers. Guests in tuxedoes, formal gowns, or kitangas perused the silent auction items displayed around the room.

A young woman took Sarah's arm. "I have the necklace for you to model." She placed the sparkling blue necklace around Sarah's neck and paraded her around the room so that potential bidders could get a closeup look. Sarah was glad to sit down when it was time for dinner to be served.

She didn't feel much like eating. Pieter would not return her gaze. He didn't seem to have much of an appetite himself and excused himself after just a few bites. Eva explained, "He's working the room. He is quite good at this."

Ana asked Sarah for an update on Kandu. "Pieter never gives us much news. How is Keisha? And her children?"

Sarah pulled out her mobile and showed them some pictures. Mila gushed over the new smiles on the faces of the boys. Ana asked to see pictures of the new delivery room.

"And here is my new house," said Sarah. "It doubles as the classroom."

Eva batted her eyelashes, a sly smile on her face. "Did you ever have to sleep in that horrid tent?"

"No, the house was finished before I moved up there."

Dessert was served. Time for Sarah's speech. She felt a bit unsteady on the way to the podium, walking in high heels for the first time in eight months.

She reminded herself to smile and take a deep breath

before she began to speak. "Good evening. Thank you all for coming to this wonderful event. It is an honor and a privilege to speak with you. Your generosity provides vital support to Women's Health in Tanzania, a foundation committed to improving the lives of women and children in this country. I feel very fortunate that this foundation has chosen to support our project.

"The death rates for mothers and babies in Sub-Saharan Africa is staggering. Most births take place at home, attended by family members, or by traditional birth attendants. These birth attendants are respected and trusted by the people in their villages. Their knowledge and experience have been handed down through many generations, and they are experts in managing normal deliveries. But unfortunately, they are not trained to recognize and manage complications—the problems that cause so many deaths of mothers and babies.

"Our program is an experiment, teaching modern concepts and methods, training traditional birth attendants to recognize high-risk pregnancies that should be referred into a hospital. We are also training them to serve as community health workers, to address the critical shortage of health care in remote regions."

Sarah paused for a moment, looked around the room, and lowered her voice. "There is another issue. The scourge of female genital mutilation. Currently, most female circumcision is performed by traditional birth attendants. Our goal is to educate these women, so that they will cease and desist this horrid practice." A wave of applause erupted from the audience.

Sarah related the odyssey of Charmaine: how scarring from genital mutilation had killed her baby and caused a fistula that left her ostracized. Corrective surgery had restored her to a normal life, and she was studying to be a nurse. She told them about Balinda, a traditional birth attendant who learned to save lives by acquiring the simple skill of taking blood pressure. She told them about vaccination programs, babies rescued from malnutrition and dehydration, and severe infections prevented by hand washing and simple first aid.

"I am privileged to work with brave, strong women like Charmaine and Balinda. But some days, my efforts seem feeble and futile. Like I'm trying desperately to empty the ocean, one bucket at a time. It's heartbreaking to realize how many other women's lives have been broken by obstetrical fistula—shunned by their communities, unable to find work. Few of them have access to the care that Charmaine received." She paused and looked around the room. "Consider the magnitude of the problem. For every Charmaine, there are thousands more women with this problem. It is estimated that in this country, there are 3000 new obstetrical fistulae each year, far beyond our capacity to repair. More than 28,000 women in this country are currently afflicted."

She walked out to the center stage, hands folded behind her back. "It's even harder to realize that these terrible problems are preventable. Obstetrical fistulae are caused by prolonged, obstructed labor during childbirth, which, in turn, is so often the result of female genital mutilation." Sarah reached out her arms, palms upward. "Why would anyone do such a thing?" She shook her head sadly as her arms fell to her sides. "This horrible procedure is intended to make them 'better wives'." She made quote marks in the air with her fingers. "In other words, it makes them passive and less likely to wander." She closed her eyes for a moment before proceeding.

"This doesn't seem right, does it? It should be a crime, shouldn't it?" She threw up her hands. "Well, guess, what? It *is* against the law." She paced slowly across the stage. "That law has driven this practice underground. No longer a public ritual, it's performed in secret now. And, increasingly, on infants."

She paused in mid-stage. "It's never easy to change a culture. We are trying to make a difference by educating the tribal birth attendants. These women have considerable influence in their communities. In fact, they currently perform most of the female circumcisions." Sarah took a deep breath and smiled. "I am pleased to announce that the midwives in our class, inspired by Charmaine, have all signed a pledge. They will never again perform FGM."

The audience erupted into a standing ovation. When the clapping died down, and the people returned to their seats, Sarah continued.

"That applause is for Charmaine. And for all of you. Your generosity tonight will support a host of innovative approaches to improve Women's Health in Tanzania." She smiled broadly and put her hand on the Tanzanite encircling her throat. "I fully expect enthusiastic bidding on all the great items in the auction!"

Thunderous applause followed her to the table, where she was greeted with hugs, air kisses, and praise from everyone, even Pieter. Ana, in particular, held her close for a moment. "Thank you so much for coming. Pieter has spoken very highly of you and I can see why."

Mila pushed a small plate in front of Sarah, a fruit-laden slice of cheesecake. "I saved this for you."

Sarah cut her dessert into small pieces that she moved around her plate, hoping no one noticed that she did not eat a single bite.

The auction was underway, and before she knew it, Sarah was summoned to the stage again and the jewelry around her neck shone down from a huge video screen. The bidding was spirited, eventually narrowing to two bidders who seemed equally determined to win, until the auctioneer announced, "Going, going . . . sold! For six thousand Euros." An attendant led Sarah to deliver the necklace to the high bidder. As they wove their way through the room, she realized that they were heading back to her own table.

Eva beamed. "I had to buy this because Sarah's speech was so inspiring."

The attendant removed the necklace and handed it to Eva, who turned to Pieter for help. As he fastened the clasp, Eva gazed at Sarah. Her eyes narrowed, and she lifted her chin in triumph above the sparkling jewels.

When the music began, Eva took Pieter by the hand and led him to the dance floor.

Sarah couldn't bear to watch. She turned away and was startled by an arm around her waist.

"*Bon sois*, Sarah!" Jean kissed her cheek. "Wonderful presentation!"

"Thanks. I didn't realize you would be here."

"How could I miss a chance to see you? May I have this dance?"

She couldn't really refuse, but why did the band have to play such a good cover of "Unchained Melody"? It was bad enough just watching Pieter and Eva glide around the floor. Jean waved to them and said, "It's really good Eva could turn up for this. Pieter was devastated when she left him."

✕

THE LIGHT KNOCK at the door was a gentle tapping—not intended to awaken anyone, just a polite query.

Sarah was watching CNN with the sound turned off. Even after a long soak in the marble Jacuzzi, she could not fall asleep.

Through the peephole she saw Pieter—shirt collar open, bowtie dangling. She opened the door a few inches.

"Sarah . . ." He stuffed his hands into the pockets of his trousers. "I am so sorry."

Her mouth was dry as dust. Her voice wasn't working.

He shuffled his feet, stared down the corridor, not focusing on anything in particular. "I didn't know she was coming. She wanted to surprise me."

Sarah finally found her voice. "It's okay."

"Your talk was fantastic. Thank you." He gazed at her for a moment, through the crack in the doorway. "I'd better go."

She watched him walk down the hallway. "Are you sleeping with her tonight?"

She regretted the words as soon as they left her mouth, reverberating in the dim corridor.

For a millisecond, he decelerated in mid-step, almost imperceptibly—like a glitch in a videoclip. But he did not stop, and he did not speak, and he did not turn around.

CHAPTER FIFTY

SIMBA

The tiny withered infant was four months old but looked like a little old man. He could not nurse because of a ping-pong-ball sized mass under his tongue. His mother squeezed her breast to get milk into his mouth, one drop at a time. He was starving to death.

Sarah wrapped a tourniquet around his tiny arm and searched for a vein. Balinda looked over her shoulder and said, "I want to learn how to do this."

"It's not a good idea." Too many things could go wrong: infections, fluid overload, and even death if the wrong fluid was used.

"But sometimes, when you are not here—babies could die."

No veins on the infant's right arm. Or the left. Or on either foot. Sarah sighed. "I'll have to do a cut down."

"What's that?"

"I'll show you."

She sliced through the skin on the ankle and slipped a catheter into a large blue vein.

By morning, the infant looked much better, but fluids alone would not sustain him. He needed surgery to remove the mass so that he could feed. But he was so malnourished that he might not survive the journey to the hospital. Sarah pushed on the lump. It wasn't solid.

"Balinda, bring me a syringe and a sixteen-gauge needle."

The mother crouched in the corner and covered her eyes as Sarah sucked turbid yellow fluid from the infant's mouth and the ping pong ball slowly deflated. Balinda handed the baby to his mother, who cradled him her arms as he latched onto her breast and fed greedily. The mass would slowly fill up again, but he only needed a couple of weeks of his mother's milk to be in shape for surgery.

Balinda planted her feet widely on the floor, hands on her hips. "I want to learn how to do that."

"I doubt you'll ever see anything like this again."

Balinda continued to glare. "I want to learn things."

"Okay, but let's take it slowly. First, I'll teach you to draw blood." Sarah did not relish the thought of offering her own veins for Balinda's training. "You'll have to find a volunteer. To practice."

The next day, Balinda brought her husband to the clinic. "He is volunteer."

Ghalib was tense and wide-eyed, but stoic, as his wife wiped his skin with alcohol. Balinda knew exactly what she was doing. She had obviously been watching Sarah very closely. In no time, she had filled up two tubes with blood. "How shall we test this blood?"

"The usual screening stuff. Jabari can take the blood to the hospital in Lushoto."

✕

IT WAS LONG after dark. Pieter was late. Not that Sarah was eager to see him again. And he wouldn't be around that much on this visit anyway, since he and Ghalib would set out early in the morning for town hall meetings with the men in surrounding villages, talking about domestic violence. She lay awake, listening for the sound of his Land Cruiser coming up the road. What could be keeping him? An accident? A flat tire? Could he have tumbled over a cliff? She sang songs in her head to avoid dwelling on potential calamities. Then she prayed. Sometime during the night, she drifted off.

His SUV was not there in the morning. But the front flaps of his tent were open, and his rucksack was inside. Keisha was cooking breakfast over charcoal. "Daktari Pieter gone. He go with Ghalib. "

"I guess he got in pretty late."

Keisha nodded gravely. "Yes, very late. Do you want tea? Banana?"

It had been a long day. Sarah conducted an important class: how to make rehydration formula for sick infants. The medical assistant from Lushoto filled in at the clinic while Sarah taught, but he was not very efficient. There were fifteen patients still waiting when the class was over. By the time Sarah finished caring for the last patient, she was exhausted. It wasn't the pleasant feeling of surrendering to well-earned fatigue. It was muscle-aching, bone-weary, can't find a comfortable position misery. She only intended to close her eyes for a moment or two. The sun was setting when she awoke to the sound of Pieter's voice outside. She sat up, fished around under the bed with her feet to find her sandals, and staggered outside.

Pieter was sipping tea with the village elders in front of

Ghalib's little store. His face lit up when he caught sight of Sarah. "You're awake now." He scooted over and patted the bench next to him, as if nothing had changed between them.

She tried to appear nonchalant. "Did the focus groups go well?"

"I doubt that we changed any minds."

Ghalib grinned and clapped Pieter on the back. "He tell them, be like Simba."

"Simba?" Sarah was puzzled.

Pieter sighed. "You know, the male lion. He takes care of his pride."

Ghalib laughed. "But Simba, sometimes, he eats cubs."

Pieter rolled his eyes. "Not a perfect analogy."

"How was your trip to the States?"

"Good."

Keisha called out, "Foodie is ready."

Pieter downed the rest of his tea. "I'll tell you more after dinner."

Sarah didn't get a chance to eat, because she was summoned to the delivery room. The patient was young and healthy and had already borne two children without problems. A quick exam indicated the baby would not arrive for at least an hour, so she went home to get a fire going before it turned cold. As she stuffed paper and wood into the stove, Pieter knocked on the door. "May I come in?"

"Of course."

"You're still not very good at building a fire."

"I'm getting by." The flames slowly spread from the paper to the wood.

Pieter sat down, leaned forward, and rubbed his temples.

"What time did you get here last night?" she asked.

"Nearly two. I was late getting away. Major trauma case."

"Then you shouldn't have come. It's not safe, driving so late at night."

"I had to come." His eyes brimmed with something. Pity? Remorse? "Can we talk?"

She poked at the fire. "Not right now. I need to get back to the delivery."

He turned to leave, but Sarah told him to stay. "I'll be back in an hour or so. Lie down and rest."

He didn't argue. She covered him with a blanket, tucked it around his neck, and kissed his forehead. "You know, you're the best friend I've ever had."

LOVING RELATIVES MURMURED encouragement and wiped sweat from the young mother's brow. The room exploded into joy when the baby was born. A healthy birth was always a miraculous moment. If only all deliveries could be so happy.

She emerged from the bright delivery room into a moonless and overcast night, dreading the impending conversation with Pieter. Her heart sank when she opened the door. The spare cot was empty.

The fire was burning low, would not last the night. As her eyes adjusted to the darkness, she noticed that the cot was totally empty. Not even a mattress. There was a large lump in the middle of the room. It was Pieter, sound asleep. He had pulled both mattresses onto the floor, side by side.

How presumptuous. He deserved to be kicked out.

But he was here. He was hers, at least for the night.

She tried not to disturb him, slipping quietly under the

covers, but he sprang to life, as though deployed by an invisible hair-trigger tripwire, and surrounded her liked a
cozy warm duvet.

"You're like a Jack-in-the-Box." She giggled. "What
about the local sensitivities?"

"I can sneak out early."

"But on the floor? There could be bugs on the floor.
Maybe even scorpions."

"*Akuna matata*. I told them all to leave. Simba always
protects his mate."

CHAPTER FIFTY-ONE

GONE

She was disoriented for a moment or two in the dim pre-dawn light. Then she remembered. They were sleeping on the floor. The fire had long since burned out, and her breath made little white poofs in the cold air. Time to get up, no matter how warm and cozy it was with Pieter nestled against her back. She scanned the room. No noxious bugs. Nothing like the scorpion she had found last week. She had screamed for help until Ghalib burst through her door to gallantly chop the bug in half with his machete. The perspective from the floor was interesting. She could see under the beds. Nothing amiss there. The only odd thing was a rope under her bed, draped across her sandals. Or maybe it was a hose. But she didn't own a rope or a hose.

Her body recognized the danger before her mind could take it in. Her heart pounded, and her stomach churned.

Pieter stirred. "What's wrong?"

"A ss-ss-snake," she hissed.

He peered over her shoulder. "So it is. Don't move."

He rose very slowly, stepped between Sarah and the snake, and reached back to beckon with his fingers. "Stay right behind me," he whispered. She wrapped her arms around him and pressed her face against his back with her eyes tightly shut as they backed slowly toward the door in tiny steps. She could hardly breathe until they were outside, and Pieter slammed the door.

"What do we do now?"

"I'll rouse Ghalib. He has some snake catching gear."

"Catching! Aren't you going to kill it?"

"We have to contain him first. Don't go back in the house."

"Are you kidding? I don't think I can ever sleep in there again."

Pieter returned with Ghalib, both men clad in tall heavy boots and thick gloves, bearing machetes and snake tongs. Balinda brought a plastic trash can with a tight-fitting lid and a kitanga to wrap around Sarah's bare legs. So much for the discrete sleepover. Pieter must have had some spare pants in his tent.

Word of the snake had spread throughout the village, and spectators assembled to see the show, adults murmuring and children giggling. A couple of enterprising young men brought ladders, so they could observe the spectacle through the transoms.

Pieter and Ghalib stood at the door, quietly discussing strategy. They would wait until the sun was a bit higher in the sky, for better light. But if they waited too long, it would warm up and the snake would become more active.

Balinda held up two fingers. "It is two step snake." She scratched the air with fingers curled like fangs. "Snake bite." Then she straightened out the two fingers and held them in front of Sarah's face. "Take two steps," with a wave of her hand, she concluded, "then you die."

The door creaked open slowly and Ghalib stepped through. Sarah could barely breathe as Pieter followed him in and closed the door behind them.

Balinda dragged Sarah to the window, pushing aside others who had crowded around to watch. Ghalib crouched down and peered under the bed. Then he gave Pieter a signal.

It all happened very quickly but seemed to play out in slow motion: Pieter kicking the cot frame away, Ghalib thrusting his snake grabber, Pieter jumping backward as the snake lunged toward him. For a seemingly interminable point in time, he and the snake hung in the air, and life was a two-dimensional image projected onto a screen that was ripping apart with Pieter's soul tumbling into oblivion.

The snake thrashed wildly, and his head stopped just short of Pieter's leg. Ghalib had grasped its midsection and pinned it to the floor. Pieter deployed his own tongs, landing a successful grab near the head.

Sarah could not bear to watch any more. She squeezed her eyes shut, trying her best to ignore the scuffling and banging sounds, until she heard the metallic clang of the machete on the concrete floor, followed by cheers of the crowd. When she looked through the window again, a long black headless creature writhed on the floor, summoning an odd recollection of digging for worms with her grandfather.

Pieter stood over the snake. "It's a big one. More than two meters long."

"Black mamba." Ghalib clicked his tongue. "Very bad."

Balinda loaded the snake into the plastic can and carried it outside, where she was mobbed by a jubilant crowd, everyone wanting to get a look.

Pieter called to Sarah through the window. "You can come in now."

She shook her head and backed away. He came out of the house and worked his way to her through the high fives and arm bumps of well-wishers.

She clung to him. "I was so afraid. I thought you were finished."

"I was a little worried myself." He kissed the top of her head and held her close.

She whimpered, "They don't travel in pairs, do they?"

He stepped back, lifted her chin. "Are you really afraid to go back in?"

She nodded.

"We could stay at the lodge tonight."

"Don't you have to get back to the hospital?"

"They can do without me for another day." He looked up at the roof of the house. "I want to seal off those transoms. That's probably how the snake got in. Mambas are great climbers."

He drove down to Lushoto to buy some wire mesh. By late afternoon, the house was secured, and Sarah and Pieter headed to the lodge. Halfway there, Sarah's phone began to ping repeatedly with incoming messages.

"You are too popular."

"I've been out of cell phone range for a while."

"Who wants you?"

"Everyone. My mother, my sister, the hospital back home." She scrolled silently through several text messages from David. As usual, the most recent messages were displayed first and so the others appeared in descending levels of urgency and frustration, starting with, "Where the hell are you, Sam?" and ending with "Dear Sarah, please call."

She squealed with joy when she read the latest text

from her mother. "Allison had her baby! A little boy. Eight pounds, two ounces."

She checked her email in the lobby of the lodge. Her mother had sent ten photos of the new baby, and Allison had plastered her Facebook with multiple images.

Pieter peered over her shoulder. "Cute little fellow."

She opened an email from Philadelphia Memorial Hospital, a multicolored multi-page spreadsheet.

Pieter said, "That looks complicated."

"It's the schedule for next year. I'll be chief, so I'm in charge of this."

"Seems you're headed home already." He stood up. "I need a beer. Want one?"

"Sure."

He strolled to the bar, and she opened David's latest email. It began with, "*I haven't heard from you in so long. Are you okay? Please call me.*"

Pieter handed her a Serengeti and glanced at the computer screen. "Sorry, I shouldn't read over your shoulder."

"It's okay. No secrets." That was a lie. Two lies, actually, but neither intentional. She fervently wanted everything to be okay. And she wanted to share the turmoil in her soul. But a small leak of emotion could lead to a dam burst and the flood might wash Pieter away.

He said, "I think I'll go for a walk."

The screen door slammed. David's email said that he wanted to talk, sort things out, couldn't wait any longer, wanted to speak face to face, was looking to book a flight over.

Six months ago, she would have been ecstatic to get such a message. But now...

For months, she had been drawn and quartered. Okay, not quartered—bisected, her soul rent asunder by opposing forces. On the one hand, loyalty to a man who had been the center of her life for so many years. They had plans for the future. On the other hand, hopeless addiction to a man from another world who had a rich and gorgeous girlfriend.

It had all become crystal clear—in that instant when a man and a snake hung in mid-air.

A world without Pieter would be unbearable.

Decency demanded that she call David. She had to let him know that she didn't love him—not now, possibly never did, not really. Not the way she ached for Pieter. But how could she make such an announcement by email, or even over the phone?

She composed a brief email promising to call him later. She titled the message, "Proof of Life," pressed send, slammed her laptop shut.

PIETER'S RUCKSACK WAS in their room, but he wasn't. And he wasn't at the lookout or on the trail to the camp-sites. They had planned to watch the sunset together on the terrace. She sat there alone until the sun disappeared behind the mountains.

She found him in the dining room of the main house, at the family style dinner table with six other guests: two German couples and two French women. She took the seat next to him and whispered, "I looked everywhere for you."

He nodded and passed a platter of chapatis. "I was walking."

Animated multilingual dinner chatter at the table masked the silence between Sarah and Pieter. Talk was still sparse as they walked down to their room. "I lost track of time," said Pieter. "Sorry to make you worry."

"It's okay," she said, and silently cursed herself for being so stupid.

He stopped just inside the door. "We need to talk."

She didn't say a word.

"Look at me."

She felt his eyes drilling into her, could not face him.

He thumped his hand on the door jamb. "I don't know what I'm doing here. I just don't know anymore."

She sat down on the sofa, stared at her feet.

He said, "If you pull a bandage off slowly, it's torture. You feel every little hair and skin cell being teased out."

She covered her face.

"But if you just rip it off, the pain is gone in a second." He walked across the room and picked up his rucksack. For a moment, he stood with his hand on the doorknob. Then he was gone.

CHAPTER FIFTY-TWO

BAD NEWS

The poster showed the anatomy of a pregnancy, an expectant mother's body sliced in half from top to bottom. Sarah pointed at a structure in the picture and spoke to the semi-circle of women seated on the floor. "Can anyone tell me what this is?"

Dura raised her hand. "That is where the baby stays. The yoo-tare . . . What is that word?"

"Uterus. Very good."

Nasila stood up and approached the poster for a closer look. "How does the baby get out when it wanders?"

Everyone in the class "knew" that an unborn baby would occasionally escape into the mother's belly. They were all well versed in the tricks required to coax a wandering fetus back to the womb.

Sarah had clearly stated, on multiple occasions, that "wandering" was a myth—never happens. She repeated that message again, tracing her finger along the thick wall of the uterus in the diagram. "The baby can't wander. Remember? There's only one way out."

A couple of the midwives nodded their heads, slowly.

But most eyes were glazed over. They heard but did not believe.

Perhaps it wasn't worth worrying about traditional myths, as long as the women retained critical concepts of care for mothers and babies. After all, Sarah had no idea how the circuitry in her laptop functioned.

On the other hand, if they disbelieved some of her facts, how strong was their confidence in anything she said? Would they continue to do the right things after she left? Or would everything fall apart, wash away, like the elaborate sand castle that she and Allison once built in front of the family beach house. They put Barbie dolls as princesses in its turrets and failed to heed their father's warning about the tide. In the morning, it was gone, Barbies and all.

Zuri suddenly burst into laughter and pointed out the window. "The boys give their goat a ride!" The class disintegrated as everyone streamed outside.

Bulu's little nose stuck out over the side of the goat cart. The boys were not laughing or smiling. Hamid wailed, "A truck hit her. Babu says he must kill her."

Bulu struggled to get out of the cart, her front hooves flailing the air, her back legs motionless.

The boys laid Bulu on the ground, and Sarah cradled the goat's head in her lap, scratching her favorite spot, just behind her left ear.

"I'm afraid your father is right. Her back legs are paralyzed. She can't live like this."

"Please do something," Hamid sobbed. "There must be something you can do."

Balinda handed Sarah a stethoscope. "What about her baby?"

Sarah heard two strong heartbeats. "She has two kids."

"Soon babies will come." Balinda pointed to the udders. "She is getting ready to make milk."

Jamal fetched a handful of straw, and Bulu gobbled it down.

They could keep her alive another few days. Long enough for the kids to be born. The boys would lose their precious Bulu, but they could still raise her babies.

Then Sarah had a great idea.

The delivery room was packed as the students huddled around Bulu, laid out on the operating table like a sacrificial lamb. Sarah prodded the goat's belly with a needle, confirming that she had no sensation. The injury had created permanent spinal anesthesia. Perfect for a caesarian section.

Keisha shooed all the children away and sat beside Bulu's head, scratching the goat's ears and murmuring soothing words. Balinda was a superb assistant, intuitively knowing where to apply pressure and how long to cut the sutures. The gush of clear fluid from the womb elicited a chorus of shrieks. Nasila clapped her hands. "So that is where the water comes from."

Sarah pointed at the womb. "See how thick this wall is? No way for babies to wander." She passed the newborns to Keisha and stared at a syringe preloaded with a lethal dose of pentothal. The plan was to end the goat's misery quickly, right after the delivery.

Keisha filled two small bottles with milk from another goat, but the newborn kids would have nothing to do with the rubber nipples. Bulu bleated loudly, pummeling the air with her front hooves, desperate to get to her babies.

Perhaps she could nurse her babies for a little while. It was worth a try.

Sarah stitched the little goat back together, and Keisha

settled the kids next to their mother. Bulu licked the babies and they immediately began to feed. Maybe she could keep Bulu alive long enough to wean the baby goats.

The successful delivery gave Sarah a much-needed boost in morale, in the wake of Pieter's sudden retreat from her life. He had ignored every phone call, every text, every email. Obviously, he chosen Eva. When he returned to Kandu in a few weeks, she would focus on civil conversation. They would agree to stay friends.

She finally called David. The conversation turned out to be much less dramatic than she had feared. A quick trip to Africa would not be cost effective. Left unspoken was the lack of any burning desire to be together. They would allow whatever feelings were left between were them to smolder, embers below a pile of ashes, and try to resurrect a life together when she returned home.

JABARI HANDED SARAH the results of Ghalib's routine blood work. She scanned the page, almost absent-mindedly, noting the right-hand column of "N"s that indicated normal results. Only one test was abnormal. She had to read that line on the report several times, to be certain she was seeing it correctly.

Medical schools provide lectures on how to deliver bad news. There is no good way.   Sarah sat down with Balinda and Ghalib. "I have bad news." She paused a moment to let that sink in. "Ghalib, remember when Balinda drew some of your blood?" he nodded. "We sent off some of that blood for testing. It shows that you might have cancer."

The couple remained expressionless and silent.

"You know what cancer is, don't you?"

Balinda nodded. "It is bad. Will he die?"

Ghalib stared into the distance and shrugged his shoulders. "We all die." Then his eyes locked onto Sarah's. "When?"

The one-word question was a knife in Sarah's chest. She didn't have the answer, not even a good guess.

"We don't know for certain that you have cancer. We need more tests."

Belinda's eyes were downcast. "I should not have drawn that blood."

"No. It's good to know this. Otherwise, we wouldn't know until . . . " She didn't complete the sentence. His PSA level was very high, consistent with advanced prostate cancer. Therapy could relieve suffering, possibly extend his life. But it was too late for a cure.

Ghalib looked so healthy that it was hard to believe that his body could be riddled with vicious rogue cells, nibbling away at his lungs and bones.

BALINDA AND GHALIB travelled to NTMC and would stay in Sarah's house until his treatment was finished, however long that took. Sarah would have to run the dispensary herself for a while. She didn't want to think about the possibility that Balinda might not return.

CHAPTER FIFTY-THREE

OUTBREAK

Nasila did a surprisingly good job of filling in for Balinda. As a student, she contested every single concept in the curriculum. Sarah had secretly dubbed her "Doubting Nasila." But once this midwife became convinced of something, she became a zealot. For example, germs. She had an epiphany in the midst of a lecture on infection control. Not that she suddenly mastered the field of microbiology. Those details were insignificant to her. But she suddenly saw sterile technique and antibiotics as powerful magic in the battle against witchcraft. She constantly waged war against germs, scrubbing the clinic floor twice a day and wearing a mask and gloves with each and every patient. Her obsession was almost annoying. Like the morning when she stood at the clinic door and would not allow Sarah to come in. "The floor is still wet."

"But it's time to open. Look at all the people waiting."

Their standoff was interrupted by a sound in the distance, something like a siren. The sound grew closer and louder, a mournful ululating cry of human anguish. A woman trudged up the path with a small child in her arms. She tripped near the clinic door and a little girl tumbled from her arms. Sarah leapt forward and caught the child.

The little girl was stiff, stone cold, and the front of her organdy dress was caked with dried blood and vomit. The mother's eyes were crimson, and a purple rivulet trickled from her nose.

Nasila whispered, hoarsely, "This is red eye fever."

Sarah gently laid the corpse on the ground stared at her own hands.

Nasila handed her some antiseptic wipes.

"Lock up the dispensary," said Sarah. "Put on full protective gear. We're in containment mode."

The meager lukewarm spray from the solar heated shower did little to wash away Sarah's sickening sense of dread. Foamy water swirled on the concrete slab before flowing under the cloth "door" and out onto the ground. No sewer. No septic tank. She flooded the area with bleach. Hopefully that would suffice to wipe out the evil pathogens.

She had given explicit instructions, and Nasila carried out her assignments to a tee. By the time Sarah's shower was over, the little corpse was double wrapped in plastic, and stashed between large stones, about fifty yards downhill from the village. The mother was provided a place to rest nearby: a straw mat on the ground and a blue tarp supported on poles to provide shade. Aneshia's husband, the acting chief elder while Ghalib was away, recruited the men of the village to build a barricade of shrubs and thorns around the containment zone.

Jabari gave Sarah a lift to the cell phone "hot spot" so that she could call the district hospital in Lushoto for back up. The medical officer knew about the outbreak. It had begun with the death of one woman. The funeral was typical African, relatives wailing and throwing themselves on the body. Several mourners had become sick, including the mother and child who had shown up in Kandu. The government had dispatched special health workers to the area and had requested emergency assistance from WHO. An ambulance would be dispatched to pick up the body and the sick woman. Sarah requested more containment gear in case other victims showed up in Kandu.

The view across the Rift Valley still took Sarah's breath away. She wondered how many times, throughout millennia, had epidemics swept through the region. It was a marvel that humankind had somehow survived.

The mother died before Sarah returned. Nasila oversaw wrapping and stowing the body, and dealt with the woman's husband when he arrived in Kandu, wailing and pounding on the door to the dispensary, demanding the bodies of his wife and child for a proper burial. She managed to calm him down and served him a cup of tea.

Sarah asked, "How did you get him to settle down?"

"I tell him, no, you cannot take them. They must be tested. You must wait two weeks. He was angry, but now he says he will wait."

"Two weeks? Why did you tell him that? They'll burn the bodies. He'll be even angrier in two weeks when he finds out you tricked him."

Nasila jutted her chin toward the man. "He will be dead before then."

FEVERISH PEOPLE STUMBLED into the village like stragglers of a zombie army after the apocalypse. The thorny enclosure had to be expanded twice. Dura was dispatched with Jabari to visit surrounding villages, preaching the gospel of barrier protection and infection control. No funerals. All the sick should head to the hospital in Lushoto. The other students joined Sarah. Garbed in the armor of gowns and gloves, they provided what comfort they could, cleaning up bloody vomit and diarrhea and dispensing water and Panadol. Facemasks blunted odors that would otherwise overpower. Men in hazmat suits appeared from time to time to transport the living to the hospital and the bodies to some mass grave or fire; Sarah was hazy about the precise destination. Village men stood guard, lest anyone try to spirit a corpse away for a funeral.

It was worse in the daylight, when Sarah could not escape their eyes. At night, they were faceless lumps on the ground.

After three days, WHO established a containment unit near the hospital in Lushoto. Patients were transported to that village of white domed tents, and the task of decontaminating Kandu began. The air was saturated with chlorine and smoke from burning straw mats. When the village had regained some semblance of normalcy, Aneisha cooked a hearty meal. But the smell of death still lingered, an invisible putrid fog. The first bite of food weighed like stone in Sarah's stomach.

Nasila peered at Sarah's eyes. "You don't eat."

"I'm not very hungry."

"I think so you are sick. Jabari can take you to Lushoto."

The blood in her veins became ice water at the thought of that tent city full of the dying. "I think . . . I'm just tired. That's all." She staggered home and tumbled into bed. Too weak to build a fire, she fell into a deep sleep, awoke later in the bone chilling night, and wrapped herself in blankets, shivering uncontrollably. Then she was drenched in sweat.

The dead little girl in her frilly dress hovered above her like a hologram.

A bright shaft of morning sunlight pierced the room as Nasila opened the door. "Daktari, you—"

"Don't come in." Sarah tried to shout, to sound commanding, but her voice was weak and raspy. "No one . . . come in. I don't want . . . anyone else . . . be sick." Her chest rattled and wheezed. Breathing left little energy for anything else. "Tell Jabari . . . call Betje . . . take me . . . to hospital."

"Jabari not here. He gone to Lushoto."

The door closed, and Nasila's footsteps faded away. Sarah leaned over the edge of the bed as blood erupted from her mouth. She did her best to clean up, gathering the mess with a towel and pushing it under her bed. The bucket next to her little washstand held just enough water to wash her face and rinse her mouth.

Keisha appeared at the door bearing porridge and bananas, silhouetted in the setting sun.

"Stay away," Sarah croaked. "Don't want . . . you get . . . sick. Don't let . . . children come."

Keisha nodded and backed out, her eyes shining. She had seen what happened to people with the red eye fever.

Sarah's mouth was parched. Her head was pounding, ready to explode and she struggled for each breath. Why hadn't she gone to the hospital? When would Jabari return?

The fever patients haunted her. Hands reaching, grasping at her gown, voices murmuring with suffering or gratitude. A little boy of three or four had cried because he was thirsty. It was futile—everything he drank came out one end or the other—but Sarah gave him water anyway. He smiled briefly and nestled on his mother's breast. Did he know his mother was already dead?

The possibility of her own death loomed large, inexorably approaching a likely probability. She remembered a news story, years ago, about a disabled passenger plane. The pilot managed to keep it aloft for an hour or so. In the wreckage, among the bodies, were hand written notes. Final messages to loved ones. What would she write if she had a pen and paper?

Her mother would grieve. Allison would weep. David—maybe he was used to being without her. And Pieter . . .

Her life didn't flash before her eyes, but the boundaries of dreams, reality, and memories blurred. She was a child again, her mother wiping her forehead with a cold cloth.

She recalled her father's funeral. Faith and knowledge are not the same. In the candlelight, with the organ and the soothing words of the pastor, it had been so easy to believe that her father had slipped through some veil into a peaceful place. But now, alone in this dark cold room on a mountain, reality was stark. There was no veil. Her father's soul had vanished without a trace.

Is there really a heaven?

Her brain was too foggy to contemplate the metaphysical. Much easier to ponder practical details. She pictured her own funeral, her mother beside Allison with her newborn baby. It would be expensive to get her body back to the states. Cremation would be cheaper. They could spread her ashes here, on this remote mountain, where everything seemed to make sense. She had flown across the ocean to get away from something but couldn't remember exactly what that something was.

She tried to pray, struggled to go through the Lord's Prayer in her head. But she kept dozing off before she could finish.

I'm not breathing.

How long had it been since she took a breath? She gasped and panted. Cheyne-Stokes breathing. A terminal sign. She had learned about it in physiology class, freshman year of medical school, David down in front, taking profuse notes, Sarah dozing in the back row.

She saw herself as a child, kneeling by her bed, hands folded.

Now I lay me down to sleep
I pray the Lord my soul to keep
If I should die before I wake . . .

BALINDA'S VOICE WAS far away, part of a dream. "*Pole sana*, Sarah. You are so sick."

It wasn't a vision. A woman gazed at her through goggles. A mask covered her smile with the missing tooth, but there was no mistaking the voice. It was Balinda.

Sarah's lips were cracked and dry, and her throat was clogged. "Why are . . . you back so soon?"

"The test was wrong. Ghalib does not have cancer."

Sarah smiled, tried to speak. What began as laughter morphed into an endless fit of violent coughing as Balinda's face faded away.

I am Viking Princess, borne aloft by my grieving subjects who have covered me in flowers. My velvet robe drips over the edges of the palanquin.

There is no tunnel. Just a blinding light, a powerful wind, and a deafening roar.

I hear my father's voice, clear and strong above the noise.

"Hang on, Sam!"

Not the withered wraith of a man, with sunken eyes and a swollen belly, but the strong young man who taught me to swim by walking backward through the water.

"I've got you, Princess."

His arms reach out and we glide off the mountain, over the cotton batting that fills the valley. Straight on toward the second star to the right.

CHAPTER FIFTY-FOUR

RESURRECTION

otal blackness. She couldn't see, couldn't breathe, couldn't move. *So this is death.*

But there was sound, a rhythmic beeping. A gust of air flowed into her lungs with a whoosh, and she felt a cool cloth on her face.

Sarah struggled to open her eyes and the ventilator squawked and honked as she tried to speak. After a few blinks, she focused on her mother's face.

"Shh, shh. You're going to be okay. You're in a hospital." Sarah rolled her eyes, and her mother laughed. "Silly me. Of course, it's a hospital. You're in Nairobi. David went back to the hotel to rest. He should be back any minute. You're no longer shedding virus. They've backed off the sedation to get you off the ventilator."

She drifted in and out of bizarre dreams until adhesive tape was ripped from her face. David's voice commanded, "Take a big breath." A searing pain ripped through her throat as the breathing tube was pulled out.

David rested his head on her belly, "Sam, we thought you were gone."

Her mother had received a call in the middle of the

night. "No one expected you to live. I got on the first available flight. David came the next day."

Blood samples had been shipped off to a lab in Europe and to the CDC, but the virus had yet to be identified. David had his own theory. "Rift Valley fever can cause the red eyes, but it's spread by insect bites. Not human to human transmission. I'm betting on some strain of nairovirus."

"It hurts," Sarah rasped, "when I breathe." She flapped a hand toward her right side.

"It's a chest tube," said David. "You bled into your chest." He said that the outbreak had been deadly, more than 80 percent of the patients had died. Sarah's survival was attributed to a blood transfusion from someone in Kandu. Someone who had survived a similar outbreak.

It had to have been Balinda.

For the next two days and nights, David never left Sarah's side, fetching her bedpan, helping to feed and bathe her.

"You have such nice legs," he remarked as he dried her ankle. "It was the first thing I noticed about you. You always came to biology class at the last minute and walked all the way up to the back row."

"You were always down in front, taking lots of notes."

He fluffed her pillow. "I watched you come in every day. I liked it when you wore a dress instead of jeans."

"You were too shy to talk to me."

"You were shy, too. Until the frog incident."

Sarah had pity on a frog that she was supposed to pith. She hesitated, and it escaped, zig-zag hopping around the lab. The entire class joined in pursuit of the errant amphibian. David finally caught it, but not before bumping his head under a bench. He performed the execution since Sarah could not bring herself to hurt the frog.

The nurse came in with a tray, and David cranked up the head of the bed to feed her.

"What kind of soup is this?"

"I'm not sure, maybe spinach. It's sort of green. How does it taste?"

"Warm and salty. Not much else."

"You don't need much else right now. I don't think your gut will tolerate real food." He fed her like a baby, scraping drips of soup from her chin.

Sarah licked her lips. "Remember our first date?"

"Yeah. That little iconic Italian restaurant."

"Red checked table cloths and drippy candles." She sighed. "Very romantic."

"Corny. But the lasagna was great."

The meal sapped all her strength. She could barely speak, and her chest ached.

"You're white as a sheet. Need a pain shot?"

The nurse injected clear fluid into her IV, and she gradually slipped into oblivion. Sometime in the night, she awoke. David was sound asleep, slumped in a chair. Still her rock, still tethered to her, through thick and thin. Maybe they would make it after all. Sometimes good things come from bad times.

He went back to the States the next day. They had not discussed the future. She had not even asked who was taking care of Whiskers. They would pick up the pieces when she got home. Like repairing a broken teacup.

Soon she was out of bed, walking slowly, leaning on her IV pole. Her mother followed behind, carrying the large bottle that was connected to the tube in her chest.

The pain of removing the tube was unbearable, even under the haze of morphine. She could have sworn that someone had ripped out her lung.

With each day, she became physically stronger but progressively despondent. Morphine blunted the physical pain but did nothing for her mental anguish. She had deserted comrades on a field of battle. How many had died? What about Nasila? What about the little boys and Keisha?

She kept a close eye on the clock and rang the call button whenever it was time for another pain shot. One day, the nurse said it was not time yet.

"But I need it now!"

Her mother grabbed Sarah's hands and coaxed her to lie back down. "I think you're getting dependent on the morphine."

It wasn't fair. The morphine was the only thing that made life bearable.

AN AMBULANCE DELIVERED them to the airport. It was strange to ride through a bustling city that Sarah had never seen, despite spending three weeks there. Her mother pushed her through the arrivals hall in a wheel chair. At the check in counter, Sarah signed her shiny and slim new passport.

"What happened to my old one?"

"You came into Kenya in a life-flight helicopter. Who knows where your passport is? Or your ring, for that matter."

Sarah stared at her bare left hand. Why had she not noticed it before? Funny—the loss of the passport cut her more deeply. The record of her life, full of stamps from far flung countries.

Her mother patted her shoulder. "We've still got you. That's all that matters."

CHAPTER FIFTY-FIVE

TEXAS

Allison beamed with pride over the little bundle in her arms. "Want to hold your nephew?"

"Of course." Sarah sat down, and Allison handed her the baby.

"You have to be careful and support his head because—"

"Do you have any idea how many newborn babies I've held?"

Allison laughed. "Oh, yeah. I forgot."

It made sense for Sarah to recuperate in Houston. David was full steam back at work, with few free hours in any given day, while her mother and sister had plenty of time on their hands. Little Charles, the newest member of the family, was a joy and still at a very portable stage in life. Allison carried him against her chest in a snuggie as she and Sarah went shopping for a new laptop and smartphone. All the data from her laptop were recovered from the cloud, but so many pictures were left behind in Kandu, on her little Samsung phone.

Her mother urged Sarah to check out a picture she had posted on Facebook. "I took it at the Nairobi airport. You got 136 likes."

"Yuck. I'm in a wheel chair, and I look like I've been in a concentration camp." The long list of likers included Mila, Pieter's sister, who had posted a sweet comment and shared the picture with her own friends. Which explained how Eva had come to "like" this picture of Sarah, posting, "*Veel beterschap*," ("get well" in Dutch). Eva also sent a friend request.

Sarah knew better than to friend Eva. Nothing good could come of it. But curiosity got the better of her. Scrolling through the photos on Eva's Facebook page was painful—so many selfies with Pieter. One had been taken on a familiar beach with a curving sandy cliff, teeming with tiny crabs.

Sarah took a deep breath, shut down Facebook, and immersed herself in the mindless and tedious task of sorting out junk mail. A welcome diversion from self-pity. She conscientiously and mechanically answered all the get-well messages.

In the midst of this mass of correspondence was a missive from Ameera, with pictures of a new baby girl. "Her name is Sarah. Did you know that the names Sarah and Ameera both mean 'princess'? So she is named for both of us."

Margo wrote that she was engaged to Israel. They would move to Nairobi in August. "I will do a trauma fellowship, and he will get an MBA. We hope you can come for the wedding."

Her mother suggested spending a few days at the family beach house.

Sarah was surprised. "I thought you sold it."

"I took it off the market. Couldn't let go. I'm glad I didn't. Allison and Mike have had some nice weekends there. You and David should go there when he comes down next weekend. You two could use some time alone."

✕

BABY CHARLES WAS still asleep when they arrived at the beach house. Allison tucked him into his porta crib, and the three women sat out on the deck gazing out at the waves. Allison recalled building sand castles. "Remember the really huge one? With the drawbridge?"

"I was just thinking about that, the other day. It just washed out to sea. Along with the Barbies."

"I have a theory about those dolls. They're not biodegradable, right? So I figure they must be in that huge mass of plastic shopping bags at the bottom of the Gulf of Mexico."

A baby's cry drifted out the window. There was a brief delay before Allison popped out of her chair. "Whoa! I almost forgot I had a kid."

Summer came early to coastal Texas, so it was quite warm when Sarah and her mother set off for a stroll on the beach. A pink Frisbee drifted past—a rogue toss from a group of chattering children. Sarah chased it into the surf but was stopped in her tracks, doubled over by a stabbing pain in her side.

Barbara jogged to her daughter. "Are you okay?"

"I'll be fine in a minute." She straightened up slowly as she caught her breath, gazing out across the water. "Does this place make you miss Dad more?"

"Not really. I carry him around with me, all the time. I remember things he would say, how he would laugh. That's what happens when you lose someone you love. They become a part of you."

The pink Frisbee floated in and out with the surf, slowly drifting eastward until a little boy scampered out to fetch it.

Barbara massaged Sarah's shoulders, kneading tight muscles. "Grief comes in waves. Sometimes it washes over you, makes you feel like you can't move." She patted Sarah's back. "Joy comes in waves, too: Little Charles, bringing you home alive . . ."

Allison met them at the door to the beach house. "David called. You left your cell phone inside."

Sarah returned the call from her bedroom.

"Hi, Sam. How are you feeling?"

"Better every day. Still can't run. Mom and I take long walks twice a day. We're looking forward to seeing you next weekend. What time does your flight get in?"

"Well . . . you see, I think I may not be coming, after all."

If only she could see his face, as she could when they talked via Skype. Funny—they had better communication when they were on opposite sides of the world. "Why not?"

"I guess . . . I'm just a chicken." He sighed. "Oh, Sam, we just . . . I really meant to come down there, to tell you in person. But I don't think I can do that."

Sarah stared out the window at the children laughing with their Frisbee. The white caps on the waves glowed pink and orange in the setting sun.

"Sam, can you hear me?"

"Yes."

"I didn't want to tell you in Africa. Not when you were so sick."

Whatever he had to say, she did not want to hear it.

But he said it anyway. "Carla's pregnant."

CHAPTER FIFTY-SIX

PHILADELPHIA

P hiladelphia Memorial Hospital was surreal. Bright lights and shiny floors. And way too many computers. Before she could take care of patients, Sarah had to spend two days in the computer lab, learning the new electronic health record.

It was achingly lonely. No one around the hospital knew what to say to her. The apartment was spooky without David. She took long walks and went to a few movies by herself. And had one-sided conversations with her cat.

She ran into Jeff one night in the operating room, while she was removing a spleen and repairing a colon perf in a patient with multiple gunshot wounds. Jeff was putting the face back together. He said, "We're callin' him Swiss Cheese Man, because he has so many holes. Look at this. His jaw is shattered, and I can put my fingers through his neck and out under his tongue."

"That's pretty gross, Jeff."

They went to the cafeteria for coffee after the case.

Jeff stirred three packs of sugar into his cup. "Would you do it over again? Go to Africa?"

"Yes."

"Almost dying? Breaking up with David?"

Sarah blew on her coffee and took a cautious sip. "It was an incredible experience. I found out who I am—what I really want to do with my life." She laughed softly, "Of course, I could have done without getting so sick. But as for David . . . I guess we weren't really meant to be."

"Most people thought you guys were already through before you left. I mean, why else would you go? And then he started hanging out with Carla."

"That's kind of creepy—to think people were talking about us."

"I'm sorry. I shouldn't have brought it up."

"It's okay." She twirled a lock of hair. "It actually feels good to talk about it. It's been so awkward. People smile sympathetically, and then murmur to each other when they think I can't hear."

"You're so much hotter than Carla. What was he thinking? And now she's big as a cow."

Sarah giggled. "She's pregnant, Jeff. She's supposed to be big. I've run into David in the hospital a few times, and it's always weird. Once I was waiting for the elevator, and when the door opened, there he was. We had to ride together for three floors and neither of us could think of anything to say. Until he got out. Then he said, 'Have a nice day.' Can you believe he said that?"

"Are you dating anyone?"

"I'm just not interested right now. I've had enough."

"What about that Dutch guy? Over in Africa. You guys seemed pretty tight."

Sarah's cheeks burned, but she tossed her head. "You mean Pieter? Nothing going on there."

"Really? I saw him here, a couple of months ago."

"Hmm. I know he was speaking at NIH. Maybe he paid a visit to Dr. Marshall."

"Why don't you come over to my place Saturday night? I'll cook some steaks and we can watch a movie."

CHAPTER FIFTY-SEVEN

GOOD ADVICE

How was your date with Jeff?"

Sarah frowned. Diana must have heard something from her husband, Chet, who played squash with Jeff once a week.

"I didn't know it was supposed to be a date. I thought I was having dinner with a friend."

"He's very sorry."

Sarah gazed around the deserted hospital cafeteria. Not too many people hanging around at midnight. Just the cleaning lady with her pushcart. Diana was waiting to deliver a baby, and Sarah had just finished an appendectomy.

"So, you're the messenger?"

Diana flushed. "No. Chet just told me what he heard from Jeff."

"Jeff knew that Chet would tell you, and that you would tell me."

The "date" had started out well enough. They had pleasant conversation over dinner, mostly sharing their Kilimanjaro climbing experiences. But they couldn't decide what to watch on TV. Then Jeff said, "Who needs to watch anything anyway?"

He had trouble comprehending the word "no." Fortunately, Sarah had remembered a phrase that Pieter had advised her to use if she ever found herself in such a situation. Just before she slammed the door on her way out, she told Jeff to go fuck himself.

"He wants another chance. He says he'll take it slower next time."

Sarah snorted. "He couldn't be slow enough for me. I'm just not interested. Ever."

"It must be hard for you. David—"

"It's not the end of the world." Sarah was sick of people feeling sorry for her. Someone was always trying to fix her up with someone. "What really hurts is everything I left behind in Africa. I didn't get to finish teaching the course, and I haven't had a chance to get back there. I wanted to do something great, but . . . I just bombed out."

"But you know you made an impact. Maybe you didn't get to teach everything you intended, but they learned a lot. And they'll teach others." Diana stared into her coffee cup, "I saw a woman die from eclampsia yesterday."

"Really?"

"Yeah. First one I ever lost. She just came in seizing. No prenatal care."

"No insurance?"

"She had insurance—just no doctors in her town—out in Malloy county. They shut down the community hospital. No one wants to practice there."

"Wasn't Janet was looking at a position in Malloy?"

"Yeah," said Diana. "The problem was malpractice insurance. She figured she'd have to deliver twenty babies before she collected enough money to cover a one-year premium. And that's not counting overhead, you know, nurses, receptionists, office rental."

Sarah's phone pinged with a text, and she bounded out of her chair. "Gotta go. Incoming gunshot wound to the chest."

A PALE YOUNG woman rolled into the ED on a stretcher. A junior resident listened to her chest. "No breath sounds on the left." Sarah grabbed a knife before he had time to ask her to put in a chest tube.

The incision was bloodless.

Until she popped the tube into the chest cavity.

A bright red geyser erupted through the tube. "I need a big long Kelly clamp!" She slashed between the ribs and thrust her hand into the chest, searching for the pulsations of the aorta. The hemorrhage stopped as soon as she clicked the clamp into place. "Let's go—straight to the OR."

A nurse with an iPad grabbed the rail of the stretcher. "I haven't finished my charting." Sarah nearly ran her over.

The patient was still alive when they reached the operating room. An hour later, Sarah leaned against the wall, watching in stunned silence as the tubes and tapes and monitors were removed from the body.

The junior resident broke her reverie. "Have you ever cross-clamped an aorta before?"

"Sure. Three times. In the simulation lab. This is the first time in a live patient."

"That was so cool."

"It would only be cool if she were still alive. Where's the family?"

Sarah's footsteps echoed in the dim and cavernous waiting room as she approached the row of chairs in the far corner, where the sister of deceased woman sat with a sleeping baby in her lap. Two little girls played at her feet.

Sarah sat down. "I'm so sorry. We weren't able to save your sister."

The woman stared in disbelief. "But we had a restraining order." The infant began to cry, and the woman lifted him over her shoulder. "It's my fault. She was afraid to leave him. I thought she'd be safe at my house."

"I'm sure you did all that you could. Are these your children?"

"These two are mine." She tipped her head toward the children at her feet. "And this baby is . . . well, I guess he's mine now." She shook with two violent sobs, and then the tears began flowing. "She left the diaper bag in the car. That's why she went out to the driveway."

"I'm so sorry." Sarah gave the woman a handkerchief, embroidered with lavender jacaranda blossoms.

CHAPTER FIFTY-EIGHT

SOCIAL MEDIA

Allison was glued to her laptop. "You never like anything I put on Facebook."

Sarah smiled at the infant in her lap. "I prefer to look at little Charlie in person."

"His name is Charles."

"He's too cute to be a Charles. How about Chuck? That's what Mom always called Dad."

It had been a busy day of sightseeing—attractions that Sarah and David had never visited during all their years in Philadelphia: the Rocky steps, the Liberty Bell, the Rodin Museum.

"You haven't even changed your status. It still says you're in a relationship with David. And you never post anything. You only pop up when someone tags you, like this nice picture. You look gorgeous. Where was it taken?"

Pieter's sister Mila had posted a picture taken at the gala: Sarah in her sky-blue gown, standing between Mila and Eva—Eva beaming in the lipstick-red dress. Pieter gazing blankly into space.

"That was in Dar, when I spoke at that gala."

"I wish I could have been there to hear you. You're an amazing person."

"I don't feel amazing. I've really messed up my life."

"Don't be silly. You're better off without David. Kind of a control freak, wasn't he?"

"In retrospect—maybe so."

"You're stronger now. More independent."

Sarah gazed at the infant in her arms, wondering if she would ever have a child of her own.

"When are you going back to Africa? You left a lot of stuff behind."

"I've been . . . putting it off."

"Susie told me your project is coming along just great. She just finished her second round of interviews and focus groups. You should be eager to get back there."

Sarah sighed and closed her eyes. "I'm afraid of what I might find. Maybe . . . maybe the clinic has fallen apart, and it's just like I was never there. Maybe I nearly died for nothing."

"Yeah, I guess that would really suck."

"There are worse things that can happen to you than dying, you know."

Allison leaned forward, squeezed her sister's shoulder. "Don't say that."

"Dying isn't so bad. It's the pain and shit that gets you to the point of dying that's terrible. And when you get that far . . . sometimes you don't really want to come back, you know? Because you're tired and you think, like, is it really worth it?"

"Don't say that, Sam."

"It's the people left behind, the people you love. That's what makes you want to come back."

"Did you have a near-death experience?"

Sarah nodded and whispered. "I saw Dad."

"You dreamed about him?"

"It wasn't a dream. It was real."

"Did you see a bright light, a tunnel?"

"There was a bright light, but no tunnel. Just noise and wind. Strong wind."

"How did he look?"

"Young, like when we were little kids."

Allison stared out the window for a moment. Then she sniffed and scowled. "Charles needs changing." She handed Sarah the laptop and took the baby.

Sarah scrolled through other pictures on Mila's FB page. There was a selfie with Pieter in Washington DC, in front of the Capital Building. Another in front of the Liberty Bell. Jeff was right—Pieter had been in Philadelphia. The caption was in Dutch. Sarah clicked on "Translate" to see the message in English: "Planning a big party to welcome my brother home at the end of September."

Eva had liked it.

Allison sat back down on the sofa with fresh smelling baby Charles. "I'll go to Africa with you, if it helps."

"Thanks, but I'll be fine alone. I'm getting motivated right now." She read Mila's post again and snapped the laptop closed. "I'll go in October."

CHAPTER FIFTY-NINE

RETURN TO TANZANIA

D r. Obaye leapt out of his chair. "Karibu, Sarah. *Karibu sana.*" He clasped her hands. "How wonderful to see you looking so well. Please, sit down."

"I'm glad to be alive, and glad to hear that all my students survived the outbreak."

"Indeed, they did. And many others, too, thanks to your work. The virus has still not been definitively classified. It may be a more virulent strain of Crimea-Congo fever. The women you trained played a huge role in containing the disease. They prevented a major outbreak."

"I wish I could say that I wasn't surprised by how they handled things. I mean, that's exactly the kind of outcome we hoped for, someday. But hope and realistic expectation . . . those are two different things. For these women to have achieved so much, I would have to say, this is beyond my wildest dreams."

"My dear, Sarah. You were a catalyst." He settled back into his chair.

"Ameera and I are applying for an NIH grant for a bigger study, training programs in other remote parts of the country. The Stanford foundation has already pledged some support."

"So, can we look forward to seeing you back in Tanzania? To carry on this work?"

"Maybe. I'm not sure. I'd like to come back. Right now, I'm finishing up my surgery training. I'll definitely keep involved from a distance."

"You are very welcome here, any time."

A THRONG OF giggling and chattering village children surrounded the van. The midwives, clad in matching orange and green kitangas, formed a semi-circle, clapping and singing, "Karibu, Sarah, *karibu sana, karibu sana*, Sarah."

Balinda, tears streaming down her face, murmured, "You are alive, you are alive, you are alive." She wrapped her arms around Sarah, and they swayed back and forth to the rhythm.

"I'm only alive because of you. You gave me your blood. Thank you so much."

"It is we who thank you." Balinda stepped back to show off her crisp white lab coat, tracing the blue letters embroidered above the chest pocket. "I am clinic assistant. Come, let me show you the dispensary."

Much had changed in the six months since Sarah was life-flighted out of Kandu. Just as Pieter had predicted, Sarah's house had helped the village recruit a permanent medical officer, someone who lived in the village four days each week. The dispensary had been refurbished, with new exam tables and cabinets. There was even a landline telephone, so it was easy to communicate with outside hospitals.

Jabari was now the official hospital courier, ferrying patients and lab samples. Sarah had donated her Rav4 for this purpose, and Rasheed had taught Jabari how to drive. (Ameera said her husband deserved a medal for bravery.)

Another change: Rasheed had installed a system to pump water to a spigot in the center of the village. No more toting water up the mountain.

The midwife course had not died after Sarah's dramatic medivac extraction. Pieter and Ameera had organized volunteer doctors and midwife faculty from NTMC to complete the course. And after the course ended, the graduates formed a sisterhood of community health care workers. They met each Saturday and adopted the orange and green kitangas as their uniforms.

Dr. Obaye was right. Sarah had been a catalyst, unleashing talents and passions.

Balinda produced a large cardboard box containing all the things left in Sarah's house. Her old passport was buried among clothes, linens, and a few toiletry items. At the bottom of the box lay the small cellphone she had used for calls and messages within Tanzania. She plugged it in to recharge while she enjoyed a cup of tea at Ghalib's shop. Hamid and Jamal found her there. "Come with us. We have a surprise."

They jogged ahead, leading her through the village, around houses, cow pens, and past a goat roasting on a spit. Sarah asked, "That's not one of Bulu's kids, is it?"

"Oh no," said Hamid. "Her kids are fine. And so is Bulu."

"What? She's still alive?"

Jamal giggled. "That's the surprise. Look over there."

Bulu trotted toward them, her rear legs supported on a small platform with wheels. Sarah knelt down and scratched the little goat behind the ears. "Who built this contraption?" she asked, even though she knew the answer.

"Pieter made this from pieces of the cart." Hamid pointed to the wheels. "See?"

Jamal sniffed. "Pieter gone."

Hamid patted his brother on the back. "But he will come back. He promised."

When her little phone was fully charged Sarah switched it on. Still no cell service here in the village, but she could scroll down through old text messages: *"Ready in the OR."* *"Need you in L&D."* *"Want to go get a pizza?"* One text message made her stop breathing for a moment.

"Hi. This is Pieter." The first message that he had sent her—on that night when she had been so very sad and desolate.

And there were the pictures she thought had been lost forever: Ameera's wedding, David atop Kibo, patients, shots from her safari, multiple images of Spike. But not there was not one single picture of Pieter on her phone. It had all been so . . . subterranean. They hadn't wanted anyone else to know. She stowed the cellphone in her pocket and asked Jabari for a lift out to the escarpment. The view across the Rift Valley was just as stunning as she recalled. In the mist, she could barely discern the little blip that was Kilimanjaro. A ping from her pocket startled her. The phone that had been dormant for months rose from the dead with a new text message. From Pieter.

"I heard you were in town. Can we have a drink together? Maybe lunch?"

He had sent the message just one day before. Sarah stared at the words, double checked the date. He was supposed to be back in Amsterdam.

CHAPTER SIXTY

LUNCH AT KIBO VIEW LODGE

Pieter was waiting at a table when Sarah arrived. "I ordered you a beer. Serengeti. Your favorite, right?"

His eyes were as blue as ever. His hair was longish, curling a bit over his ears, so he must not have been home to Amsterdam recently.

She forced herself to smile, but her chest ached, and her cheeks burned. It was difficult to breathe, let alone speak. "It's really, really good, to see you."

"I was surprised you got my text. I didn't expect you to have that phone. Didn't know if it would even work. It was sort of like sending a message in a bottle."

"I didn't know you were still around."

"There were some untied strings."

"You mean, you had to tie up some loose ends."

He grinned. "I know you like to correct my idioms."

"Did you get the latest draft of the grant proposal?"

"Yes. It looks good. I'll email you some edits."

"Thanks." She began to relax. "I had a good visit to Kandu. The dispensary's developed into a decent little health clinic."

The server took their orders—cheeseburgers, of course.

Pieter updated her on things around the hospital, most of which she already knew: Margo in Nairobi, Ameera's new baby, Teddy going to school to become a medical assistant. Then he asked when she would be heading home.

"I'll be on the KLM flight tonight. And you?"

"I head back to Amsterdam tomorrow."

"I accepted that faculty position for next year. I'll have protected time to get a degree in global health."

"That's great. Your future is all set."

As usual, he cut his hamburger into quadrants that he ate in clockwise order, using a knife and fork.

"You still eat it the wrong way." She grabbed her cheeseburger with both hands, and they both laughed when mustard dripped down onto her chin.

"It's good to see you looking healthy. We were all worried about you."

"I was *so* sick. There are days and days that I just don't remember. I was on a ventilator, and I even had to have a chest tube!"

"I know. I put it in."

Sarah stared at him. "You? The chest tube?"

He nodded.

"But . . . . so, you were there?"

"You don't remember?"

"I just remember Balinda."

"I brought her and Ghalib back. Turns out he didn't have cancer after all."

"I do remember hearing that. Funny what stays with you."

"We weren't going to go up there so soon. Health advisory said we should wait. But Betje called. She was worried about you."

"No one told me. I had no idea. I . . . I'm so sorry. All that blood from my chest. You could easily have caught the virus."

He smiled. "You should have seen the isolation suit. I felt like a spaceman."

"I heard I got some blood. Was it from Balinda?"

"Yes."

Sarah picked at the label on her beer bottle. "I had a near death experience. You know, the bright light, dead relative thing. I saw my father. He told me to hang on."

Pieter chuckled.

The label tore, and she put the bottle back down. "I know, you don't believe in that stuff. You think it's just hypoxia."

"That was me. I remember telling you to hang on."

"But . . . he called me Sam. You never call me Sam. You thought it was a dumb nickname."

"Maybe I wanted you to be strong."

"And he said, 'I've got you, Princess.'"

"I said that when we loaded you into the chopper. You were thrashing around. I had to give you some morphine."

He leaned back and pulled a small box from his pocket. "I have something for you."

She opened the box and gasped. It was a diamond ring.

"Don't you recognize it? I knew it would be stolen if I left it on your finger."

The stone caught the sunlight and cast rainbow sparkles on the tablecloth.

"You can be a marked woman again. That should make David happy."

Tiny words inscribed inside the ring read, *Sarah and David Forever.*

"I should have given it to your mother. It just didn't occur to me at the time."

"You saw my mother? You mean, you were in Nairobi?"

"I rode with you in the chopper. You don't think I would let you go there alone, do you? I came back before David got there."

"He's already collected on the insurance for this. Probably used the money to buy an engagement ring for Carla."

"Carla? Did you break up with David?"

"Actually, he dumped me."

"For the lab lady?"

"She got pregnant. He was very apologetic, said something about how she lied about being on the pill." She laughed hollowly. "Anyway, now I'm a free agent."

Pieter poked French fries around his plate with his fork. "Are you seeing anyone?"

"No. Not interested."

He looked at his watch and pushed his plate away, leaving a quarter of his hamburger untouched.

Sarah put the ring back in the box and stuffed it into her purse. "I'll give it back to his mother. She'll be happy to see it."

"I should be going." He signaled to the server to bring the check.

"Mom never told me you were there at the hospital."

"She didn't know me."

"Why didn't you tell her who you are?"

"How should I have introduced myself?" He tapped his chin, thoughtfully. "How about, 'Hey, I used to fuck your daughter?'"

The server brought the bill, and Sarah reached for it.

Pieter snatched the check from her hand. "It was my

invitation." He stood up, dropped a few bills onto the table, and smiled thinly. "It was good to see you."

He walked away. Just like that. The waiter began to clear the table.

It hit like a 10,000-volt shock. She would never see him again. She caught up with him in the parking lot, grabbed his sleeve, threw her arms around him. It was like hugging a mannequin.

"I love you," she whispered.

He patted her shoulder—twice—and then he was gone.

She stared at the ground as he started the engine and backed out. Tires crunched on and she heard a clunk as he shifted into first gear. Then second gear. She stood still until the engine noise faded away.

CHAPTER SIXTY-ONE

THE PROMISE OF TANZANITE

S arah checked her face in the rearview mirror, wiping mascara from her cheeks, then sat in the driveway until she gained control.

Ameera sat on the terrace, nursing baby Sarah under a jacaranda tree that was just starting to bloom again.

"Thanks for letting me use your car. Shall I make us some tea?"

The baby was fast asleep in her bassinet when Sarah returned with steaming mugs of fragrant ginger tea.

"How was your lunch with Pieter?"

"Fine."

"Well, that's a short answer."

"It was a short lunch." Sarah's jaw tightened as she stirred her tea.

"I'm sorry."

"You knew about us, didn't you? And we thought we were so discrete."

"The way his face lit up every time you came into the room. The way you always blushed. Yes, it was pretty obvious."

"Nobody told me that he was with me in Nairobi. That he saved my life."

"I just assumed that you knew. I'm so sorry."

"It's okay."

"Does he know that you broke up with David?"

"I told him." Sarah sighed. "You know, he had my ring —kept it so it wouldn't be stolen."

A pair of wailing toucans landed on the jacaranda tree.

Ameera set down her teacup. "Someday you will meet someone else. When the time is right."

"You should arrange someone for me. I haven't been doing such a great job picking men."

SARAH'S HOUSE WAS deadly silent. The refrigerator was open, unplugged, and empty, suitcases all packed. She made one last methodical check of all the drawers and cabinets. That's when she found it. The blue shirt. Crumpled in the back of the closet. Pieter's favorite: faded chambray. He always rolled up the sleeves to hide the frayed cuffs.

I should toss it in the trash.

But it was soft against her face, and it smelled like him.

Out on the veranda, a gentle breeze laced with jasmine flowed down from the mountain. Billowing clouds obscured both peaks. The glider tweeted like a little bird as she slowly rocked back and forth. Spike jumped up beside her, looking quite fit, apparently still well fed by the neighbors. A large white-breasted crow splashed in the bird bath. Margo said the crows were evil invaders from Zanzibar. But Sarah thought they were marvelous. Beautiful and arrogant, seemingly clad in tuxedos. She mentally photographed the flowers, tall crotons, the toucans, the weaver birds, the jacaranda.

Her reverie was broken by raucous squawks. It was her ibis. The bird landed a mere twenty feet away, finally posed close enough for a clear photo. But her camera was packed away, which was just as well. Turned out, the bird wasn't really green after all. At least not green all over. He was mostly gray-brown. She must have been captivated by the malachite sheen on his wings.

The bird flew off and joined a flock passing by. There were thousands more just like him in the skies of East Africa.

Tires crunched on the gravel in her driveway. Tumaini was way too early. She wasn't ready to leave, didn't want to forgo precious last moments in the garden, so she ignored the knock on the kitchen door. When she heard footsteps coming around the house, she closed her eyes, pretending to catnap.

"Sarah?" Pieter stood on the steps. "Sorry to run off like that. Very rude of me."

She rubbed her eyes and swallowed a couple of times before finding her voice. "It's okay."

"I would offer to take you to the airport, but I guess—"

"Tumaini's taking me."

"Right, of course, he would want to see you off." He turned toward the mountain that was still cloaked and leaned against the post at the end of the porch, his tall, lanky form silhouetted by the distant clouds. "Kilimanjaro's not showing up to say goodbye."

"Yep, I've been stood up."

He chuckled softly. "No one ever called Kibo a gentleman." His shoulders heaved as he took a very deep breath, eyes still aimed at the mountain that he could not see. "Did you mean it? What you said . . ." He twisted his head toward her, ever so slightly. "In the parking lot, I mean."

"Yes."

He whirled around. "You don't act like it. Didn't even tell me you were coming back. I had to hear that from Margo. So I changed my ticket and—"

"You dumped me. Remember? You totally blew me off." She flung her arm in a sweeping gesture that startled the cat, who jumped down and ran into the hedge. She pumped the glider faster and faster, the gentle tweets of the hinges giving way to screeching groans. "I mean, you just . . . The last time I saw you, you were stomping out of the room and—"

"You wouldn't talk to me." He plunked his foot on the glider, halting it so abruptly that Sarah almost flew off into the garden. "You wouldn't even look at me. You just kept staring down at your friggin toes."

He plopped down beside her, resting his elbows on his knees. "By the way, how are your toes?"

"Back to normal." She lifted her foot so that he could admire her freshly lacquered toenails, then started the glider gently rocking again. "What was it you wanted to talk about? That night, at the lodge."

"I . . . wanted some advice." He sat up and cleared his throat. "About a job. I interviewed for a job in Philadelphia."

"A job. You mean, you would move to the States? What about Eva?"

"Eva?" She might as well have brought up the price of broccolini in Siberia.

"Eva. Your 'friend'." Sarah released her grasp on the blue shirt that lay in her lap and made air quotes with her fingers around the word friend. "The friend who was glued to your side at the gala."

"That was so awkward. It wouldn't have been so bad if you hadn't been wearing that stupid ring. Why couldn't you just have worn it on your right hand? And you left the party with-out speaking to me. Then you locked me out of your room."

"I locked you out?"

"At first, I just thought, okay, the key card won't work. The red light kept flashing." He waved an invisible card at an imaginary door. "I knocked and knocked but you wouldn't answer. I knew you were in there. I could hear the TV."

"I did open the door, remember?"

"That was later. And you only opened it a couple of inches. I must have been pretty drunk by then—tequila shots in the bar with Jean. You looked disgusted with me."

"I only heard you knock once. Maybe I was in the Jacuzzi the first time. I didn't expect you to show up. I thought you were with Eva."

"No way. You're my girl. Wasn't it obvious?" He reached over and squeezed her hand. "Is that my shirt?"

"It smells like you."

"Sarah, Sarah, you little thief." He wrapped his arms around her, pulled her close.

"I missed you so much," she sobbed. "I could never stop thinking about you."

The kiss made everything suddenly right, like a river flowing into a dry lake bed, drenching rain on dry, cracked earth, the wind that blew away the clouds, and the sun to shine down and turn everything green again. She pressed her face against his chest, feeling his heartbeat. "I'm not going to leave. I'm staying here with you."

"You have to go home. You have a job. So do I."

"Then I'm going with you. I'll move to Holland."

"You aren't serious, are you?" He pulled back and stared. "You'd leave it all? All those years of training? Just one more year, and you'll be a full-fledged surgeon."

"I'm serious."

"I wouldn't want you do that. You'd regret it."

"Then what?"

"I'll follow you."

"You'll come to America? Just like that?"

"No, not just like that. I can't just not show up for work next week. I have to give them some notice. And I'll need to find work in America."

"Is that job in Philadelphia still available?"

He shrugged. "Maybe. If not, I'll find something else."

Sarah giggled. "Just come stay with me. Be a kept man."

"Sure, I can boil your eggs. Burn your toast."

Pieter rode along with Sarah to the airport. Tumaini turned up the volume of his old cassette recorder and they all sang along. Halfway there, Kilimanjaro broke through the clouds and a rainbow plunged into the side of the mountain. It was a spectacular backdrop for the first portrait of Sarah and Pieter, together as a couple. Tumaini snapped the picture with Sarah's little Samsung phone. "Daktari Sarah. This rainbow was a sign. You will come back to us."

SOMEHOW, PIETER CONVINCED the woman at the security desk to let him into the airport, even though the e-ticket on his smartphone was for the next day. Maybe it was his lopsided grin. Sarah waited alone in the long check-in line, because Pieter said he wanted to stroll around a bit. She missed him terribly as soon as he walked away. She wondered why he wandered and worried about what might happen once he got to Amsterdam. Hadn't he said that Eva was "a bit clever?"

Pieter returned just in time to hoist her bags onto the scale. Then he made a strange request.

"I want to buy something in the duty-free store. Can I use your boarding pass?"

The clerk pulled a small bag from under the counter. He took Sarah's boarding pass and Pieter's credit card and completed the transaction.

The bar was packed with folks enjoying one last round before the long flight to Amsterdam. It was standing room only and spaces between the chairs were crowded with roller bags and backpacks. Pieter guided Sarah to a table right next to the bar. As if on cue, three young women surrendered their seats, and the bartender brought out two glasses of sparkling rose wine.

Pieter raised his glass, "This is the closest thing they have to Champagne." He took a sip, then opened the small box from the duty-free shop bag.

It was a ring. A large, deep blue Tanzanite, surrounded by small diamonds.

He pulled it from the box. "It's not a proper engagement ring."

"Let me get this straight. Is this a proposal?"

"Yes, well, sort of. But you don't have to say yes or no right now." He cleared his throat, shifted in his seat. "Or ever. And either way, I would want you to have this."

Sarah stared at the ring. She had known Pieter little more than a year, had not seen or spoken to him for months, but the thought of going through life without him was unbearable.

Pieter leaned forward. "You could just wear it on your right hand."

Sarah smiled and stretched out her left hand.

"Can I take that as a yes?"

The bar crowd erupted into applause.

Sarah was the last person to go through security. Time for one last kiss as her backpack went through the scanner. She paused at the door leading out to the tarmac. Pieter waved through the glass wall and his lips formed words. "I love you."

A woman in the next seat asked the usual questions: What did she do in Africa? Did she go on a Safari?

Sarah gazed at the ring. "I was just tying up some loose ends."

Pieter said that it wasn't a "proper" engagement ring. How wrong. It was perfect. Tanzanite: a precious stone that only shows its true colors after exposure to intense heat. A gem found nowhere else on earth—only in the country that they both loved. Tumaini was right. They would be coming back.

ABOUT THE AUTHOR

DR. GAYLE WOODSON is a world-renowned throat surgeon. As one of the first few women to be trained in the Johns Hopkins Surgical program, she began her career at a time when female surgeons were regarded as oddities. She has lectured on six continents and done medical outreach in Central America, the Middle East, and Africa. Recently semi-retired, she now divides her time between Florida, Newfoundland, and Tanzania with her husband. They have four children, four grandchildren, and a Springer spaniel.

SELECTED TITLES FROM SHE WRITES PRESS

She Writes Press is an independent publishing company
founded to serve women writers everywhere.
Visit us at www.shewritespress.com.

To the Stars Through Difficulties by Romalyn Tilghman. $16.95,
978-1631522338. A contemporary story of three women very
different women who join forces in a small Kansas town to create
a library and arts center—changing their world, and finding their
own voices, powers, and self-esteem, in the process.

Faint Promise of Rain by Anjali Mitter Duva. $16.95,
978-1-938314-97-1. Adhira, a young girl born to a family of
Hindu temple dancers, is raised to be dutiful—but ultimately, as
the world around her changes, it is her own bold choice that will
determine the fate of her family and of their tradition.

Magic Flute by Patricia Minger. $16.95, 978-1-63152-093-8.
When a car accident puts an end to ambitious flutist Liz Mor-
gan's dreams, she returns to her childhood hometown in Wales in
an effort to reinvent her path.

Arboria Park by Kate Tyler Wall. $16.95, 978-1631521676. Stacy
Halloran's life has always been centered around her beloved
neighborhood, a 1950s-era housing development called Arboria
Park—so when a massive highway project threaten the Park in
the 2000s, she steps up to the task of trying to save it.

Again and Again by Ellen Bravo. $16.95, 978-1-63152-939-9.
When the man who raped her roommate in college becomes a
Senate candidate, women's rights leader Deborah Borenstein must
make a choice—one that could determine control of the Senate,
the course of a friendship, and the fate of a marriage.

A Drop In The Ocean: A Novel by Jenni Ogden. $16.95,
978-1-63152-026-6. When middle-aged Anna Fergusson's research lab is abruptly closed, she flees Boston to an island on
Australia's Great Barrier Reef—where, amongst the seabirds,
nesting turtles, and eccentric islanders, she finds a family and
learns some bittersweet lessons about love.